Northern Exposures

BOOKS BY ERIC WALTERS

Long Shot
Hoop Crazy!
Tiger in Trouble
Full Court Press
Rebound
Caged Eagles
The Bully Boys
The Money Pit Mystery
Three-on-Three
Visions
Tiger by the Tail
The Hydrofoil Mystery
War of the Eagles
Stranded
Diamonds in the Rough
Trapped In Ice
STARS
Stand Your Ground

Eric Walters

Northern Exposures

HarperCollins*PublishersLtd*

For my wonderful daughter, Christina

Northern Exposures
Copyright © 2001 by Eric Walters.
All rights reserved. No part of this book may be
used or reproduced in any manner whatsoever
without prior written permission except in the
case of brief quotations embodied in reviews.
For information address
HarperCollins Publishers Ltd.,
55 Avenue Road, Suite 2900,
Toronto, Ontario, Canada M5R 3L2

www.harpercanada.com

HarperCollins books may be purchased for
educational, business, or sales promotional use.
For information please write:
Special Markets Department,
HarperCollins Canada,
55 Avenue Road, Suite 2900,
Toronto, Ontario, Canada M5R 3L2

First edition

Canadian Cataloguing in Publication Data

Walters, Eric, 1957–
Northern exposures

ISBN 0-00-648531-6

I. Title.

PS8595.A598N67 2001   jC813'.54
C2001-930202-9
PZ7.W34No 2001

TC 9 8 7 6 5 4 3 2 1

Printed and bound in Canada
Set in Monotype Garamond

Chapter One

The ringing of the telephone jolted me out of sleep. I opened one eye and stared at the offending instrument on the night table. It rang again. Beside it sat my alarm clock glowing out the time in angry red numbers: 8:58 a.m. That was far earlier than I ever wanted to see on a clock on a Saturday morning. The phone rang a third time. I figured it was my mother on the other end of the line. I knew that even though it was the weekend she was at her office and had probably been there for at least a couple of hours already.

I guess I was sort of used to all the hours she put in—especially when she had a big trial coming up. What I'd never gotten used to was her insistence that everybody else, especially me, should be up and working early every morning. She liked to say that she did more before noon than most people did the whole day—somehow I didn't think that was something to brag about. Even when she didn't have work to do she would often get up just to watch the sun rise. She said she was a "morning person."

Again the phone rang. Obviously my father wasn't home either or he would have got it himself. I wondered if he'd even come home at all last night. He'd mentioned at dinner last night that he had eight patients who were due to give birth on the weekend, and then he was called out to the hospital just as we started dessert.

Again the phone rang. It had to be my mother, for sure—persistence was one of her strengths.

I reached over and grabbed the phone. "Yes, Mother, I'm up. I was just in the shower," I lied.

There was a long pause on the other end of the line. "Umm . . . my name is Norm Rippon. Can I please speak to Kevin Spreekmeest?" a man asked.

It was my turn for stunned silence as I swallowed hard to regain my voice.

"Is there a Kevin Spreekmeest at this number?" he asked.

"Yes . . . I mean, no!"

"I'm sorry, I don't understand."

"There isn't a Kevin Spreekmeest here. You want me, I'm Kevin Spreekmeester," I explained.

"Spreekmeester? My form clearly says Spreekmeest."

"Form! That would explain it. There are never enough spaces on forms for me to write out my whole name."

There was silence, and I could picture him counting the number of spaces on his form.

"So your name is actually Spreekmeester. I'll just make a correction."

"Thanks," I said.

I hated to have my name butchered and I was pretty sensitive about it. It was hard when I was a little kid to have a name that was longer than I was tall. The scariest thing, though, was that I was almost Spreekmeester-Pawlowski, the hyphenated name my mother went by after she married my dad.

"Well, Mr. Spreekmeester, I'm calling to inform you that you are the grand winner of our contest!"

"I am!" I exclaimed. "Oh that's . . ." I let the sentence trail off. I'd been fooled by one of these telephone solicitors before. They pretend you've won a prize when really all they're trying to do is sell you something.

"I don't want to buy anything," I said coldly. Being woken up was bad enough. Being woken up by somebody trying to sell me something made it even worse.

"But I'm not selling anything. You've won first prize in our contest."

"I don't even remember entering any contest," I argued. This had to be some sort of con. I may have been thirteen years old, but I wasn't stupid.

"Didn't you enter the *Mississauga News* photo contest?" he asked.

That tweaked my memory. "Yeah, I guess I did."

"Your photo was the winning entry!"

"My photo won?"

"Yes, it was the unanimous choice. The judges were awed by your ability to produce a collage effect without manipulating the negatives or using a darkroom. You're obviously a very talented photographer."

What was he talking about? I didn't know anything about photography. I'd only entered the contest—something called "Capturing Mississauga"—because it meant I could ditch school to wander around and shoot pictures for the day. My friend Ian had arranged the whole thing, right down to forging both his and my parents' signatures so we could enter. Like Ian had said, "A day doing almost anything beats the heck out of a day in school."

I thought about the contest. All the people who were entering—and there must have been at least fifty or sixty of us there—showed up at the newspaper office at 9:00 in the morning and were given a specially marked roll of film. The idea was that you had twelve hours to take the twenty-four shots, then you turned it back in and they developed the pictures. Which of course meant that we didn't even get to see the pictures we took. What made it even better was that Ian and I took the whole roll of pictures in less than two hours and were completely free for the rest of the day.

"The judges thought your repeated exposure technique was sheer genius!" the man said enthusiastically. "I won't even ask how you came up with that idea!"

That was a good thing, because I really didn't know what he was talking about.

The guy continued to drone on about taking pictures, and it wasn't just that I didn't know what he was talking about, I wasn't even sure that all the words he was using were English!

I couldn't wait to tell Ian about this. He wouldn't believe that I had won and he'd probably figure that I was just putting him on, the way he was always putting me on. Ian was a real joker and he loved to make people look stupid . . . Wait a second . . . what an idiot I was! There was no way I could have won that contest. Not only did I not know anything about photography, but I'd used a broken-down old camera that I wasn't even sure worked. This couldn't really be anybody from the newspaper contest. It had to be Ian playing another one on me. He said I had "sucker" permanently printed on my forehead. Sometimes I thought he was right, and I was getting tired of it.

"Hello, are you still there?" asked the man, startling me out of my thoughts.

"Yeah, I'm still here . . . Ian."

"Ian? No, my name is Rippon, Norm Rippon," he said, sounding confused.

I had to admit that it certainly didn't sound like Ian. But that just meant that Ian had got somebody else to do it for him so I wouldn't recognize his voice. I could picture Ian sitting right there beside the guy as he made the call.

"Tell Ian he can't fool me," I said. Then I thought that Ian wouldn't be satisfied just to hear one end of the call. He had to be listening in on an extension.

"You can't fool me, Ian!" I shouted.

"I'm sorry, but I don't understand," the man sputtered.

"Sorry is right. You're a sorry excuse for an actor."

"But I'm not an actor!" he protested.

"You're right about that . . . you're no actor," I snapped, although he'd certainly had me fooled at first. "Just put Ian on!"

"There isn't anybody here named Ian . . . I work for the *Mississauga News!*"

"Fine, and there isn't anybody here named Kevin," I said, and I slammed the phone down with such force that my alarm clock jumped off the night table and fell to the carpeted floor.

I bent down to pick up the clock.

"What an idiot, waking me up to play some sort of stupid joke on—"

The phone rang again. I grabbed it before the first ring had finished.

"Mr. Spreekmeester, it sounded like you hung up on me."

"Good guess," I said as I slammed the phone down once more. I stood up and started to walk out of the room, and the phone rang a third time. I spun back around and picked it up once again.

"Just give up!" I shouted.

"I can't give up! I need to advise you of your prizes and I have to arrange a time today to come over to your house to interview you for an article."

"And are you going to bring Ian over too?" I asked.

"I've told you, I don't even know anybody named Ian . . . but I will be bringing along a photographer. Your picture will be on the front page of the paper."

"Won't that be a thrill and a half," I said sarcastically.

"And I need to meet with you as soon as possible. Could I come over this morning?"

"Yeah, whatever ... knock yourself out," I said, and I returned the phone to the cradle again. I started off for the bathroom but I'd gone no more than three steps when the phone rang once more! This had gone way beyond annoying!

Angrily I snatched the phone from the cradle. "Why don't you get bent!"

There was silence.

"And why would I want to do that, Kevin?" my mother asked.

Chapter Two

I knew I had to say something back to her, but the words just stuck in my throat.

"And what exactly does 'getting bent' mean?" my mother asked.

"It doesn't mean anything! I didn't know it was you!" I exclaimed.

"I should hope not. Just who did you think was calling you?"

"I thought it was Ian," I blurted out.

"Ian," she said, and I could picture her slowly shaking her head.

My mother really didn't like Ian, and she seldom missed a chance to explain to me that he was the "wrong sort" of kid for me to hang around with. When he was over at the house she was polite to him, but I could always pick out that special tone in her voice and look in her eyes that let me know how she *really* felt.

"And why exactly should Ian get . . . what was that delightful term you used?"

"Bent," I mumbled quietly.

"Yes, bent."

"It's nothing, really, I was just goofing on him."

"Because I'm of the opinion that Ian would benefit more from getting straightened out—"

"You're not supposed to pick on my friends," I said.

There was silence on the other end of the line. The only thing my mother hated more than being wrong was having it pointed out to her.

We'd been going to a family therapist for the past three months—me, my mother and dad. We'd spend an hour a week in his office sitting in comfortable chairs and talking. One of the things we talked about was learning how to "fight fair," and that included not picking on people. It was explained to me that we were in therapy to "open up the lines of communication" and to try to "make our family function even better." No matter what anybody said, though, I knew what this was really all about. My parents wanted to know why my marks had fallen so badly and why I'd stopped taking piano and art lessons, dropped out of Tae Kwon Do, and didn't want to play rep soccer any more. And of course once they found out the answer they were going to want somebody to fix it—which meant fixing me. Then everything would be back to the way it was before. Well, that wasn't going to happen.

"Fine, I won't say anything against your friends." She paused. "But it is fair for me to ask what he did to cause you to be mad at him."

"He woke me up this morning," I said.

That was true, although I wasn't about to tell her what he did. Of course I realized I was breaking one of the therapist's rules too—I was lying by telling half the truth—but there was no way I could tell her about Ian playing another practical joke on me.

"Funny, Ian doesn't strike me as a morning person. I'm surprised he's awake already," she said.

"Are you kidding? Ian loves to get up early on the weekends

so he can get all his homework and chores finished," I explained. At least I wasn't telling another half truth: this was an out and out lie.

"I guess I shouldn't be surprised. My inability to predict what that boy is going to do is one of the things that worries me most. I just wish—"

"Mom!"

"Fine, fine, I'll stop talking about him," she said, and I knew there was less chance of that than there was of me actually having won the photo contest.

"I guess your father is still at the hospital or he would have answered the phone," she said.

"Must be." If I'd said I didn't know then she would have known that I hadn't been up and doing chores.

"When he gets home could you get him to . . . hold on for a second, I have another call." There was a click, and the sound of elevator music filled my ear. I hated to be put on hold, but conversations with my mother, if they went on for more than a few minutes, generally were interrupted one way or another.

"Sorry, Kevin," she said when she came back. "I've got an important call on the other line and I have to go. Give your dad a kiss for me and hopefully I'll see the two of you at dinner, or at bedtime at the latest. Bye bye."

"Yeah, I'll see you—" The line went dead before I could finish the sentence. I put down the phone.

I tried to decide which I should listen to first, the grumbling in my stomach or the pressure on my bladder. The bladder won out so I stopped in the washroom before heading for the kitchen.

Heading down the stairs I yelled out for my dad. There was no answer, which meant he was definitely at the hospital. My mother worked long hours mainly when she had a case coming to court, but my father was always working. He said he'd take a break when people stopped having babies, and there was no danger of that. I used to be amazed by how everywhere we went he ran into a patient or former patient. I remember when I was little I actually thought his first name was "Doctor" because so many people called him that.

Entering the kitchen I opened the cupboard and pulled out a box of Cheerios. I put my hand into the box and grabbed a fistful of cereal, stuffing it into my mouth. This was the best way to eat cereal. No bowl and no spoon also meant there was no cleanup. But I needed something to wash it down.

As I went to open the fridge my eye was caught by the "To Do" list taped to the door. There were the usual items; the "make bed," "tidy room," "walk dog" sort of jobs. Nothing unusual and nothing I couldn't finish off in less than an hour.

Then my eye drifted over to a plastic laminated "Weekly Schedule." Each day was clearly marked off along the top row. There was a colourful border filled with pictures of kids playing sports, drawing, working at computers, dancing and doing schoolwork. I ran my fingers across the columns. Each square where an activity could be listed—where all my activities *used* to be listed—was empty. There were faint markings, a line here and a speck there, which were the remnants of hundreds of lessons and games and practices and classes. Now there was nothing. I couldn't help but smile.

I pulled open the fridge. On the top shelf was a pitcher of milk and half a dozen containers holding a variety of juices. My mother had got a juicer for her birthday and she'd taken to making juice out of anything that vaguely resembled fruits or vegetables. I liked OJ as much as the next guy but these concoctions weren't even labelled and it was like playing Russian roulette. Better to go for a sure thing.

I bent down and rummaged behind the leafy vegetables, hoping to find what I was looking for. Finally my hand came across a familiar shape hidden at the back that my eyes couldn't see. I pulled it out.

"Yes, we have a winner!" I said aloud as I pushed down on the tab and a *phiiffff* escaped the can of Coke. I took a long swig, swished it around to get rid of morning mouth, and then swallowed.

My dad, who wouldn't even think of smoking or drinking alcohol, was addicted to Coke. Of course he mainly drank it at home or when he was sure that nobody, especially not his patients, could see him guzzling the stuff. He said he had to be a good role model, and he wouldn't want people to see him irresponsibly consuming something that wasn't healthy. It's pretty bizarre when your dad is a closet Coke drinker.

I grabbed another handful of cereal, crammed it in my mouth and took a sip of Coke. The pop and cereal made an interesting taste combination. If it hadn't been for the fact that I didn't want to have to do any dishes, I would have tried a bowl of Cheerios with Coke on it. Now *that* would be the breakfast of champions.

Reaching into the cereal box again, a few toasty Os escaped and fell to the ceramic-tile floor. That sound was instantly followed by the clicking of toenails as my dog, Winnie the Poodle, reacted. How a fifteen-year-old, half-blind dog could have heard that sound from halfway across the house was pretty amazing. She snuffled around at my feet until she had located each and every piece. She then looked up at me and turned her head to the side, as though she was giving me a look of disapproval.

"I don't need you to look at me that way too!" I said. "This breakfast is a healthy part of a balanced diet and has many important nutrients . . . like sugar and food colouring."

Winnie didn't look convinced.

"Here, knock yourself out," I said as I dropped an entire handful of cereal to the floor. She scrambled around wildly, trying to stop the oats from escaping . . . Escaping . . . I wanted to make a phone call to Ian before he had a chance to escape! I threw down another handful of cereal to Winnie and ran back to my room.

I hit number one on my speed dial. I thought maybe he'd still be on the phone, so I was relieved when it started to ring. Three . . . four . . . five . . . come on, Ian . . . six rings . . . maybe I should hang up, or—

"Yeah," a voice mumbled.

"You jerk!" I yelled into the phone.

I heard him clearing his throat. "Kevin . . . what time is it?" he asked, putting on a voice like he'd just woken up.

"It's thirty minutes after your call got me out of bed," I answered.

"What are you talking about?"

"Your fake phone call. Did you really think you could fool me?" I demanded.

Again he cleared his throat. "First off, I don't *think* I can fool you, I *know* I can fool you. I've done it a dozen times. Second, I don't have the vaguest idea what you're talking about."

"Yeah, right. Who did you get to make the phone call? He wasn't very good."

There was a long, long pause at the other end. "How about we start at the beginning now. Why don't you relax and take another sip of your Coke."

"How did you know I had a Coke?" I asked in amazement.

"I'm part of the Psychic Hotline," he joked. "And this call is costing you three dollars and seventy-five cents per minute. Would you like to know about the girl you'll marry one day and how she she'll leave you for your much more interesting best friend?"

"Shut up and answer the question! How did you know I was drinking a Coke?"

"Easy. It's Saturday morning, and may I add far too early on Saturday morning, and neither of your parents are home—"

"How did you know they weren't . . ." I let that sentence end because the answer was so obvious: they were hardly ever home.

"Duh, Kevin, it doesn't take a psychic to guess that one. So I figured since you were alone, up early, and got to bed late, you needed a Coke to jump-start your head. So, did you get in trouble for getting in past curfew last night?"

"Not yet. My mother said we had to wait until she and my dad could sit down together and discuss how they should handle it."

Ian and I and a couple of other guys had been out hanging at the mall and then the arcade. I'd missed my eleven o'clock curfew by almost an hour.

"Boy are you lucky your parents are going to wait until they can sit down together before they punish you."

"How do you figure that?" I asked.

"Well, by the time the two of them coordinate their schedules to meet and talk about it you'll be in first-year university and they won't be able to ground you." He laughed, and I started to laugh along.

I knew he was wrong, though. We'd talk about it in two days when we had our regular session with the therapist. While there were lots of things my parents didn't seem to want to talk about, what I'd done wrong was always a welcome subject.

"So you were trying to tell me a story," Ian said.

"Like you don't know," I snapped.

"Exactly, like I don't know. Tell me what happened."

"Come on, just admit that I saw through your plan."

"Okay, I admit you saw right through my plan . . . now could you tell me what plan that was?"

"Don't act stupid," I told him.

"Who's acting? You've seen my marks. Now just tell me what I was supposed to have done."

"Yeah, right. You almost had me going for a while, though," I confessed.

"Good to hear."

"That guy did sound convincing," I reluctantly admitted, "and for a split second I almost believed my photograph had won the contest."

"And what contest is that?" Ian asked.

"Quit acting—"

"I told you, I don't have to act stupid," Ian interrupted.

"The *Mississauga News* photo contest. For a second I honestly believed that I'd won."

There was complete silence on the other end.

"Ian?"

"Yeah, I'm here, I'm just having trouble believing what you said. Are you telling me somebody called and told you that you won the photo contest?"

"Of course that's what I'm saying, and of course you know that already because you put somebody up to it," I said.

"Maybe you're a bigger fool than even I gave you credit for," Ian said.

"What do you mean? You didn't fool me, I knew it was you!"

"I've got to tell you, in complete and utter honesty, that I have nothing to do with this," he said, and he did sound genuine. "But you had to be a fool to believe, even for a microsecond, that you could have won that contest. Somebody else, and I don't know who, is putting you on."

"So it isn't you?" I asked meekly.

"No. I wonder who the joker is."

Before I could answer, the doorbell rang. "I have to go. Somebody's at the door."

"Okay, give me a call later on, like after I'm actually awake, and we'll figure out what to do this evening."

"Sounds good," I said.

I hung up the phone and raced down the stairs to get the door. It rang again as I pulled it open. There was a man wearing a tie and trench coat standing on our porch. He looked like he was either going to try to sell us something or change our religious beliefs. Either way I wasn't buying.

"Good morning, I'm here to see your father," the man said.

"My father isn't here right now."

"Oh, I thought he'd be here. Do you know when Mr. Spreekmeester will be home?"

Obviously he knew our name, but equally obviously he didn't know my father very well if he called him "Mister" instead of "Doctor."

"I don't know when he'll be back, he's at the hospital," I said.

"The hospital! My goodness, did something happen?"

"Something's always happening. He has babies to deliver."

"Oh, I see . . . he's a doctor . . . I didn't know that. I was just talking to him this morning and we got disconnected, and then the line was busy, and I need to see him as soon as possible. I just took a chance and came over. Are you expecting him home soon?"

I shook my head. "There's no predicting."

"Oh dear, oh dear," the man said, and he looked at his watch. "I have a photographer coming to take his picture and I have to interview him."

"For what?" I asked, wondering if this man was from some medical journal. My dad was always getting write-ups about the work he was doing with high-risk pregnancies.

"Your father won a very important contest."

"A contest?" I asked, and my whole body suddenly went numb. "A photography contest?"

"Yes."

I swallowed hard. "Are you . . . are you Mr. Rippon?"

"Yes, I am! Before he went out did your father mention I was speaking to him?"

I shook my head. This was unbelievable. I'd actually won the contest!

"You weren't talking to my father. You were talking to me."

"You?"

I nodded my head. "I'm Kevin Spreekmeester!"

"You're the person who won the contest?"

I nodded my head.

"I don't believe it!"

"But I am," I said more emphatically. "Honestly!"

He reached out and pumped my hand. "I wasn't doubting that you were Kevin Spreekmeester. What I can't believe is that somebody could be so talented at such a young age. This is wonderful! What a story it's going to make!"

"I really won?" I asked, totally baffled.

"Of course you did."

"And you're really going to write about me winning the contest?"

"Front page, accompanied by a full-colour picture. It's going to be great. By the way, did I mention the prizes you've won?"

"Prizes?"

"For starters, you've won a brand new camera! Thirty-five millimetre, zoom lens, built-in flash, wide-angle lens. But I guess you're pretty attached to the camera you used for the winning entry."

"Not really," I said. I'd tossed it out the day after the contest because it smashed to pieces when it dropped out of my locker and hit the floor.

"There are thirty-five rolls of film and all developing costs."

"That's nice." Since I usually took about a roll of film a year, that would last me until my forty-ninth birthday.

"And of course there's the grand prize. An all-expense-paid five-day photo-safari to Churchill, Manitoba, to photograph polar bears!"

"Polar bears? Churchill, Manitoba?"

"And not only will you be there, but you'll be working with one of the best wildlife photographers in the world! Isn't it exciting!"

That wasn't the word I had in mind.

"You'll be leaving in late October."

"But I have school," I protested.

"I'm sure your parents won't mind you missing a few days of school for such a wonderful opportunity."

Obviously he didn't know my parents at all. What were they going to say about any of this? They didn't even know I had been in the contest . . . or missed a day of school . . . or had Ian forge their signatures so I could take the day off to be part of the contest in the first place.

I heard a car door slam. If it was my father I'd get the answer sooner than I expected . . . or wanted. A man with half a dozen cameras strung around his neck turned the corner of the house.

"Oh, good, the photographer is here. Let's take some shots and then get on with the interview."

Chapter Three

"Now who's trying to fool who?" Ian demanded as he walked down the hall away from me. It was Monday morning, and we were on our way to our first class of the day.

"Nobody's trying to fool anybody! I really *did* win the contest!" I insisted as I followed after him.

"I've got to give you credit, though. That was a creative twist—you really had me convinced that you thought it was *me* trying to play a joke on *you*!"

"I *was* convinced! I thought it was you for sure. But I was wrong! Nobody was trying to trick me! I really, *really* won the photo contest!"

"Huh! The only way I'm going to believe you won is when I see your picture in the paper."

"That won't be until tomorrow night . . . but what about if I show you some other proof?" I asked.

"Like what?"

For the first time Ian had stopped walking away from me. Ian is shorter than I am, and thin as a rail, but he has a way of making me feel about two feet tall.

I took my pack off my back and lifted the flap. "How about

this?" I asked as I pulled out my new camera. It was still in the box, and I handed it to him.

"Nice camera," he said as he opened the package. "But all that means is you have a new camera. No proof there that you won anything."

"Then how about this, then?" I handed him the certificate that entitled me to all the free developing from a local camera shop.

He studied it carefully. "This is good, really good. What did you do, make this with your computer?"

He handed it back to me and I looked at the certificate. I knew it was all legit, but I also knew I *could* make something just like this without too much trouble. I still had one more ace up my sleeve.

"Here's the proof you wanted," I said as I pulled out a large envelope.

"What is it?" Kevin asked.

"A blow-up of my winning photograph. This is what will appear in the newspaper."

"This I have to see," he said as he took the envelope from my hand, opened it and pulled out the photograph. "What is this?"

"It's what's called a collage. It's a collection of photos that are made on the same negative."

"And you think this is proof?" Ian asked. "So you have some picture . . . big deal! You could have ripped this off from some geek in the Camera Club."

"Look a little closer. Recognize anything?"

"Well . . . there's city hall . . . and the statue of the muskoxen . . . and the Square One mall . . . and this looks like Jack Darling Park . . . and this is . . . me."

"That's right. Those are the last five pictures I took that morning."

"You really *did* take this picture . . . I mean pictures."

"All five of them."

"But how did this happen? How did they all get on one picture."

"I've been trying to figure that out since I first saw it myself. I even went to the library and took out some books on photography."

"And?" he asked.

"Best I can figure my camera wasn't working right and when I tried to advance the film after taking a picture it got stuck. So the different images in the picture are a combination of the last shots I took. Notice how some of them are more faded than the others?"

"Yeah, some are hardly there at all."

"Those are the pictures I took first."

"And this one here, of city hall, is the clearest picture because it was the last one you took before we handed in the film," Ian said.

"Exactly!"

"So . . . so . . . you really did win the contest?"

"That's what I've been trying to tell you. Unfortunately, I won't be able to use the grand prize."

"Why not, it looks like a good camera," Ian said, turning it over in his hands.

"The camera is one of the prizes, but not the grand prize."

"What's the grand prize?" Ian asked.

"A trip. To Churchill."

"Where is that?"

"It's a small town way up in northern Manitoba on the shore of Hudson Bay."

"That's the grand prize? If they really wanted to give you a trip they should have sent you on a cruise, or to Club Med or DisneyWorld."

"That would have been neat, but none of those places have polar bears."

"And Churchill does?"

"The biggest concentration of polar bears in the world. Every year in October they gather on the shore and forage for food and wait for the ice to form so they can go out to hunt for seals," I explained.

"Okay." He shrugged. "But why do they even want you to go where there are polar bears?"

"To take pictures. To work with this world famous photographer guy."

"And they couldn't have him help you take pictures of Mickey Mouse instead?" Ian joked.

"It's supposed to be very exciting, but like I said, it doesn't matter, I won't be able to take the trip anyway."

"Why not?"

"First off, I'd be going by myself."

"That would be a problem. Your parents have just got used to letting you go to the washroom by yourself," Ian joked.

"Very funny." It would have been more funny if it hadn't been so close to the truth. "Besides it would mean missing a week of school."

"That ends that. We both know how they feel about school," Ian agreed. "Did they just say no or did they give you a lecture to go along with it?"

"I haven't asked them yet," I said quietly.

"Yet? It's not like they'll say yes if you just wait long enough."

"It isn't that. I'm afraid they'll ask me a lot of questions that I don't want to answer. Things like how I got out of school for the day."

"I see your point. Try to keep my name out of it if you can," Ian requested.

"I'll do my best to keep your part a secret."

"Unfortunately your best probably isn't going to be good enough. When your mother starts asking me questions I feel like a criminal in court instead of a kid in your kitchen. Does she always act like she's cross-examining a witness?"

"It gets worse when she's in the middle of a trial, like she is now. Sometimes I'm almost afraid to ask her to pass the milk in case she objects to my question."

"Were they at least happy about you winning the contest?"

"You don't understand," I said. "I haven't told them anything yet."

"You'd better tell them soon. It'll be better coming from you than them reading it in the paper, or having somebody call and tell them about it. You said it was going to be in tomorrow's paper, right?"

I nodded. "I have to tell them."

"You can do it tonight . . . assuming they're coming home?" Ian said.

"Tonight's our time together," I said quietly.

Ian nodded in understanding. He was the only one I'd told about our family therapy sessions. Maybe because Ian's family made ours look almost normal by comparison.

It wasn't that I was ashamed of going to therapy, but I didn't like people to know my business. This was private stuff. Besides, I didn't think everybody would necessarily understand why we were going to see a social worker. Some people might have thought we were crazy or something. Crazy we weren't—although in my mind we were clearly *something*.

Chapter Four

I took a chair on one side of the waiting room while my mother sat across from me. She was dressed in her best lawyer costume—perfectly tailored suit guaranteed to intimidate the opposition—and not a hair was out of place. She made me feel downright shabby in my messed up jeans and sweatshirt, but guess who was more comfortable.

While I tried to amuse myself by browsing through magazines that were almost as old as I was, Mom busily worked away at the notes she was preparing for the upcoming trial. A couple of times she muttered things to herself, and once she made a call on her cellphone. The only hint that she wasn't in her office was that occasionally she'd look up and give me a little smile. She glanced at her watch every few minutes, and her expression clearly showed her annoyance. Our session was scheduled to start soon and Dad wasn't there yet.

The door to the office opened and the sounds of friendly conversation and laughter preceded the people coming into the waiting area—a man and woman and a girl, their daughter I assumed, who was about my age. I'd been watching them week by week coming out of their session as we waited to go into ours.

I could remember when they used to come out of that door scowling and glaring at each other and hardly even talking. Then they actually seemed to be getting worse. A couple of times I could hear yelling right through the door, and a few times one or the other, or all of them, came out in tears. We used to look downright good compared to them, and I wondered why we were even there when it was obvious that therapy was meant for families like them. Then things started to change. At first it was just little things. And for awhile when they moved forward one week they'd slide back the next. But then the changes became more obvious and didn't go away. Whatever was wrong with them was becoming right. Meanwhile, we seemed to be staying the same. Nothing was changing. Sure, things weren't getting worse, but they certainly weren't improving, either.

Dan James, the therapist, followed out behind them and they said their goodbyes. It was all so friendly and positive. He turned to us, and I thought his eyes flashed disapproval when it registered that my dad wasn't there.

"Come in, please," Dan said, gesturing to his office. "Will your husband be joining us?"

"I'm sure he will be here shortly," my mother answered as she gathered up her papers, put them into her briefcase and stood up. "You know that babies—"

"Don't rush for anybody," Dan said, interrupting her to complete the sentence I knew he'd heard more than once. Dan had a slight smile on his face. That wasn't unusual. Except for the rare times when we were talking about something serious he always wore the same friendly, cheerful expression. He sort of reminded me of a dolphin. If I'd still been taking drawing classes I'd have done a caricature with his face on the body of a dolphin. I'd actually started to draw him that way once but crumpled up the paper and threw it away before I was finished.

Dan hadn't said a word about it, but I knew he disapproved of my parents' being late or absent. He'd emphasized in the first few meetings that this had to be a priority for all of us if it was going to work. Then he'd said it again in the second session, and the third. Yet despite what he said it was more unusual to have all of us there, and there on time, than to have somebody missing for at least part of the session.

Just as Dan was getting ready to close the door to his office I heard the outer door open, and a few seconds later my dad rushed in all out of breath.

"Sorry for being late, but you know babies—"

"Don't rush for anybody," the three of us said in unison.

My dad smiled. "Exactly!"

We all settled into our seats.

"So, how have things been going?" Dan asked.

"Don't ask!" Mom said. "I have a big trial coming up and I'm not even near to being ready and . . ." She let the sentence trail off. "You mean around the house . . . with the family, right?"

Dan just nodded his head and gave her a dolphin look.

Then Mom said, "Maybe before we get started tonight I should mention that this will have to be our last family session . . . at least for the next two or three months. The way this trial is shaping up I simply won't have the time."

While the timing of the announcement was a surprise, the fact that she was making it was completely predictable. The only question I'd wondered about was which one of them was going to bail out first.

"That's unfortunate," Dan said, with his usual gift for understatement. It was a good thing the man wasn't being paid by the number of words he spoke or he'd be livng in a cardboard box and eating out of the dumpster behind McDonald's.

"It is, but just because I'm not able to make it doesn't mean my husband and son can't still attend," she added.

"You've probably noticed that I'm often hard pressed to be here myself," my father said.

I stifled a laugh.

"So perhaps a break would be good," my dad went on. "It might even present an opportunity for Kevin to come here by himself. What would you think about that, Kevin?"

I'd opened my mouth to answer his question before I thought about just how much trouble I'd be in if I honestly said what was on my mind. I closed it again.

"I'm afraid I wouldn't be able to see Kevin alone," Dan said.

"Why not?" my dad asked. "The time slot would still be available, and if money's the issue because you don't charge as much for individual as you do for family counselling—"

"We'd be willing to pay the difference," my mother interrupted.

Dan shook his head and his smile faded a notch. "We contracted for family therapy."

"Surely a contract can be broken . . . after all, I'm a lawyer, so I know how to do that." My mother chuckled and my father laughed along with her.

"Sorry, it doesn't work that way," Dan said. "If you want, I can refer you to a variety of therapists who would be willing to see Kevin." He paused and turned directly to me. "If that is what Kevin wants."

My parents' eyes focused on me as well. I knew what they wanted me to say, and I knew that what I wanted was the exact opposite. I didn't say anything, and they all waited for my answer. Actually, as far as I was concerned, they could have waited right through our hour and into the next session and they'd still have been waiting for an answer.

"I think it really doesn't matter anyway," my mother said. I knew she'd say something if I left it long enough. She hated silence.

Dan gave her a "go on" look.

"We've been coming for over three months and I haven't seen any changes," she said.

"I have to agree," my dad added. Another big shock, him agreeing with her.

"So things have stayed the same," Dan said.

I knew from experience that this wasn't him agreeing with them but simply repeating the last thing somebody said. That's just one of those things that therapists do—sort of the equivalent of a dolphin jumping through a hoop.

"Exactly. No improvement," Mom said.

Dan nodded his head. It was such a natural action for him that I wondered if he nodded in his sleep. "Have things gotten any worse?"

"I don't see how they could," my dad answered.

"Then I must apologize to all of you," Dan said.

"Apologize?" Dad asked.

"Yes. I had no idea things were so bad that they couldn't get any worse. I must have totally misread the situation. Perhaps it would be wise to terminate the family counselling and I'll arrange for you to see a good marriage counsellor."

"Marriage counsellor!" my mother practically shrieked. "Why would we need a marriage counsellor? Things are just fine between us!"

"Better than fine," my dad blurted out. "They're wonderful . . . even better than wonderful!"

"I just thought that since the two of you are so incredibly busy you probably don't have much time to be together, and—"

"It's not the quantity of the time but the quality that counts," my mother argued.

"And we do have quality time," my father agreed.

"Okay," Dan said, looking perplexed. "The marriage is fine—I'm sorry, better than wonderful—so . . ." He let the sentence trail off. "I think I understand." He nodded more vigorously. "You must be having financial pressures. If the sessions are too expensive I can make arrangements to reduce your payments and—"

"We have no problems whatsoever in that area!" Dad practically yelled.

"My husband is a very successful physician and I am a partner in a major, I repeat *major*, law firm. I don't know how you could get such an idea!" my mother replied icily.

"We are very, very well off," my dad concurred.

Dan shook his head solemnly. "I'm not having a very good day, apparently. So the marriage is wonderful, your finances are in great shape. I've only got one more guess . . . and at this point you must know I'm just guessing. One or both of you must hate your job."

"That is the most ridiculous thing you've said in all the time we've been in these meetings," my dad bellowed.

"I *love* my career! Being a lawyer, preparing for a big case, presenting in court, the game of cat and mouse between yourself and the other lawyer is a thrill that you probably can't even understand!"

"And as for me," my dad said, "being a doctor is much more than a job. It is exciting and rewarding and something that I never get tired of doing."

Dan looked perplexed, and the dolphin grin was completely gone. "So your marriage is wonderful, you've got lots of money, and you both love your careers more than anything else. Does that pretty well sum it up?"

"Yes, it does," my dad said emphatically.

"Exactly. That's the first thing you've gotten right tonight, Dan. You're just not yourself at all. Maybe you should be seeing a therapist." Mom smiled and gave one of those "aren't I clever and superior" looks that made me want to scream.

"Maybe I should, because I'm still lost. Everything is great, but you both think that things couldn't possible get any worse. So what is it that is so terrible?"

I could see the wheels spinning around in my mother's eyes, but she was, on this rare occasion, unable to give an answer. She opened and closed her mouth a few times, and it reminded me of somebody working a pump before water starts to flow out of it.

"It's just that . . . just that . . . well, Kevin missed curfew the other night."

"How late were you, Kevin?"

"About fifty minutes."

"That is unfortunate, but certainly not terrible. And how were you consequenced?"

"Consequenced" is the word therapists use when they mean punishment.

"He hasn't been, yet," my father said.

"There won't be a consequence?" Dan asked.

"Of course there will," my mother announced. "Rules and laws have to be followed or society will crumble!" She sounded as though she were arguing a case before a judge.

"We just haven't had a chance to sit down as a group and discuss it until now," my dad said, coming to my mother's rescue.

"Oh, I see." Dan nodded his head, and the dolphin face was back in place. "So you were late last night."

"No, I was on time," I said.

"Was it the night before, Kevin?"

"No, it was Friday night."

His expression changed, so he now looked like a confused dolphin. "But that was three full days ago and you still haven't had a chance to sit down?"

"I've got this trial coming up—"

"And I've delivered fourteen babies since then," my dad added, interrupting my mother.

"Life is busy. But there must be more to this problem than Kevin simply being late."

"Of course it's more than that," my dad answered. "It's just that Kevin isn't . . ."

The sentence trailed away to nothing, but everybody in the room knew what he was going to say. Kevin still isn't doing anything except hanging around with his friends and watching TV. Kevin's marks are still in the 60s instead of the 90s. Kevin hasn't been *fixed*.

"You don't think he's getting any better," Dan said.

That was what my father and mother were thinking, everybody knew that, but now that the words hung in the air they seemed far more painful.

"Is that it?" Dan asked. "If the therapy was going well then you'd assume that Kevin would become more like himself again."

"I don't know if I'd put it quite that way," Dad said. "But that would be nice."

"Yes, it would," Mom agreed.

"And your opinion, Kevin?" Dan asked.

"I . . . I . . . don't have one," I lied.

"Come now, Kevin, surely you must have an opinion," my mom pressed.

I did, of course, but nothing either of them wanted to hear, nothing that would do any of us any good. The truth was, I didn't need to be fixed because I wasn't broken. All I needed was a break, from them and from all the activities and all the expectations they put on top of me all the time.

My dad leaned forward and put a hand on my shoulder. "We want to hear whatever you have to say, son. You look so distracted."

I looked at him, and then at my mother, and finally at Dan. All eyes were on me.

"Kevin?" Dan asked.

I needed to stop them all from looking at me. I took a deep breath and then swallowed hard. "I guess I do have something I want to say."

"Go on, please," my mother said.

"I won."

"You won, what?" Mom asked.

"The contest. The photo contest."

"What photo contest?"

"The *Mississauga News* photo contest. I beat out hundreds of other people to win the grand prize."

Maybe there weren't really hundreds of people in the contest, but I didn't care. I knew that the more people they thought I'd beaten the more impressed they'd be. They started to pepper me questions and as I went on to explain things I could see that old look returning to their eyes.

"I'm proud of you, son," my dad said as he reached out and shook my hand.

"That goes for both of us," my mother added.

"I also want to add how happy I am, too," Dan said. "But of course the reason I'm happy has absolutely nothing to do with you winning."

"It doesn't?" I asked.

He shook his head. It was a welcome change from the nodding. "I'm happy because you made an independent choice to pursue an interest that was important to you. In my opinion, that is half of what these sessions are about."

"It is?" I asked.

"Certainly. And of course the other half is to help your parents understand that you need to be free to pursue those independent interests. But of course, you all knew that."

31

I didn't, and judging from the look on my parents' faces they didn't either.

"And that's been one of the pleasures of being your therapist. You've been able to see this from a mature and reasonable point of view. Some people would have been foolish enough to assume that we were somehow here just to fix Kevin. Isn't that silly?" Dan asked.

Both of my parents laughed nervously and avoided making eye contact.

"I didn't even know you enjoyed photography," Mom said, breaking the tension.

"Perhaps we can get you a new camera," Dad suggested.

"Or enrol you in a photography course," Mom said.

That was just like them. Couldn't I just *do* something instead of having to take lessons and practise and try to become the best?"

"You don't have to do any of that," I said.

"Of course we don't have to, but we want to," Dad said.

"No, I mean you don't have to because those things are part of what I won."

"They are?" they both said in unison.

I reached down to my backpack on the floor beside my chair and pulled out the new camera. I handed it to my dad.

"Wow, is this a beauty or what?" he said.

"And there's free film and developing, too."

"Excellent," Mom said. "All you need is some expert instruction. I'm sure there must be something offered through the city, or one of the local colleges."

"That's been taken care of too," I said.

"It has?" Dad asked.

"I get to work with a photographer . . . a world famous photographer . . . if you'll let me."

"Well of course we'll let you! It sounds like the chance of a lifetime!" my mom said.

"You're sure?" I asked hesitantly.

"Of course!" she exclaimed.

I nodded. "Thanks, it means a lot to me. I guess I'd better start getting all my stuff ready then."

"Ready for what?" my dad asked.

"Ready for the trip. I leave in less than two weeks."

Chapter Five

There was a deafening silence. I could almost hear my parents thinking, but nobody seemed to be able to make any sound. I figured that each of them thought they'd heard wrong and was waiting for somebody else to question what I'd just said.

"Pardon me?" my mom asked.

"My flight leaves early in the morning on October twenty-fourth and I arrive around six that night."

"Your flight!" my dad exclaimed.

"Arrive where?" my mom asked.

"Churchill, Manitoba. And actually it's two flights ... one from here to Winnipeg, and then a second plane takes me to Churchill."

"What are you talking about?" My mom sounded confused and angry.

"That's the grand prize. I get to work with a famous photographer for a week in Churchill, Manitoba."

"But why are you going there?"

"To photograph polar bears."

"You aren't going anywhere, young man!" my dad said firmly.

"But—"

"But nothing!" my mother said, interrupting me. "You are not going off on some wild goose chase!"

"It's polar bears."

"You know what we mean! Besides, at least geese don't eat people!" Dad exclaimed. "I've seen lots of dog bites in my time, and I can only imagine how much bigger a bear bite would be. Those animals must weigh at least 150 kilograms!"

"Females can weigh almost 400 and a male can be as big as 700 kilograms," I said. "At least they are when they come off the ice, but they'll be a lot smaller this time of year."

"Sounds like you know a lot about polar bears," Dan said.

"I've been reading about them. That and photography. I took out some books from the library and I've been surfing the Net, I found a lot of websites."

"It's wonderful that you've taken such an interest," Dan said.

"Interest or no interest, this trip is completely out of the question," my dad declared.

"Definitely," my mother agreed.

"Why?" Dan asked.

My mother stared at him in total disbelief. "You think we should let him go?"

"I was just wondering why you two are so strongly opposed," Dan said.

"We're opposed to letting our little boy go thousands of kilometres away on his own."

"I'm not a little boy!" I protested.

"That's not what I meant to say," my father apologized.

"That *is* what you said, though," Dan pointed out.

"My husband just meant that he's still too young to go off by himself. Especially flying that far away."

"So the issue is Kevin going alone," Dan said.

"Exactly!" my father said, and my mother nodded wholeheartedly in agreement.

Dan nodded his head but replaced his smiling dolphin look with his puzzled dolphin look. "Then I guess that one of you needs to go with him."

"I can't go, I have a trial coming up! I can hardly afford to waste the time coming *here*," my mother said.

"Do you think it's a waste of your time coming here?" Dan asked.

"You know what I mean," she said. "I don't mean it's a waste, I just mean that my time is so limited and I have so much to do."

"I see," Dan responded, and I was willing to bet that he really did understand. "Perhaps you can go," he said to my father.

"I couldn't possibly get another doctor to cover my practise on such short notice and I have an ethical responsibility to my patients."

More of a responsibility to his patients than he does to me, I thought.

Dan nodded his head again. "So basically you're both incredibly busy . . . so busy that Kevin has to miss out on a wonderful opportunity."

"We both have obligations," my mother protested. "Blaming us for our business isn't fair, Dan."

"Nobody is blaming you," Dan said, "and you're right, it isn't fair . . . it's not fair to Kevin that he's denied a trip because nobody can find the time to go with him."

"Surely you don't think we should let him go without us?" my father questioned.

"I'm not saying that."

"Then you don't think he should go?" my mother asked.

"I'm not saying that either," Dan replied.

"Then what exactly are you saying?" my father demanded.

"I'm saying that since these sessions began you've both wanted Kevin to take an interest in something again, to be involved in more activities, to look toward his future and to be more responsible." Dan paused, and they both nodded in agreement. "And now that he's done all of those things you're going to take it all away from him. It just doesn't seem fair to me. Does it to you, Kevin?"

I looked up at Dan and he winked at me. Game, set and match for Dan. I'd always heard that dolphins were very intelligent animals.

Chapter Six

The plane set down with a jolt and the wheels screeched as the rubber bit into the asphalt of the runway. Anxiously I looked at my watch—it was almost 2:30. My connecting flight, the one to take me from Winnipeg to Churchill, would be leaving in just over thirty minutes. Originally there'd been a three-hour layover between flights, but my plane out of Toronto had a mechanical problem that delayed our departure. Then, to make a bad thing even worse, the flight itself took longer than expected because, as the pilot announced, we were "encountering strong headwinds."

I knew there was only one flight each day to Churchill—if I missed this one there wouldn't be another one until the following afternoon. My parents had been concerned about me being alone in the airport between flights for three hours. I could just imagine how they would be worried about me spending the night by myself in an airport! Not that they'd know. They didn't even know my plane had been delayed.

My mom had said her goodbyes to me the night before because she knew she'd be up and out and at work before I was awake. My dad had driven me to the airport, but just as we were pulling my luggage out of the car he was paged. He called over a porter and asked him to get me to my flight. He then pressed a wad of "emergency money" into my palm, gave me a hug goodbye and raced off to get to the hospital.

I looked at my watch again. I needed to be the first person off this plane. As it taxied down the runway toward the terminal I stood up and reached for my carry-on luggage in the overhead compartment.

"Kevin, you need to stay seated until the plane gets to the terminal."

I looked over to see the flight attendant, Tammy, standing there with a big smile on her face. She reached over and placed a hand on my shoulder, easing me back to my seat. My seatmate, a balding, middle-aged man in a wrinkled business suit, continued to snore away at my side.

"The pilot has a rule—he likes the plane to get to the terminal before the passengers," she joked.

Nervously I laughed along. She'd talked to me a lot during the flight, asking me questions and being friendly and even bringing me two Cokes instead of one, because she said the little bottles they served on the plane were so tiny. The first time she'd talked to me I couldn't even mumble out a reply. She was . . . a woman. And not a woman like your mother, or like anybody's mother that I'd ever met, but like somebody from like a movie or a rock video or TV or a poster or—

"Are you so tired of me already that you need to rush off the plane?" she asked.

"No!" I barked out, and I felt myself blush. I'd spent half the flight playing around with little fantasies like me saving the plane—and her—from hijackers. And then I'd run into her again some time—like maybe ten years later when I was twenty-three or twenty-four, and there'd be this magical connection.

"It's just that I've got to catch a flight," I mumbled.

"That's always a concern when a flight is delayed. Let me have a look at your ticket."

I fumbled around in my pocket. The ticket was crumpled and worn from me holding it so tightly in my hands for the last hour of the flight. Somehow I'd thought that if I held on to the ticket the plane couldn't leave without me. That made about as much sense as me saving the plane from hijackers. I handed it to her and she smoothed it out and examined it closely.

"Oh dear," she said. "Oh dear!" Suddenly she reached up and opened the overhead compartment. "Which is yours?"

"The green and white bag," I said. Even though I didn't play rep soccer any more I still really loved my old soccer bag.

She pulled it free. "Come with me," she said as she hurried down the aisle.

I stumbled after her unsteadily, swaying with the motion of the plane along the tarmac. Tammy was standing at the front hatch, and as I stopped in front of her she handed me my bag.

"This is not good at all. The gate your flight leaves from is the farthest away from where we arrive. If you want to make it to your plane you're going to have to leave your luggage."

"Leave my luggage! But I need my luggage!" I protested, knowing how mad my mother was when I so much as left my lunchbag at school.

"You'll get your luggage, you just won't get it until tomorrow. Give me your baggage checks and I'll make sure your bags are sent to you."

I felt hesitant, and I think it showed on my face.

"Do you have everything you'd need for a night in your carry-on bag?"

I tried to think through what was in it. There was my new camera, all the rolls of film, some schoolwork I needed to complete, my CD player, a dozen of my favourite CDs, a week's supply of socks and underwear, a toothbrush and paste, a new pair of thermal gloves and a hat my mom had bought for me at the outdoor store. The salesman had insisted upon the hat. It was really expensive, but he said a hat is the most important piece of outdoor gear because 90 percent of body heat is lost through your head. If that was really true I figured I could go outside naked in a blizzard if I had on a really, really good hat.

"I guess I have enough . . . but—"

"Don't worry. I'll personally take care of everything. Besides, what's more important, getting *you* on the plane or your *luggage*?"

While I had hoped to get both on the plane, it was hard to argue with what she was saying.

"Kevin, I'm going to draw you a map of the airport on the back of your ticket."

I leaned closer so I could see what she was sketching. As she started to explain I inhaled deeply, and the scent of her perfume filled my nostrils. She smelled as wonderful as she looked.

The plane bounced slightly and her hair—long, blond, puffy and poofed—brushed against me. I felt myself blushing again. She didn't seem to notice that I was having trouble following what she was saying. I was nervous enough around girls my age, and now I was standing oh so close to a woman—an older woman. She must have been twenty-two or twenty-three years old.

"Does that all make sense?" she asked.

"What?"

"Do you think you can follow those directions?"

I looked back down at the crude, squiggly map on the back of the ticket. It didn't seem to make much sense at all.

"Sure, no problem," I lied, too embarrassed to admit that I hadn't heard a thing.

She flashed me a brilliant smile and I felt my feet get all melty. Then she gave me back my ticket and her hand touched mine. The melty feeling migrated down my legs until my knees felt rubbery.

"Give me your baggage checks and I'll make sure your luggage is on tomorrow's flight."

I unzipped the side compartment of one of my bags and took out the checks. She took them from me just as the plane bumped to a stop. I placed a hand against the wall to steady myself, and she turned around and began to unlock the hatch. I looked past her head and out the adjacent porthole. The terminal loomed large. It was dim and grey, and a light snow was falling from overcast skies.

Tammy popped open the door. "Get going! Follow the map and you'll just be able to get there on time!"

I hesitated for an instant.

"Go!" she yelled, and she grabbed me by the arm, propelling me out the door. I rushed down the covered walkway. Just as I was about to go around a corner and disappear I turned around and took one last look back. Tammy gave me a big smile and a wave.

"See you later!" I yelled, and then, lowering my voice dramatically so there was absolutely no chance she'd hear me, I added, "Like in my dreams."

I continued along the passage. It was slightly uphill, and between that and the weight and awkwardness of my bag I wasn't moving very quickly. I pushed open a pair of double doors at the end and burst into the terminal.

"Excuse me!" a woman said abruptly as she nearly bowled me over. She hurried off, a big suitcase on wheels trailing behind like it was her pet.

I looked around. Somehow in my mind I'd figured that since Winnipeg was so much smaller than Toronto the airport would be smaller too. That didn't seem to be the case. It was gigantic! At least you'd have thought it would have been less busy, but I was wrong about that as well. People, carrying and pulling their luggage, hustled and bustled all around me.

Which way did I need to go? I looked down at the map on the back of the ticket. Whatever Tammy's talents were, drawing maps wasn't one of them, and I couldn't figure out anything. Maybe I was looking at it upside down. I turned it around, but that didn't help. Why hadn't I listened more closely, or asked her to explain things again? It was probably like my mom said about men—they'd rather die than ask for directions, read the instructions or look at a manual.

Then I remembered something Tammy had said: my gate was at the farthest end of the terminal. To the left I could see where the building ended while in the other direction it continued into the distance. Was that the right direction? I looked at my watch. The plane would leave in fourteen minutes. If I didn't move I was guaranteed to miss the flight. I headed to the right.

All along the building on one side there was a continuous line of long counters. Behind each were uniformed employees of the different airlines, serving the passengers standing under each sign. Between the counters were sliding doors opening up to the different gates. My first flight had arrived at gate three, and now the sign between these two counters said "Gate Five." I needed to get to gate sixteen. Maybe I wasn't close, but at least I was heading in the right direction.

Mounted above my head were TV monitors that displayed the flight information—arrivals and departures and the times and gates. I tried to scan the list while I continued to walk. I didn't think I had time to stop. I passed by gate nine. Another glance at my watch: nine minutes left. Not only did I not have time to stop, I did not have time to walk this slowly. I picked up the pace.

I passed by a cafeteria, some shops and a seating area. There were a bunch of uncomfortable-looking chairs bolted to the floor. I wondered just how bad it would be to spend the night balled up in one of those. Hopefully I wouldn't have to find out.

Up ahead was another gate. I tried to read the number . . . no that couldn't be right. I stopped in disbelief. It said "Gate One"!

"You look lost, son."

I turned around. A man—a porter wearing a red coat—stood there with one hand on a baggage trolley.

"I am . . . I've got to find gate sixteen."

"Are you booked on the Adventure Airlines flight?"

"Yeah, I am . . . how did you know?"

"It's my job to know things like that. I've been carrying bags at this airport for the better part of thirty years. And I also know that gate is pretty darn far from here, and," he looked at his watch, "your flight's scheduled to leave in just a few minutes."

"I've got to get on it!"

"Then you'd better get moving. Listen up. You run like crazy in that direction," he said, pointing back the way I'd come, "until you come to a gift shop."

I remembered passing right by the gift shop and glancing in the window.

"You hang a right there down a narrow little corridor. When you get to the end of the corridor you go off to the left. Look for a big sign advertising Diet Coke. Gate sixteen is just to the right of that sign."

"Great, thanks!" I blurted out, and I started to run, but he grabbed me by the arm.

"Tell me back the directions. There's no point in running unless you remember where you're running to."

"Umm . . . gift shop, right . . . corridor, narrow . . . then a . . .
a . . ."

"Left."

"Yeah, a left, and then . . . to the right of Diet Coke."

"Good, now get going! I'll radio to communication and tell
'em you're coming. Maybe they can hold the flight a minute,"
he said, pulling a walkie-talkie out of his pocket.

I started off at a full run.

"Good luck!" I heard him yell after me.

Quickly I started to pass the landmarks I'd just seen. If
anything, there seemed to be more people moving, or simply
standing, and I had to dodge around them. I could feel sweat
starting to drip down my sides under my coat and I had to fight
the urge to slow down. I thought about what the coach used to
say to me at soccer practice—and the way he'd say it—if I let
up even a little when I was doing my laps. "Rep isn't for wimps,
Spreekmeester. Step it up!" This gate couldn't be any farther
than the distance I used to run before each and every practice,
so if I could do that without stopping, I could do this.

Just as I was beginning to think I'd somehow missed the gift
shop, it appeared, and I turned down the corridor. There were
people in front of me, moving slowing.

"Excuse me!" I yelled as I squeezed between them and the
wall and continued running.

I heard someone mutter something directed toward me,
which only gave me incentive to move even faster. I popped
out the end of the corridor and almost headed to the right
before I re-remembered what the porter had said and veered
off to the left. Up ahead I could see gates and big billboards
mounted high on the walls. I scanned them, looking for Diet
Coke. I was just beginning to worry that maybe they'd changed
the ad when I saw it! I had never been so happy to see a bill-
board in my life.

Just beside the gigantic ad was a small door. Getting closer I could see the lettering. All at once I was grateful and disappointed. It said "Gate Sixteen," which I wanted, but the waiting area was completely deserted. There was nobody there, not even an attendant taking tickets. I'd got there, but the plane had already left.

I wanted to simply stop, but it was as if my body was on autopilot and I continued to coast toward the door, hoping beyond hope that the plane was still there but already knowing it wasn't. There was a small window and I peered through it. They'd even taken away the boarding corridor. All I could see was the dim, grey sky and the snow, which had started coming down much harder. I dropped my bag to the floor and looked at my watch, although I knew what it was going to tell me: it was after 3:30.

I felt a sudden tightness in my chest and my jaw began to shake ever so slightly. What was I going to do? I'd missed my flight and I was stranded, alone in a strange city, thousands of kilometres from my parents. I had to fight not to slump to the floor to join my bag.

Chapter Seven

"Excuse me," came a voice from behind me.

I quickly turned around. There was a young man standing there. Tall and gangly, he was wearing a backwards baseball cap and a heavy parka. In one hand he was holding a bag about the size of my carry-on luggage and in the other a large cooler, the kind people use for picnics.

"Can I get by you? I have to get to my plane," he said, gesturing out the door I was still blocking.

"It's gone," I said.

"It's what!" he practically shouted as he leaped forward and peered out the window. "Thank goodness. You had me worried for a second. It's still there."

"It is?" I shouted.

"Yep. Over there to the right. Take care," he said as he opened the door and headed out.

I picked up my bag and grabbed the door before it closed again. He was at the bottom of a long set of stairs that led down to the tarmac from the terminal door.

"Wait!" I yelled as I started down after him. The steps were steep and metal and covered by a sprinkling of snow and I had to hold onto the rail to avoid taking all of them in one bounce. "Is that Adventure Airlines?"

"The one and only. Are you on this flight?"

"If it's the one going to Churchill."

"Direct flight. Come on, we better hurry."

The plane wasn't that big, and it sat on the tarmac away from the terminal, so I hadn't seen it when I'd peered out through the tiny window. It was a small plane painted in bright colours, and on the tail fin was the image of a snarling polar bear. This was obviously the right plane. Its lights were on, and the engines—two large propellers, one on each wing—were slowly turning. There was a small set of stairs on wheels propped up against the open back door of the plane. A woman, wearing a heavy parka and big black boots, stood at the bottom.

"So what happened this time?" she asked the guy as we reached the bottom of the ramp.

"Couldn't help it. The car didn't want to start, and then I got a little lost."

"You've lived in this city for over a year and you still can't find your way around. You're hopeless!"

"But you have to admit I'm getting better. I'm hardly late at all."

"You have a point there. So, who's your friend?" she asked, gesturing to me.

"Ahhh . . . this is my good friend . . . um . . ."

"Kevin," I said. "Kevin Spreekmeester."

"Yes, Kevin Spreek . . ."

"—meester."

"Yeah, Spreekmeester. Can you take extra special care of him this flight?"

"We take extra special care of everybody," she said. "Maybe he'd even like to sit with you?"

"Good idea," he said. "Well, Kevin, do you want to sit with me?"

"Sure . . . I guess so." He'd certainly be better company than that snoring guy on the last flight.

"Fine, then hand Wendy your ticket and let's get aboard."

She took the ticket from me, ripped off the top sheet and handed the rest back while the guy stood at the top, waiting.

"Watch your head," he said, and he ducked to get through the hatch. Although I wasn't nearly as tall as him even I had to tilt my head slightly to the side to enter. This wasn't a very big plane at all.

"By the way," he said, holding out his hand, "I guess we should be formally introduced. My name is Gavin Davidson, but my friends all call me Crash."

I wanted to ask him why he was called Crash, but I was the last person in the world to give a guy a hard time about his name.

"Good to meet you, Kevin. Is this your first time going to Churchill?"

I nodded. "It sounds like you go there a lot."

"All the time," he answered as he walked up the aisle toward the front of the plane.

I started to count the seats as I followed after him. There were two seats on each side of the aisle and seven rows. Each seat I passed was occupied. It looked as if he was going to sit in the very first row.

"And you're always late?" I asked.

He turned around and stopped. "She was exaggerating. I'm on time much more often than I'm late."

"But aren't you afraid they'll leave without you?" I asked.

He shrugged. "Not particularly."

He kept going forward and opened the door to the cockpit. What was he doing? I stopped dead in my tracks.

"Are you coming?" he asked. He was standing in the cockpit now, holding the door open. I could see all sorts of lights and dials glowing behind him.

"We shouldn't be going in there."

"We have to. I've never figured out how to fly a plane from back there."

"Fly the plane! You . . . you mean . . . you're the pilot?"

"Co-pilot. Come on in and meet the captain."

I walked through the door and into the cramped cockpit.

"Kevin, this is Captain Sam Bishop."

The captain reached out his hand and we shook. He was dressed like a real pilot in a uniform with wings on his chest and pilot's cap on his head. He was older, probably old enough to be Crash's father, or maybe even his grandfather.

"And now that I've met Kevin, maybe he can introduce me to *you*," Captain Bishop said to Crash. "You look vaguely like my co-pilot, but he went missing and we haven't been able to locate him."

"I'm sorry, I'm sorry," Crash said. "But which would you rather have, a co-pilot who is always on time or one who's a great flyer?"

"I'd like both . . . and in your case I'm not sure I have either."

"Come on, Sam, don't be mad at me. Compared to what I've heard about you when you were my age, I'm practically a candidate for sainthood."

Captain Bishop started to give him an angry glare, but his lips curled into a smile and he chuckled. "One of these days, Crash . . . and it could have been today. I was just getting ready to leave without you. Would have left if the tower hadn't given me a call. It seems we had a lost passenger, a young man about thirteen, who was rushing to make our flight."

Crash pointed a finger at me. "You mean Kevin?"

"He's the only one on this plane who's even close to

thirteen . . . not including you. Only reason we waited a few minutes longer."

Crash reached over and gave me a slap on the back. "I knew I liked this kid. Do you mind if he sits up front with us?"

"Not at all. Right after takeoff he can take my seat. Until then, why don't you strap yourself in back there." He pointed to a seat tucked in behind the door.

I sat down and eased my bag off my shoulder. I'd been running so hard all the way that I'd kind of forgotten how heavy it was. I tucked it under the seat as the two of them started talking and fiddling with different buttons and dials. I tried to follow what they were doing and saying, but I got lost in the jargon.

"Here we go," Crash said. "How about if I take the controls for takeoff?"

"She's all yours," Captain Bishop said. "But remember, she's not the youngest any more. You have to treat her as gentle as you do your mother."

"This plane is about the same age as my mother, but not nearly as tough."

"Whatever," Captain Bishop snarled. "Tower, this is flight seventy-four, can we please get clearance to leave gate sixteen?"

I assumed there was an answer given back through the head-phones that I couldn't hear.

"Roger. We will proceed to runway zero-two-two and get into the line waiting for takeoff."

Crash pushed forward on a series of levers and the roar of the engines increased. The plane began to vibrate and rattle and then started to move. I looked out through the front window and watched as we spun away from the terminal. The snow was falling harder again and it pelted down against the windshield of the plane.

"Any idea what the weather is like along the route?" Crash asked.

"High winds, pockets of snow, low ceiling and limited visibility," Captain Bishop replied.

"Did you call up weather control?"

"'Course not. It's always high winds, pockets of snow, low ceiling and limited visibility this time of year. Asking me about the weather makes about as much sense as asking me whether it's going to get dark tonight."

Up ahead I could see the tail of a large jet. I'd been on planes many times before, but I'd never seen takeoff from the cockpit before. We pulled in a short distance behind the jet and came to a stop. This was really exciting, and I felt a strange sort of tingling in the back of my head.

"I think I know where it is this time," Crash said as he took off his headphones and got out of his seat.

He opened a cabinet and rummaged around in it. Then he pulled out a large roll of duct tape, ran off a big piece and snapped it off with his teeth. He reached up and applied the big hunk of a tape to a seam on the wall. What was he doing?

"I was listening real carefully when I revved the engine, and I'm positive this is where that rattling is coming from."

"As confident as you were the last time?" Captain Bishop asked, pointing toward another piece of tape stuck directly over his head. "Or that time?" he said, gesturing to another one. "Or—"

"I know, I know, but this time I'm sure," Crash said. "I've got to find that rattle before I'm forced to leave the plane mid-flight."

"I still don't know what rattle you're talking about," Captain Bishop said.

"I don't know how you can miss it. It's driving me crazy!"

Captain Bishop just smiled and didn't say anything.

At that point I noticed that there weren't just those three pieces of tape: it was like the whole of the cockpit was wallpapered with duct tape. There were dozens and dozens of pieces stuck everywhere.

"Since you're standing anyway, why don't you go back and check that everything's secured for takeoff," Captain Bishop suggested.

"Sounds good. I'll hit the can while I'm back there," Crash answered. He opened the door and headed back into the passenger compartment.

"Kevin," Captain Bishop said quietly, "I need you to keep a secret. Can you do that?"

I shrugged. "Sure, I guess."

"Marbles," he practically whispered.

"Marbles?"

"Shhhh!" he hissed at me. "Marbles. Four of them are in that vent right above your head."

I looked up at the metal vent. It was held firmly in place by four large pieces of duct tape.

"But why would there be marbles in there?"

"Because I put them in there. Crash is a good pilot, but he spends too much time talking and not enough listening. I had to do something to make him more sensitive to the sounds of the plane. I'm trying to make him a better pilot." He paused. "Besides, it's as funny as can be watching him trying to figure it out." He started to laugh. "And you've got to promise me that you won't you tell him, and that you'll pretend not to hear it either. Okay?"

"I guess so," I answered.

"Good boy. Now why don't you slip on those extra headphones and you can listen in on the tower conversation while I move us forward in line."

Chapter Eight

Takeoff was amazing. The sound of the engines was tremendous and the plane vibrated and rattled—well, at least the marbles rattled. As we rolled along the runway picking up speed Crash joked that he was thinking about deliberately crashing the plane, just so the federal authorities could search through the debris and find not only the cause of the accident but the source of the rattle. I knew he was joking, but it wasn't the sort of joke I wanted to hear from somebody who was flying a plane.

Shortly after takeoff Captain Bishop suggested that he and I trade seats. He settled me into the co-pilot chair—warning me not to touch anything—and then he took the seat I had been occupying. Within twenty minutes Captain Bishop was asleep, and snoring.

"Would you like me to give you the guided tour of what we're passing over?" Crash asked.

"Sure, that would be nice."

"Lost in the darkness below us out the left side—or, as us technical plane people call it, the non-right side of the craft—there's a river, a series of ponds and small lakes, assorted rocks of differing sizes, muskeg and of course evergreen trees. And if you look out the right side of the plane—which, of course, is also known as the non-left side—you'll see a river, a series of small lakes, some rocks of differing sizes, and muskeg and . . . of course . . . evergreen trees. That ends the tour. That's all there is for the whole flight."

I couldn't help but smile. As Crash turned to adjust something on the control panel to the far side he turned his head, and the back of his cap, which was actually the front, was facing me. For the first time I read what was written there. In small, neat letters it said simply, "Fly Naked." Somehow that didn't fit what I'd expect an airline pilot to wear, but it certainly suited Crash.

"Stupid engine," he muttered under his breath.

"Something wrong?" I asked anxiously. I'd never been on a plane that was powered by propellers, and they just didn't seem as safe to me as jet engines.

"Nothing serious. The left engine doesn't sound quite right. I think it's getting the wrong mixture of fuel to air."

"It's going to be all right, though isn't it?" My level of anxiety was rising. I wanted to keep all that scenery that was below us, below us.

"There's no problem. Besides, we have a second engine. Even if this one died, the plane could fly just fine on one engine."

"It can?"

"No problem. I can turn one of them off if you want to see—"

"That's okay! I believe you, honestly!"

Crash smiled. "And believe it or not this old bird isn't even a bad glider."

"What do you mean?"

"Gliding means flying without any engines. It's before my time, way before my time, but there was a flight fifteen years ago where this plane was landed with no engines. One engine died in mid-flight, and then when she was coming in for the landing at Churchill a flock of Arctic terns crashed into the plane, taking out the second engine. The pilot brought it in anyway. It was such a perfect landing that nobody on the plane even knew anything had happened."

"Wow, he must have been some fantastic pilot!"

Crash gestured back toward Captain Bishop. "He still is. Best I know."

Crash mumbled something under his breath again. "I need to adjust that engine. It's bothering me even more than those marbles in the vent."

I felt myself visibly blanch, but I tried not to show anything. "Don't worry. I know all about the marbles in the vent."

"But how . . . ?"

"I took the whole cockpit apart one Saturday and found them."

"But why didn't you tell Captain Bishop that you found them?"

"Respect."

"I don't understand."

"I told you just a little bit about Sam. The man's practically a legend, and if he wants to play a joke on me, who am I to deprive him of his fun? Could you put your hands on the stick for a minute?"

"The stick? What stick?"

"The wheel."

"Oh . . . sure . . . I guess I could," I answered, carefully placing both hands on the wheel.

"It's on autopilot anyway so it should stay level, but I like to make double sure when I leave the pilot's seat. You're in charge."

"I'm what?" I practically yelled.

"Shhhhh! You don't want to wake up Sam. He may be a

legend in the air but he's pretty grumpy when he's woken up from his nap."

"But I can't fly a plane!" I protested in a hushed tone.

"First off, you're not really flying it, and second, have you ever tried to fly one before?" he asked.

"Of course not!"

"Then how do you know you can't?"

Before I could answer he spun his seat around and got up. I wanted to say something, but for the life of me I couldn't think what I was supposed to say. Instead I clutched the wheel tightly. I watched as Crash went to the side panel and began fiddling with different buttons and levers. Even I could tell that the engine was responding to his efforts by making slightly different sounds. The plane shifted slightly to one side, and all at once I grabbed the wheel tighter, my stomach tried to force its way up my throat and the marbles rattled noisily. I was beginning to hate those marbles.

"There, that's better," Crash said as he slumped back into his seat. "Now the engine's making the right sound."

I listened. I thought that maybe I could hear what he meant. Either way, I just felt relieved to have him sitting beside me again.

"Could I ask you a question?" I said.

"Sure."

"I was just sort of wondering—"

"About my name?" Crash guessed. "It's just a nickname, part of a long and boring story. I've never crashed a plane, car or snowmobile in my entire life. Satisfied?"

"Yeah . . . but how did you know—?"

"That you wanted to ask that question?"

I nodded.

"Because that's the question everybody wants to ask a pilot

named Crash, just like really tall people are always being asked if they ever played basketball."

"Have you ever thought about maybe going by another name?" I asked.

"Sometimes. What's your last name again?"

"Spreekmeester."

"Have you ever thought of changing your name?"

"It's my name!" I protested, although there'd been lots of times I'd wished I'd been a Smith or a Lee or anything that contained less than half the letters of the alphabet in it.

"Well then, how about if you change your first name?"

"What's wrong with Kevin?"

"Nothing. It's just, with a last name that long and unusual, you need yourself something a little shorter and spiffier for your first name. Something like . . . like . . . I don't know . . . maybe Biff, or Buck or Elvis."

"Elvis?"

"You're right, that's no good. It has as many letters as Kevin and people would expect you to wear sequined outfits, grow really long sideburns and eat a lot. But you should think about getting yourself a good nickname."

The door to the cockpit opened before I could answer and the woman who'd taken my ticket, Wendy, popped her head in. Now that she didn't have her parka on, I could see that she was a real knockout. She had to be a bit older than Tammy, the future love of my life, but she was small and pretty, with dark brown hair and eyes to match.

"Can I get anything for you three?"

"Sam would like a pillow," Crash said, gesturing to the peacefully sleeping pilot. "Buck, do you want anything?" he asked.

It took me a second to realize he was talking to me. "I guess a pop would be good. Do you have any Coke?"

"That's all we have," she answered. "This is a non-smoking, non-Pepsi flight."

"As it should be," Crash agreed, "as it should be."

"And can I get anything for you?" she asked Crash.

"You know perfectly well what you can do for me. You can agree to go out with me on a date."

"Don't you ever give up?" she asked.

"No. Persistence is one of my most endearing qualities."

"Maybe your *only* quality. Crash, you're way, way too young for me."

"You're only as old as you act," he countered.

"In that case you must be twelve."

"How can you say that?" Now he sounded hurt. "People tell me I'm very mature for my age."

"Well, if you *are* twelve then you're a very mature twelve-year-old. Why don't you just stop wasting your time? I wouldn't go out with you if you were the only man in all of Manitoba." She turned to leave. "But I'll be back with Kevin's Coke in a second." She closed the door.

"That was very encouraging," Crash said.

"What was?"

"Didn't you hear what she said?"

"Yeah, that she was getting me a Coke."

"Not that part. The part about how she wouldn't date me if I was the last man left in Manitoba."

"And that's encouraging?"

"Definitely! She used to say she wouldn't go out with me if I was the last man in Canada, and now I'm down to only one province! By this time next month it might be the only person in Winnipeg and then maybe the only one in Churchill and finally ... who knows? You've got to follow your dreams, right?"

"I guess so. Was your dream to be a pilot?" My parents

always wanted to know what people wanted to be "when they grew up," and I had to admit that it had become a fascination for me too. I still wondered what I wanted to be.

"As long as I can remember that's been my dream. Someday I hope to fly the big birds."

"You mean like the jumbo jets?"

"Exactly, although I guess I shouldn't complain. Compared to what I used to fly this *is* a jumbo jet," he said.

"What were you flying before?"

"My own plane. One propeller, five-seater. I did charter flights up north."

"Around Churchill?" I asked.

"Nope. Churchill isn't even up north. It's just a few kilometres above the treeline. The north doesn't really start until you hit the Arctic Circle, and Churchill is hundreds and hundreds of kilometres south of there."

"But if Churchill isn't up north, then why are there polar bears there?" I asked.

"They're migratory animals. They have no choice but to come south because all the ice melts in the summer."

"So just where are you from?" I asked.

"A little place you've never heard of and couldn't pronounce. It's right on the Arctic Ocean."

The flight attendant came back through the door holding a can of Coke. "I hope you weren't expecting it in a glass."

"No, this is fine. Thank you," I said as I took the can from her.

"Sure you don't want anything, Crash?" she asked.

"I do want something," he said, and he flashed her a big smile.

"The answer is no!"

"I'm confused . . . you won't tell the passengers to fasten their seatbelts because we're coming in for a landing?" he asked.

"Of course I will!" she exclaimed. "I thought you were going to ask me out again."

60

"Please," Crash said as he turned back to the instrument panel. She looked embarrassed and left to inform the passengers.

"I thought I'd play hard to get for a while," Crash said, and then he laughed to himself. "You see those lights up ahead?"

I peered hard through the windshield. At first I couldn't see anything except the darkness and snow, but then a few flickers of light became visible in the far distance.

"Those red and white lights dead ahead are markers for the airport and the runways. The red flashers over to the left are on the top of the grain elevators."

"I didn't think they could grow grain up here."

"You're right about that. The growing season up here is about as long as winter in Florida. The grain gets shipped up here by rail and exported. Churchill is an ocean port, at least for the few months of the year when the bay isn't covered in ice."

"What are the winds like?" Captain Bishop asked. I hadn't even noticed that he was awake.

"Coming from the northwest. Strong, but nothing that should give us any problems."

Captain Bishop got up. "Mind if we trade seats, son? I wish I could let you stay up there right through the landing, but it doesn't seem too smart for there to be *two* kids at the controls when we try to touch down."

I got up quickly and he took his seat.

"Better belt yourself in, Kevin," Crash said, ignoring the shot from Captain Bishop.

I quickly strapped myself in, tightening the belt up snugly around my waist. As I did so I could hear the engines change tone and we tilted slightly forward, the marbles rattling noisily. While I couldn't see anything but grey, dark sky out of the windshield from where I sat, I could feel us descending, and both my ears felt funny. Then all at once I could see the lights of the airport, shining bright, and the markers outlining the sides of the runway. The ground rushed up to meet us and I braced myself for the wheels to hit. I was surprised when there was nothing but the sound of the engines being cut back and I could hear the wheels rolling along the tarmac.

"That was a great landing! I didn't feel a thing!" I exclaimed.

"I told you," Crash said, "the old goat is a great pilot . . . of course, that only makes him the second best on this plane."

Captain Bishop chuckled softly to himself and I laughed along with him.

Chapter Nine

The plane bumped along the runway, and not just the marbles but other parts of the plane rattled, rolled, shook and vibrated noisily.

"Why so rough?" I asked, my voice vibrating in tune with the ride.

"Ice on the runway. It forms into little pressure ridges," Captain Bishop explained. "They all run in the same direction because the wind is almost always blowing that way."

Crash picked up a microphone. "Thank you for flying 'Bear Air' with Adventure Airlines and welcome to Churchill, Manitoba, the polar bear capital of the world. The outside temperature is a balmy minus-five degrees and there is a gentle breeze blowing out of the northwest at fifty-five kilometres an hour. While awaiting the bus to take you to your lodge, we strongly suggest that people stay together and don't stray far from the plane. Enjoy your time in Churchill." He put down the microphone.

It was dark, and snow was blowing across the tarmac. I figured it would be easy to lose sight of the group. "Do you want people to stay close because you're afraid somebody will get lost?" I asked.

"That could happen, but we're more concerned about somebody getting found," Crash said.

I gave him a confused look.

"Found by a polar bear," he explained.

"There can't be bears here at the airport!" I exclaimed.

"There can be polar bears anywhere around Churchill this time of year. Just last week there was a mother and her six-month-old cub just over by the terminal," Crash said.

"He's joking, isn't he?" I asked Captain Bishop.

"They were over by the building, lying down in the snow right beside the entrance."

"What happened?"

Captain Bishop started to laugh.

"We had a planeload of foreign tourists on board and not one of them could speak a word of English," Crash told me. We see the bears and start screaming at them! We were trying to warn them of the danger and move them away. Instead, they think we're trying to show them the bears and they figure this is a photo opportunity. So every last one of them suddenly whips out a camera and starts taking pictures! And instead of backing away they start moving closer and closer. Worst of all, they almost surrounded the poor bears, so even if they'd wanted to get away they were practically going to have to run over somebody! If it hadn't been so dangerous, it would have been funny!

"It *was* funny!" Captain Bishop exclaimed. "The tourists were all clicking away, and Crash was jumping up and down and screaming at the top of his lungs!"

"They just ignored me!" Crash said incredulously.

"Not all of them. Two or three of them started to take pictures of Crash!" Captain Bishop chortled.

"It was like they thought I was doing some sort of native dance to welcome them to Churchill. Then one of them handed his camera to his buddy and he started walking right up to the bears so he could get his picture taken with them. I was positive he was going to get killed."

"Was he all right?" I asked.

"He got lucky. The manager of the airport heard Crash yelling and carrying on and he came out with his rifle just in time," Captain Bishop explained. "He took two shots at the mother bear and sent them running."

"Did he hit her?" I asked.

"Both shots," said Crash. When the first one hit, the bear jumped up in the air like she'd been stung by a bee, and then when the second bullet found its target she took off. She was running so fast the little one could hardly keep up."

"But how fast could she run after being shot?"

"Fast . . . it's not like the bear was hurt."

"But you said she was shot twice?" This made no sense.

"She was . . . but with rubber bullets."

"I don't understand," I said.

"Here, let me show you." Captain Bishop got up from his seat and went to the cabinet where Crash had got the duct tape. He took out a small brown box. "Almost everybody up here has the first two chambers of his gun loaded with these."

On the side of the box it said "Vulcanized bullets." Captain Bishop opened up the box, removed a bullet and handed it to me. It was made of rubber!

"I've never heard of rubber bullets before," I said.

"It's to save the bears. You hope you can chase the bear away without hurting it. It's not just that they're a protected animal, everybody up here has a lot of respect for the bears," Captain Bishop explained.

"Not to mention respect for all the dollars that the polar bears bring to Churchill. Over ten thousand tourists come up here every year to see them," Crash added, as he continued to fiddle with the dials and controls of the plane.

"It would hurt like crazy if one of these hit you ... could even give you a concussion or blind you if it hit you in the eye," Captain Bishop told me. "But it would hardly hurt a bear at all. But that's enough gabbing, this plane isn't going to unload itself."

I followed Crash through the door. Except for a couple of very old women who were still waiting to leave the plane, it was deserted. Wendy stood at the open door talking to another older gentleman and Crash and I squeezed by and went down the stairs that had been rolled up to the plane to allow the passengers to disembark. At the bottom was a little knot of people, all securely tucked inside their parkas, hoods pulled up, gloves and hats on.

"Want to lend me a hand, Kevin?" Crash asked.

"Doing what?"

"Unloading the luggage."

"Sure, no problem."

Crash undid some latches on the side of the plane and a panel dropped down, making a ramp. He climbed up and into the belly of the aircraft. I looked around. Aside from the plane, the huddle of passengers and a few lights extending back down the runway, there wasn't anything else to see. Was this an airport or a farmer's field? Where were the other planes, the ground crew to help unload the luggage, the terminal? Even more important, where were the people who were supposed to meet me?

I strained to see through the dark and falling snow and could just faintly make out the outline of a building. If this was the terminal, it looked about the size of a house—a very small house. At least if they were there I'd have no trouble finding them.

Standing there watching I realized how cold it was and how badly dressed I was for the weather. I put down my bag, opened it up and pulled out my new hat and gloves.

"Good to see you putting those on," Crash said. I could hear his voice but couldn't see him in the darkness. "I hope you have a warmer jacket and boots in your luggage." I was wearing my favourite old jean jacket.

"I do," I said quietly. "I just wish I had my luggage."

Crash poked his head out. "What do you mean, you wish you had your luggage? Isn't your luggage in this hold?"

I shook my head. "It's in Winnipeg."

"You left your luggage in Winnipeg! Why would you do that?"

"I didn't have a choice. My plane from Toronto was late and then I had to rush to catch this flight. But it's okay, Tammy will be getting it on tomorrow's flight up to Churchill."

"Who's Tammy?" Crash asked.

"She was a flight attendant on my other flight."

"Flight attendant . . . Tammy . . . is she very attractive, in her early twenties, with long blond hair?"

"Yeah! Do you know her?"

"No," he said.

"But . . . how do you know what she looks like?"

"I don't. I was just describing what I *hoped* she'd look like." Crash disappeared into the hold of the plane again.

"Catch!" Crash yelled, and a bag came hurtling at me out of the darkness. I put my hands up just in time to soften the blow as it hit me in the midsection. I'd hardly had time to drop it to the ground when a second one, much larger, came sliding down the ramp. At least this one wasn't airborne. I took it off the bottom of the ramp and placed it beside the smaller bag.

Crash poked his head back out. "Kevin, when I get back to Winnipeg I'll make it my personal mission to get your luggage."

"Thanks, but I'm sure Tammy will get it to the plane."

"You're probably right, but first thing tomorrow I'm going to go out and find her."

"Gee, thanks."

"And this Tammy," Crash said, "she's really good looking, right?"

"Yeah."

Crash broke into a big smile.

All at once it dawned on me just who Crash was trying to help. I figured I'd better make other plans for my twenty-fourth birthday party.

"And I won't stop until I find Tammy, or at least a reasonable imi— Darn!"

"What's wrong?"

"Some people have left the group and are walking off on their own."

I turned around. Three people, wrapped like all the rest in thick parkas, were walking away from the group. They were already almost lost in the darkness about fifty paces away and moving farther down the runway.

"Can you do me a favour, Kevin, and bring them back? If a bear doesn't get them, they might freeze to death."

"Sure, no problem."

I thought this was the only airport in the world where you could walk on a runway and worry more about being eaten by a polar bear than being hit by a plane. I hurried after them—after all, I didn't want to get too far from the plane myself.

"Hey!" I yelled.

A few of the people nearby turned in my direction—I seemed to be seeing the same old people all the time—but the wandering threesome didn't hear me. The wind was strong, coming right at me, and it felt as though my words were blown back down my throat to lodge somewhere in the lining of my lungs. Instead of falling, the snow was blowing sideways. My face was stung by hundreds of little needles of snow and ice that were whipping around. And what with the wind, the snow and the little ridges of ice lining the runway I wasn't able to run very fast. Thank goodness for two things: I was wearing my running shoes instead of the boots my mother had insisted I bring; and the threesome seemed to be moving very, very slowly, so I was gaining on them pretty quickly.

"Wait!" I screamed, and one of them turned around. He nudged the other two and they stopped as well.

I ran up to them. Peering out of the tunnels formed by the hoods of their parkas were three old faces. What was with all these old people?

"Yes, son?" came a woman's voice from one of the parkas.

"You have to come back. You can't wander too far from the plane," I explained.

"Who said anything about wandering?" a man barked. "Just 'cause we're old doesn't mean we're lost—"

"Russell, please, he's just trying to help," the woman interrupted, putting a hand on his shoulder. The man mumbled something that was lost in the wind, but all three started back with me.

"Besides, he must know what he's doing . . . he works for the airlines."

"I don't work for them."

"Do you live up here, son?" the woman asked.

"No, I'm just up here to take pictures of the polar bears."

"How lovely. Our whole seniors tour is here to take pictures too."

Seniors tour! That explained why everybody I saw was old. Maybe everybody on the whole plane was old!

"You must be cold," she said.

"No, I'm fine," I lied. It looked like I might just test that theory about the importance of a good hat because the wind was cutting through my pants and jacket like I really *was* standing there naked.

"Where are you staying in town?" the woman asked.

I thought about the name of the place on my travel papers. "It's called the Northern Lights Motel."

"That's where we're staying, isn't it, Russell?"

He grumbled out a "Yes."

"Maybe we'll see you there," she said.

Great, me and a bunch of seniors. This was going to be really exciting.

I shepherded them back to the plane and then went to help Crash again. He'd already taken all the luggage off the airplane and was straightening the bags into a line. Just as I got to his side I heard the sound of an engine and turned around to see the headlights of a vehicle—a big vehicle—coming toward us. It got louder and closer, and then just as I thought it was going to take out the waiting crowd of seniors it swerved, came alongside the plane and slowed to a stop. It was a large yellow school bus. The doors flew open and a man wearing a bright orange vest climbed off.

"Perfect timing!" Crash said to me. "I could really use your help to move the bags over to the bus. Normally I'd ask the passengers to take their own bags, but on these seniors tours it's safer if I do it myself. The last thing we want is for somebody to keel over with a heart attack. I'd rather carry their luggage than carry the person who *owns* the luggage."

"Does all the stuff go on the bus?"

"Well, since your stuff isn't here I'm assuming it all goes there. Who's picking you up, anyway?"

"It's written on my travel papers."

I took off my gloves and rummaged around in my pocket. I pulled out the tattered papers, which almost got away from me in the wind, and handed them over to Crash. As he studied them I quickly pulled my gloves back on. I was amazed at just how fast my fingers were becoming numb. And it wasn't just my fingers—the ends of my toes were freezing and I thought that this was probably the first time in my entire life I wished I was wearing boots instead of high-tops.

Crash started to laugh.

"What's so funny?" I demanded.

"How old are you?" Crash asked.

"Almost fourteen."

"Are you sure you're not older?"

"People usually think of me as being a little older," I said proudly.

"A little! I was thinking about fifty years older!"

"Fifty years?" I echoed.

"Yeah, you must be at least in your sixties, because you've been booked on the seniors tour!"

Chapter Ten

"What do you mean?" I demanded. Nobody had said anything to me about being part of a seniors tour. This was definitely not what I'd had in mind.

"You know how everybody on the plane is old?" Crash said.

"Yeah."

"Well, you're one of the old people." He started to chuckle to himself.

"That can't be right," I argued.

"Right or wrong, this is your group. Come on and I'll introduce you to your tour guide."

I trotted behind Crash as he went toward the man with the vest. Now my brain felt as numb as my fingers.

As we got close I realized that this guy was huge. He towered over not just me, but Crash as well. What also struck me was how he was dressed. The orange vest, which was unbuttoned, was on top of a shirt that wasn't even tucked into his pants. On his head was a funny-looking fur hat with earflaps, and extending down his back was a long ponytail of jet-black hair. His boots were his only concession to the weather. They were thick-soled, which made him seem even taller, and they came up to his knees. His face was hard and looked as if it had been carved out of granite by the wind and snow. His hands were free, although a pair of big black mitts was clipped onto the belt of his pants. Even I was dressed better than him, but he seemed oblivious to the driving snow, wind and cold.

In a loud voice he greeted everybody, introducing himself as Charlie McGinty. His voice was deep and booming and seemed to chase off the driving wind. He then ordered everybody onto the bus.

As they started to file on board, Crash tapped him on the shoulder.

"Charlie," Crash said, and the man spun around to face us. "I'd like you to meet somebody."

We shook hands and my hand just disappeared in his. "Pleased to meet you. What brings you to Churchill?" he asked.

Crash answered before I could. "He's part of your tour."

Charlie's brow furrowed. "Can't be. This is a seniors tour."

"He's a very young senior." Crash chuckled, but judging from the expression on Charlie's face he didn't think this was funny.

"How old are you, boy?" he demanded angrily.

"Umm . . . almost fourteen." Why was he mad at me?

"Almost fourteen makes you thirteen! I need to talk to your parents. Where are they?"

"Umm . . . back in Mississauga, I guess."

"They're not here? What do they think this is, a babysitting service or something?"

"No, I just—"

"I'm a photographer and a tour operator! I haven't got time to take care of any kid! Especially one who hasn't got any more sense than to dress like he's headed to the mall!" he hollered loudly.

"It's not his fault about the clothing. His luggage got sent to the wrong place," Crash explained, lying for me. "He'll have his arctic gear by this time tomorrow."

"He'll have frozen to death by this time tomorrow. I've got half a mind to just pop you back on that plane and send you down to your parents!"

Maybe that wouldn't have been the worst thing.

"Come on, Charlie, give him a break!" Crash said. "He's a good kid, and he'll more than carry his own weight."

"You keep out of this!" Charlie threatened. "All you do is fly 'em up here. I've got responsibility for 'em all the time they're here. Why are you up here anyway, kid?"

"To take pictures of the bears," I stammered.

"So is everybody else. Why did your parents send you here alone?"

"It wasn't even their idea . . . I won."

"You won what?" he asked, and then all at once his eyes lit up and his face softened. "The photo contest . . . you're the winner of that newspaper contest?"

I nodded.

"Kevin Spreekmeest," he said.

"Spreekmeester," I corrected him.

He shook his head. "All they sent me was the name, and it sounds like they didn't even give me all of that. I just figured you were a senior and that's why they put you in with this group."

"I'm sorry."

"Nothing for you to apologize for."

"So are you going to keep him or what?" Crash asked.

"Of course he can stay! He's not a kid, he's a photographer. I always have room for a real photographer, and he must be a darn fine one to win a big contest like that!" He bent down and motioned for me to come closer. "And I've got to tell you," he said in a voice just above a whisper, "I get tired of wasting my time talking to these people who don't know which end of their expensive cameras to look through. It's going to be a pleasure to have you along."

He slapped me on the back and I almost tumbled forward from the force of the blow. Unfortunately what he had said had struck me even harder. He was expecting me to be a photographer, a good photographer, and of course I wasn't. It wasn't even that I was a bad photographer as much as a non-photographer—and he'd only need to talk to me for a few minutes before he'd realize just how little I knew about taking pictures.

"You'd better get on board the bus," Charlie said.

I smiled in relief and trotted off to join the others. I had one foot on the step when I looked back and saw Charlie, the driver of the bus and Crash, with a bag under each of their arms, starting to put the luggage into the bus. My feet were feeling awfully cold and the big toe on my left foot was throbbing a bit. I turned around and went over to the pile of luggage. Then I picked up two bags and started back to the bus.

"Hey, you don't have to do this!" Charlie said, as we met in the middle. He tried to take the bags from my hands.

"I know," I said, holding the bags firm. "But I want to."

"I told you he'd carry his own weight," Crash said.

Charlie released his hold on the bags. A smile creased his face and he nodded his head ever so slightly as he headed off to grab more bags.

I pulled my legs up to get my feet off the frozen metal of the floor. They felt like two frozen hunks of meat. What with waiting for the bus, standing around and then loading the bags, my feet had gone from cold, to aching, to numb, and then all the way to a total lack of feeling.

Charlie dropped down beside me and his weight bounced me into the air before I settled back down into the frozen vinyl bus seat.

"You weren't exactly what I was expecting," he said.

Neither was he, but I didn't think I should mention that.

"How long you been taking pictures?"

"A while," I answered. After all, a few weeks is a while.

"You must be pretty good to win a big photo contest."

"I'm all right, I guess."

"Don't be so modest," he said. "Don't hide your light under a bushel."

I had no idea what that meant, but modesty had nothing to do with it. Maybe if I kept on helping with things like the luggage he wouldn't be as mad when he did find out I was a terrible photographer.

"I've been taking pictures since I was ten, but I didn't win a darn thing until I was almost twenty. That was when I knew for sure I was going to be a photographer. After that, I started to get my photographs published in magazines—you know, *National Geographic* and places like that. Eventually I got pretty well known for my wildlife shots. I've been all over the world on photo assignments, but Churchill is my home."

That really made me wonder what was so great about Churchill since Charlie chose to stay there rather than go somewhere warm like, I don't know, Africa? Africa was sounding pretty good just about then.

"How about you?" Charlie asked me.

"How about me what?"

"Do you want to be a photographer?"

"I'm not sure what I want to be." My mother always said I should be a doctor like my father, and my dad always said I should be a lawyer like my mother. Those were about the only two things I was sure I *didn't* want to be.

"Being here will help make up your mind. If you don't want to be a photographer after a week up here then you're destined to be something else. Here we are!" he exclaimed as the bus pulled to a stop.

I looked out the window. "This is the motel?" I asked. All I could see was a small white house.

"Nope, the motel is down the way. This is my brother's place. Tell him I sent you to get some winter gear."

"I don't understand."

"Clothing. A parka, some boots, things like that," he explained.

"But my stuff is coming up tomorrow!" I protested.

"A promise won't keep the cold away until then. Once you're dressed he'll drive you over to the motel. We're just going another few blocks down Kelsey."

"But shouldn't you come in and introduce me or something?" I asked.

"Introduce you!" he hooted. "Who do you think lives there, the Queen of England? It's just some of my family."

"But what if they're not home?"

"Lights are on and I can see smoke rising from the chimney. Besides, even if they weren't there you could just go inside and make yourself at home and wait."

"But I can't just walk into somebody's house!"

"You're not just walking in, I'm inviting you in."

"What if it's locked?"

"This is Churchill. Every door in the place is open. We all know each other up here."

"But—"

"You got more 'but's than the backsides of a whole herd of caribou!" he interrupted. "Go!"

I stood up and moved by him. The bus door opened up and a wave of snow was pushed in on a gust of cold air. I stopped and turned around.

"Go!" he ordered in a harsher tone, and with a harder look on his face.

I bounded down the steps, and before I could take three paces forward I heard the bus door close and the snow crunching underneath its wheels as it started away. A gust of wind caught hold of me and pushed me toward the house, and didn't let go until I was standing directly in front of the door. I lifted up a hand and gave it a thump.

I waited for an answer and tried to think what I'd say—"Hi, Charlie sent me for clothes," or something like that. There was no answer. The only sounds were the whistling of the wind and a steady bumping sound. I turned toward the noise. A shutter on the window was partially hanging free, and as the wind surged around it rhythmically hit against the side of the house. Maybe that was why there was no answer—my knock had got disguised as just part of the percussion of the shutter. I lifted my hand and knocked again. My hand hit harder, and a stinging feeling travelled up my arm at the same time I heard the banging in my ears. I waited. Still no answer. I couldn't just stand out there, but despite what Charlie had told me I couldn't just barge into somebody's house. I decided that what I needed to do was to give the door a couple of good solid kicks to get somebody's attention.

I drew back my foot to deliver the blow and stopped. I thought about what might happen when the solid block of ice that was my foot hit against the door. I could just envision my foot shattering into little shards. Then, as I stood there flamingo-like, balanced on one foot, a gust of wind propelled me forward, and at that same instant the door popped open. In that split second, as I tumbled into the house, I caught sight of the girl who had opened the door, but I was powerless to stop myself as I crashed into her, and we became a tangled ball of arms and legs lying in a heap on the floor.

Chapter Eleven

"I'm sorry!" I practically shouted as I struggled to disengage myself from her. "Charlie sent me! He told me to just walk in, but I didn't, I knocked, honestly!" I yelled, blurting out everything in one burst so she wouldn't call the police or something.

I managed to separate myself, quickly got to my feet and took a couple of steps off to the side. She stood up, grabbed the door, put her shoulder against it and pushed it closed, stopping the wind and snow from blowing into the house.

She turned to me with a quizzical look on her face. She was about my age, slightly shorter and with long jet-black hair, just like Charlie's. She had a full, round face and dark, dark eyes . . . she looked like she was native, like an Inuit.

"Charlie sent me here," I told her again.

Her expression didn't change.

"To get some clothes . . . you know . . . clothing . . . a parka and boots." I lifted up one of my feet and gestured to my shoe.

She didn't answer. I looked back up at her. Maybe she didn't speak English. What was the language the Inuit spoke? It was something like Inuti . . . something or other. I had to take this slower.

"Charlie," I said, saying the word slowly. Names had to be

the same in any language. "Charlie . . . sent . . . me. Do you know Charlie?"

"Charlie," she said, nodding her head.

"Yes, Charlie! Charlie sent me!" This was good. At least we were making some headway. "Charlie on bus . . . biiiiigggggg bus. *Vroom, vroom!*" I said, trying to make a sound like an engine and moved my hand to imitate a moving vehicle. "Charlie go on *bus*."

"Bus," she repeated.

"Good, excellent!" This was real headway. "Clothes. Need clothes." I wrapped my arms around myself and pretended to shiver. "Brrrrr . . . cold!"

"Parka," she said.

"Yes! Parka! I need a parka!" I figured that word must be the same in both languages.

She nodded her head and smiled.

Maybe before I went any further, I thought, I should introduce myself. I stuck out my hand. "My name is Kevin."

Instead of extending her hand she looked more confused again. Did Inuit shake hands, or was I saying something different from hello?

I pulled back my hand. "Kevin," I said tapping myself on the chest. "Me Kevin."

She nodded her head. "Loretta."

"You're Loretta!" I said excitedly. "That's a *pretty* name." But it certainly wasn't an Inuit name.

"Thanks, I've always liked it. My mother named me after her favourite country singer, Loretta Lynn," she said, in perfect English.

I felt as though I'd been kicked in the stomach.

"You speak English!"

"You picked that up, did you?"

"But you're Inuit," I stammered.

"Actually I'm Cree, but even if I were Inuit what would that have to do with me not speaking English? Even the old people speak English."

"Then why didn't you speak when I talked to you?" I asked.

"Kicks. I wanted to see how goofy you'd get." She started to chuckle. "And you surpassed my wildest dreams! Charlie on bus, *vroom, vroom*. Biiiigggggg bus!"

I felt like melting into the floor, but the ice in my feet kept me firmly anchored to the carpet.

"Are you related to Charlie?" I asked her, still a bit afraid of getting laughed at.

"He's my father's brother, my uncle. So, where are your clothes?" she asked.

"Still in Winnipeg, but one of the pilots said he'd get them for me tomorrow."

"Captain Bishop or Crash?" she asked.

"Crash . . . you know him?"

"No, I made up the names," she chided me.

"I just meant—"

"Everybody knows everybody up here. There are no strangers and no secrets when you live in a place this small."

"Crash said he'd make sure he'd get them to me on tomorrow night's flight. So I only need stuff until then."

"Maybe, maybe not," she said.

"Crash promised me!" I protested.

"He can promise anything he wants, but he can't control the weather. A lot of times they can't even land because of the winds and weather and they have to go back down to Winnipeg. Come on and we'll get you some gear."

I followed after her. "I guess this is strange, you know, somebody showing up at your door to borrow some clothes," I said, trying to make conversation.

"Nope, Charlie sends three or four tourists here each season."

"That many people lose their luggage?"

"More likely they lost their brains, because they packed their bags like they were going to the beach instead of the Arctic." She stopped at a closet and opened the door. "So what do you need, a parka, boots and mitts?"

"I don't need mitts, I've got gloves," I said, pulling them out of my pockets.

"Yeah, I see," she said, casting them a disdainful look, "and that's why you need mitts."

"These are great gloves," I protested. "They're very expensive. My mother got them at a special outdoors store."

She shook her head. "I'm glad your mommy got you special gloves, but take these just in case," she said as she tossed me a pair of heavy leather mittens."

I caught them. They were soft and big. They looked like they'd reach well up my arms. I had a feeling they were going to be seriously warm.

"What size boots do you wear?" she asked.

"Twelve."

"Twelve! Wow, that would make your feet longer than you are tall."

"Funny," I said.

"There's a real advantage to having feet that big. It'll be just like wearing snowshoes so you'll never sink into deep snow. Here, try these on," she said as she passed me a pair of black winter boots. "These are my father's old ones."

They certainly looked big enough. I sat down on a chair and started to unlace my shoes. The laces were crusted with snow and ice and it was hard to get them off. I slipped on the first boot. My foot settled in comfortably and I tightened the buckles.

"And here's a parka for you."

I looked up. She was holding something brightly coloured with geometric patterns on the sleeves. It was a girl's coat!

"I can't wear that!" I protested.

"Why not? Are you so insecure about your maleness that you can't even wear a coat that's a little decorative? I bet you're the kind of guy who's afraid to wear pink or to cry at a movie!"

"I am not!"

"Then tell me what movie made you cry!" she demanded.

I swallowed hard. "None of your business." I didn't want to tell her that no matter how many times I'd seen *Free Willy* I still clouded up at the part where the whale jumps over the breakwall to freedom.

"Stop complaining. I'll get you a bag to put your stuff in while you finish getting ready."

She laid the parka down on the carpet beside me and disappeared into another room.

I took off my other shoe and put on the second boot. Then I stood up and took a few steps. They were maybe just a little too small, but they'd do for a day. Next I took off my jean jacket and dropped it to the floor. I looked down at the parka lying beside it. There was no doubt it was a girl's coat . . . but there was also no question that it would keep me a lot warmer than my jacket. I bent down and picked it up. It was soft to the touch and I slipped it on. What did it matter anyway? There wasn't anybody I knew within three thousand kilometres of there.

"There, now that wasn't too hard, was it?" Loretta asked as she came back into the room carrying a bag.

"Charlie said your father would take me to the hotel after I got the clothes. Is he here?"

"Nope."

"Will he be home soon?"

"Could be."

"What does that mean?"

"He could be home soon or he could be home in five hours."

I wasn't waiting there for five hours.

"Is the hotel far from here?" I asked.

"Naw. Less than two kilometres, straight along Kelsey."

"Then I guess I'll just walk."

"By yourself?"

"Well, yeah, I guess so. You said it wasn't far. I'm sure I can find it."

"Finding the hotel isn't the problem, it's what might find *you* on the way," she said.

I'd heard that line before. "You mean a bear, right?" I paused. "But I'm in town. There can't be any bears in town."

Loretta laughed. "You're on the outskirts of town, but there are people who live right in the heart of town who've had bears break down their front doors or smash up their cars."

"Come on, nobody would just let polar bears walk around through the town."

"Nobody *lets* them. We have a whole Bear Patrol that guards the place. When people see a polar bear they call, and the patrol comes fast. But they can't be everywhere. Sometimes a bear sneaks in. It isn't that hard at night, especially when the snow is blowing."

"But why would the bears come into town? Wouldn't they be frightened of the people?"

She shook her head. "You don't know anything about bears, do you?"

"I read a little," I said, looking away.

"And did you read how big they get?"

"Up to about seven hundred kilograms for a male."

"And did you also read that they're the only animal in the world that is not only unafraid of humans but will actively seek them out . . . to eat?"

"Eat?"

"Like a snack. People McNuggets. For polar bears we're no

different from a seal except we're easier to catch and they don't have to spit out the fur afterwards."

"And you're saying that could happen if I walk?" I asked.

"Could. You might just get a close encounter with a polar bear."

"Can I call a cab or something? I need to get to the motel." *And away from you,* I thought.

"No cab." She gave a big sigh. "I guess there's one way." She walked over to the front door. Off to the side was a coat rack; she took down a parka and started to put it on.

"You're going to drive me?" I asked. She didn't look old enough to drive and I hadn't seen a car, although there could have been one parked around back.

"Drive? I'm only fourteen. I was going to walk with you," she said as she took off her slippers and started to lace up her boots.

I laughed. "And that's going to make me safe? Won't that just mean there's two of us for the bears to eat?"

"Not likely. Don't worry, I'll protect you."

"And how are you going to do that?" I asked in disbelief.

"Oh, I've got an idea or two," she said. She reached over and opened up a tall cabinet right beside the door.

"A gun!" I exclaimed as she pulled out a rifle.

"You noticed."

"Is it . . . is it loaded?"

"It better be or it won't do either of us any good." She opened the breech with a loud *click-click* and tilted it toward me. "A bullet in the chamber and the clip is loaded."

"You shouldn't be fooling around with that!" I exclaimed.

"I'm not fooling around with anything. I've been around guns all my life. The first time I went hunting with my father and grandfather I was only six. I bet you've never even fired a gun have you?" she snickered.

I didn't like being laughed at. "Where I come from you don't need to wander around carrying a gun."

"And just where is that?"

"Mississauga."

"Missi-whata?"

"Mississauga. It's a city . . . a big city . . . half a million people big . . . and you've never heard of it?" I scoffed.

"So shoot me!" She paused and smiled sweetly. "Oh, but I forgot, you can't shoot me because you don't know how, and besides, I'm the one with the gun," she said as she patted the barrel of the rifle. "So do you want to wait here all evening or do you want to go to your motel?"

"Motel," I answered.

"Good. Let's get going so my whole night isn't totally wasted."

Chapter Twelve

I trudged along beside her silently. I wasn't that interested in conversation anyway. I was pretty occupied craning my neck, searching for a glimpse of something big and white hiding among all the small white particles of snow flying through the air. Glowing in the near distance were the lights of the town. As we moved closer I could even make out the darkened outlines of the buildings.

I was so focused on looking up ahead that I tripped over a rock and stumbled forward. Loretta turned around and gave me a look that said much more than I wanted to hear. It wasn't my fault I tripped—the boots were clunky and heavy. Then again, at least they were warm.

The same could be said for the parka. With the hood pulled up I even managed to escape from the wind. And now that I knew how warm it was, I was finding it hard to care what I looked like. I guess it didn't hurt that it was dark and there was nobody around to impress.

"Oh my goodness!" Loretta came to a sudden stop and I almost bumped into her.

I snapped out of my thoughts and pressed in closer to her side. "What is it?" I asked anxiously. My unspoken thought was that it must be a bear.

"Don't you see it?"

"Where?" I asked, peering hard in the direction she was looking. I couldn't see anything . . . except maybe . . .

"Do you see it?" she asked again.

"I think . . . maybe . . . is it a bear?"

She snickered. "There's nothing. I was just yanking your chain."

She turned and started to walk away as my jaw dropped to the ground. I stood there, frozen in place.

Two dozen paces away she stopped and turned back to face me. "Just because there wasn't a bear this time doesn't mean there won't be one in a few minutes!" she called out. She started walking again.

What was with this girl? What had I ever done to deserve such a hard time from her? The last thing in the world I wanted to do was follow after her. But I looked around at the driving snow—snow that could be hiding anything—and realized suddenly that following her was actually the second last thing I wanted to do: being eaten by a bear was in last place. I started jogging after her.

"Anybody ever tell you that you're funny?" I asked as I caught up to her.

"No," she said, slowing down and turning partway around to face me.

"Yeah, well, there's a reason for that," I said as I continued past her and kept on walking toward the lights.

As we moved along, with the sound of her feet crunching along behind me, I began to wonder if it was such a smart thing to insult somebody and then have them walking behind you carrying a gun. Maybe it would be smarter to try to make friends. I stopped and waited for her to catch up to me.

"So what do kids do for fun up here?" I asked.

"Is that a crack?" she asked defiantly.

"No, I just wanted to know . . . honestly."

"Lots of things. We do lots of things."

"Like what?"

"Skidooing, snowshoeing, skating, hunting, swimming—"

"Swimming? I didn't think it would ever get warm enough for swimming!"

"Not in the bay . . . at the recreation centre."

"I didn't know you had a rec centre."

"You don't seem to know much. What did you think, we all just hang around our igloos and suck on blubber?"

"No, I just—"

"Why do all you people from down south think we're just a bunch of simple hicks?" she demanded.

"I don't think that you're—"

"The stupid questions we get and the stupid things southerners say and do always amaze me!"

"All I wanted to know was what you did for fun," I said apologetically.

"Well, *you* can't take part in my very favourite activity."

"What's that?" I asked

"Making fun of stupid tourists."

I wanted to say something in reply—something clever that would put her in her place—but my brain felt even more numb than my fingertips and I just trudged along in silence. Thank goodness we were almost in town. Soon I could shake my escort.

The street became wider and we soon approached buildings on both sides. These were mainly houses, but there were a few stores scattered among them. I tried to look at them out of the corner of my eye without turning my head too far either way. Without exception there were lights glowing in the windows and smoke billowed from the chimneys. A woman stood in the front window of one of the houses. She waved. Instinctively I started to wave back before I realized that of course she was waving at Loretta and not me. I could just imagine Loretta laughing at me—again. I tucked my head down and picked up the pace. The faster I got there the sooner I could leave her behind.

"This is it," Loretta said.

"*What* is it?" I asked, looking around.

"This is where you're staying," she said, pointing to a small-ish-looking building.

"This is the motel?" It didn't seem nearly big enough for all my senior buddies and me.

"It's bigger than it looks from the front. Charlie's put on a couple of extensions on the back. You can't see them from here."

I didn't see any extensions, but what I could see, now that I looked closer, was a small neon sign hanging on a strange angle in the window. It glowed out "M O T L." The "E" was nowhere to be seen.

Loretta started up the path and I followed after her, as usual. As she pushed open the front door it gave a loud *ping*—there was a bell attached to it. It *pinged* again as I managed to struggle against the wind and closed it behind us. We stood in the "lobby" of the "motel," which wasn't any bigger than Loretta's place. Actually, it looked just like the living room of her house.

"Look familiar?" Loretta asked. "My grandfather built both this place and my house."

I was getting tired of her answering the questions I hadn't even asked yet.

She pulled off her mitts and put the rifle down in the corner behind the door. Two other rifles already stood there against the wall. What was with all these guns? Was this the north or the Wild West? Loretta started to undo her parka. I did the same, except I took mine off completely. Inside, in the light, with people I'd at least talked to before, I didn't want to be seen in that coat.

90

My ears perked up as I heard voices coming from down the corridor. Loretta motioned for me to follow her. Peeking in the first door we came to, we could see Charlie sitting in a chair with his back to us. The members of the tour group were sitting in a semicircle around him and he was talking about the bears. I started to listen, but my attention was captured by the appearance of the audience. These people were *really* old!

I didn't have much experience with old people. My father's parents had died before I was born, and my mother's parents lived at the other end of the country, so we saw them only once or twice a year. I looked around the room, from person to person. They all had interchangeable grey hair, wrinkles and spots.

One of the women smiled and waved as my eyes met hers. At first I was a little taken aback, but then I recognized her from the airport runway. I gave her a weak smile and a little wave in return.

Probably alerted by the woman's wave, Charlie turned slightly around and caught sight of me and Loretta. "So, you got all set up?"

"Everything," I answered, holding up the parka ever so slightly but trying to show only the dull green lining instead of the colourful outside. I wondered if I could wear it inside out.

"Loretta?" Charlie asked, and what I heard was the unspoken question "What are you doing here?"

"Dad wasn't home so I outfitted him and walked him over," she explained.

"Thanks. Why don't you go and help yourself in the kitchen. I'll get you a drive back home in a while."

She nodded and disappeared.

"Have a seat, Kevin," Charlie said. "We're talking about the white bears."

I scanned the room. Every seat was full.

"You can come and sit here," the friendly woman offered as she squeezed in close to her husband, leaving a small space beside her on the couch. I crossed the room and settled in, making sure I didn't sit on top of her.

"What was the last question?" Charlie asked.

"I asked if you'd had any personal experience with bears walking into town," a man said.

"More than my share. You see the window?" Charlie said, pointing behind me.

We all swivelled our heads around to look at a small window at the far end of the room.

"Five years ago I had a bear smash that glass and try to climb in."

There were gasps from around the room, and I thought I saw the two people closest to the window lean slightly away from it, as though another bear might just be on schedule to appear.

"What did you do?" somebody asked.

"I'm telling you, I was of two minds. On the one hand I wanted to run and get my camera, and on the other hand I needed my gun."

"And which did you grab?"

"My gun. Dead people don't take such good pictures."

"And what happened?"

Charlie paused, and without another word I knew what the answer was going to be. "I didn't have any choice. I had to take a shot at it. Hit it in the shoulder when it was halfway through the window."

"And?"

"And it climbed back out. I had to call the Polar Bear Alert for the Bear Patrol. Nothing I can think of is worse than a wounded polar bear in town. That reminds me. The Polar Bear Alert number is 675-BEAR. If any of you see a bear in town or somebody in danger, you drop whatever you're doing and dial that number."

"Even if it means missing a great picture?" somebody asked.

Charlie started to laugh. "A true photographer . . . I'm going to have to keep a close eye on you." Everybody started to chuckle and laugh along. "That's where the real danger is on these photo-safaris. If I wanted to keep people safe I'd just keep them away from the bears, but that isn't what you came up here for, is it?"

There was a murmuring of responses from around the room.

"So the trick is to get you close enough to get the shots, but safe enough not to get hurt. Just remember, it's better to miss a shot than lose a life. These bears are dangerous. More dangerous than any other animal on the face of this earth."

"The most dangerous?" a man asked.

"Without a doubt," Charlie said.

"Well, I've been on photo-safaris around the world, and even tigers and lions shy away from people. It's only the old and injured that sometimes prey on people."

"Polar bears are different . . . not only because they're bigger than those other animals—a lot bigger—but also because every single polar bear, I repeat, *every single polar bear,* is potentially dangerous. Each bear has its own personality and temperament, and we just can't predict what they're going to do. What *can* be predicted is that, unlike every other animal I know, they won't be scared of man. Living up here on the ice, they really have never had much contact with humans, so they've never learned to be afraid. For hundreds of thousands of years the polar bear has been the master of its territory. It fears nothing, and everything it comes across is nothing more than food. To a polar bear, *you* are nothing but food, and an easy snack at that."

"And that's why they come into town, looking for people to eat?" a woman asked anxiously. She was so tiny she looked as though she wouldn't be more than a mouthful for a polar bear.

"Not people. Just food, and to them almost anything is food. Polar bears are creatures of opportunity, and a town filled with people and their garbage is a great opportunity. It's really the garbage, and the smell of that garbage, that draws the bears in."

"Do they have a good sense of smell?"

"That's the bears' best sense. A polar bear can smell a seal through a metre of snow from twenty kilometres away."

"Wow," I said softly as others used different words to express the same feeling.

"The bears have to have a great sense of smell because they tend to be fairly nearsighted. Mainly what they notice is motion. If you were upwind of a bear, didn't move and didn't make a sound, it would possibly pass within two dozen metres of you and not notice a thing." A smile grew on Charlie's face. "Not that I've ever tried it. Most people start to move before a bear has a chance to get that close."

"Believe me, I'd run," I said to myself softly, but obviously loud enough for Charlie to hear.

"Unfortunately," he pointed out, "that's the very worst thing a person can do."

"What do you mean?" I asked.

"Unless you're the fastest man on the planet you can't outrun a polar bear. For short bursts, say a couple hundred metres, a grown polar bear can run at an amazing pace. It's incredible to watch one in full flight. You wouldn't believe anything that big could move that fast."

"Do you think we'll have a chance to see one run like that?" a man asked.

"Probably not. They're fairly lazy until the weather turns cold."

"This isn't cold?" I asked. The tips of my toes were still tingling, despite the warm boots I was now wearing.

"Not to a polar bear. With their heavy fur and thick layers of fat, the whites are so well insulated that they overheat easily. You'll probably notice that right after the bears do anything too physical they'll either submerge in water or lie flat on their bellies, legs stretched out, on a patch of snow or ice, to cool down." Charlie took a big sip from his mug of coffee before continuing. "If you find yourself confronted by a bear you have to back away, slowly."

"This all sounds very scary. Maybe it wasn't wise for us to come on this trip," a woman commented to the man sitting beside her. I presumed it was her husband. "I'm afraid to walk down the street."

"I'm sure there's nothing to worry about," the man replied, patting her on the hand.

"I'm sorry if I scared you . . . although that is part of what I wanted to do. Being scared generally makes people safer. During the day, in town, you are completely safe. The Bear Patrol makes sure of that. The key is to take proper precautions in other areas. Maybe this is a good time for me to draw your attention to the sign on the wall."

He pointed to a large yellow sign which I'd noticed a few minutes earlier and had been curious about. In black lettering it said: "POLAR BEAR ALERT." Below was a large bear pawprint, with five sharp claws. On the bottom in smaller lettering it read; "Stop! Don't walk in this area!"

"These signs are placed in locations frequented by bears."

"That sounds like everywhere except the bathroom," the woman beside me said, and there was a fair bit of nervous laughter.

"Actually, I can tell you a pretty good story about a bear trying to get into an outhouse while one of my uncles was . . .

how should I say . . . busy. He was sitting there, just getting
ready to take care of the paperwork, when . . ." Charlie stopped
and looked around the room. "Maybe this isn't a story that I
should be telling in mixed company."

"Come on, son, there isn't anything you're going to say that
we haven't heard or seen or had happen to us," the woman
chided him. Others nodded their heads and encouraged him to
continue.

"After all, we're all old enough to be your parents," somebody added.

"Not all of you," Charlie said, nodding in my direction. I felt
every eye shift to me and I looked down.

"Getting back to the signs. You'll see them primarily along
the shores, especially where there are boulders and other places
for bears to take shelter. Avoiding those areas is your best bet
to avoid meeting a bear unexpectedly."

"Any other tips?" a woman asked.

"Travel in groups, make noise when you walk and avoid dark
and poorly lit areas. When we're out together on the tundra, it
is essential that nobody wanders away from the group or very
far from the tundra buggy. In the buggy you're as safe as a baby
in its mother's arms. Away from the buggy and on the ground
there's always a risk."

"What if we want to stay on the buggy all the time?" a man
asked.

"Then you're free to stay aboard and take all your shots from
there, although I think some of the best shots, especially of the
plant life, will need to be taken from ground level and not from
way up on top of the buggy. Which reminds me, I want to talk a
bit about how to get the best possible shots, so let's take a short
break, everybody can get a coffee, and then we'll have some
discussion about photography. Okay?"

That idea was more than fine with me. I'd have a chance to

get some much-needed instruction about taking pictures without it being too obvious that I had no idea what I was doing. I would just keep my mouth shut, listen and learn.

Most of the seniors got to their feet. A few of them needed a hand to rise, and while most of them moved well, there were a few who seemed only able to shuffle. A number of people went down the hall the way Loretta had vanished, I guess to fetch coffee.

I didn't like coffee at all, but I needed a caffeine fix badly. Maybe they had some Coke in the kitchen.

"Kevin?"

I turned back around to face Charlie.

"The things I'm going to talk to them about tonight are pretty basic. General stuff about composition, background, framing the subject, correct f-stops and lens selection. I'm afraid you'll probably find all of it pretty boring."

"A little," I lied. I'd have to at least understand what any of those things were to be bored by them. I'd be hanging on every word he said. The secret would be not looking like I was paying attention when I really was. Now that was a kick in the pants—in school I always had to look like I was listening when I really wasn't!

"I'm afraid I have to teach them at the level where they're at. Most of them are just beginners who need all the instruction they can get, and . . . wait a minute, I have an idea! Rather than being a student tonight, you can help me teach the others!"

My mouth dropped open. The only thought I had was wondering if he'd let me keep the parka when he tossed me out in the snow after he found out I didn't know squat about photography.

Chapter Thirteen

"But I can't do that," I sputtered. There was no way I was going to make a complete fool of myself pretending to be an experienced photographer when I barely knew which end of a camera was up!

"You can't? Why not? Don't you want to help?" Charlie asked. His face grew serious and his eyes seemed to glare.

"No, I don't mind helping," I answered quickly. "It's just that . . . I can't."

"And why is that?"

"Because . . . because . . ." *Think, think, think . . . come up with some reason!*

"Because why?" he demanded.

"Because of Loretta," I stammered. *Why did I say that?*

"What about Loretta?"

"I'm . . . going someplace with her." Another lie that made no sense.

"Going out where with Loretta?"

"To the . . . to the . . ." Nothing was coming.

"Is she taking you to the rec centre?" Charlie asked.

"Exactly!" I practically yelled, I was so thrilled that he'd given me an answer.

The granite of his face softened. "That place sure is popular with the kids. Loretta seems to spend all here spare time there, and so does every other kid in town."

"So it's okay that I go with her?" I asked hesitantly.

Charlie nodded his head. "Of course. Who am I to stop you from having some fun? After all, I'm not here to be your parent. You do what you want. Besides, I can understand you wanting to get away and be with people your own age."

Unexpectedly he placed one of his massive hands on my shoulder. He leaned close to whisper in my ear. "I really like these seniors tours, and some of the old folks are just great, but sometimes it feels a bit strange when everybody is so much older than me . . . so I can just imagine how *you* must feel. Has Loretta arranged a ride?"

"Umm, no." At least that part was true. She could hardly arrange a ride for some place she didn't know we were going. "I think we're just going to walk."

"Walk?" he bellowed, and I jumped as heads turned to face us. "Weren't you listening to anything I was talking about here tonight?"

"Every word!" I objected. If I'd been listening half as hard in school, my marks would have been back where my parents wanted them.

"Then why would you walk to an isolated spot, by the shore, at night, just the two of you?" he demanded.

"I thought it was here in town," I said. I obviously didn't have any idea where it was, but why would it be anywhere else?

"It's not in town. It's down the way, sitting by itself out by the shore. There are Polar Bear Alert signs all around it, and . . ." He paused. "But you wouldn't know any of that, would you?"

"No," I said, shaking my head furiously. "I don't know anything!"

He shook his head slowly. "Sometimes my temper gets the better of me. I shouldn't have raised my voice to you like I did. There's no reason to be mad at you."

I felt an immense sense of relief.

"It's Loretta I should be mad at!" he said, and his temper flared again. "She knows better than to put the two of you in danger like that! Darn fool girl is too proud and too independent for her own good! Always thinks she knows best. You know, you can't tell that girl anything!"

That did sound like the Loretta I knew. Well, at least it wasn't just me she was pigheaded with.

"I'm going to give her a piece of my mind!" Charlie said. He turned around and took a step toward the hall.

"No, you can't!" I yelled, and to my utter shock I grabbed him by the arm and actually spun him slightly around. I'd always heard that fear could generate super-strength, and I was definitely scared.

Charlie looked down at me, his face bearing a scowl that might have been meant for Loretta but was now aimed at me.

I swallowed hard. "Please don't talk to her," I begged.

"Why not?" he demanded.

"Because . . . umm . . . maybe I didn't really understand what she meant . . . or I got things wrong . . . or she *has* a ride . . . or . . ."

"Because she'll be mad at you," Charlie said.

"Yeah," I snorted. She and Charlie would both be plenty mad at me if they found out the lies I'd being weaving to try to get myself out of this spot.

His angry glare softened for a second time and was replaced by a smile. "Okay, I guess I understand."

"You do?" I asked, confused because I didn't fully understand it myself.

"If I go in and rag all over her then she'll know you were talking to me about the two of you heading out, and she'll take it out on you."

"Yeah," I said, nodding my head vigorously.

"And with her temper you really don't want to get her mad," Charlie said. "She's quick to anger and slow to cool."

Again, he wasn't telling me anything that wasn't obvious.

"And if she gets angry, she might not take you to the centre," he continued.

I nodded.

"But I still can't let the two of you go off by yourselves. I'll arrange for somebody to drive you there, and you have to promise you'll have her call me for a ride back. Okay?"

"Sure, of course. I really appreciate it," I said. I appreciated it a lot more, and for different reasons, than Charlie knew.

"That's no problem. And don't be embarrassed," Charlie said. "I'm not so old that I don't remember what it's like to be sweet on some girl."

"Sweet on . . . ? You think I'm sweet on Loretta?" I asked in disbelief.

"Oh, I don't know what you kids call it nowadays. Anyway, it doesn't surprise me that the two of you would hit it off."

"It doesn't?" The only way the two of us could have "hit it off" was if we both had hammers and were involved in some sort of fight.

"Nope, not at all. Maybe I shouldn't mention it, but I know that Loretta sometimes has some problems with kids her own age."

I could see that—actually, I could see her having trouble with teenagers, small children, adults and members of different species. She was one annoying kid.

"And I think she has those problems because she always acts like she's a lot older than fourteen. You know, more mature. And you seem older to me too . . . more responsible."

"Thanks," I mumbled.

"So I promise you I won't yell at her when I tell her the two of you have to get a ride to and from the rec centre."

"Couldn't I tell her?" I pleaded. I knew if they talked now my whole story would crumble into a messy pile of lies.

Charlie shrugged. "As long as you convince her that you two have to accept a ride. Do you think you can talk her into it? She's pretty stubborn."

"Don't worry, she'll agree. Besides, shouldn't you get back to your camera talk?" I gestured toward the room. The seniors who had left were all back, their cameras on their laps, hands balancing cups of coffee and fresh-baked muffins.

"Yeah, you're right, I'd better get going before somebody falls asleep. The cook is in the kitchen and she's due to leave to go home in a few minutes. She drives right past the rec centre. Tell her I asked if she could drop the two of you off on her way home."

"Sure, okay, that sounds good."

I hurried down the hall and pushed through the swinging door that led into the kitchen. Loretta was sitting on a stool by a counter. She briefly looked up from the magazine she was reading, saw it was only me, and dropped her eyes back down to the page. There was nobody else in the room.

"Where's the cook?" I asked. "She hasn't left, has she?"

"Not yet. She's in the cold cellar," Loretta replied, jerking her thumb toward a closed door over at the far side of the room. "Why are you interested in the cook?"

"Because Charlie wants her to give us a drive."

Loretta looked up from her magazine and fixed me with a steely gaze. "What did you say?"

"The cook has to give us a drive."

"Us, as in you and me?" Her tone of voice said loads about how she felt about this turn of events.

I nodded.

"And why would she need to drive the two of us anywhere?" she asked.

"Because your uncle wants her to," I replied. That part was true. Now for the lie. "He wants you to show me around the rec centre."

"Show you around or be your babysitter?"

"Show me around. He knew it would be strange for me to spend all week with nothing but old people."

"That's not my problem. I've got things to do tonight."

"You do?" I asked.

"You sound surprised," she snapped. "You don't think I have friends or that there's anything to do in this town?"

"N-no, of course not," I stammered. "I just . . . I just . . . what are you going to be doing?"

She didn't answer right away and her eyes fell to the floor. "I was going to the rec centre," she finally muttered.

"Couldn't I come along?" I pleaded.

"Don't whine! You're even more annoying when you whine!"

"I wasn't whining!" I protested. "I'd just appreciate it if you'd let me come along. I know it would be a favour . . . I'd owe you one."

"No you wouldn't," she said.

"I wouldn't?"

"No. You'd owe me three. You already owed me one for getting you those clothes, and another for walking you here. Do you have any money?"

"Yeah, I have some . . . why?" Did she expect me to pay her to take me to the rec centre?

"I was just getting ready to eat supper when you came banging on my door. If I'm taking you to the centre then you have to treat for a burger—"

"Sure, no problem!" I interrupted.

"And some fries and a drink."

"I'll pay!" I said. To get out of this situation I would have put out a lot more money than this was going to cost.

"Good! And there's one more thing."

"What?"

"You have to try to be a little less annoying."

"Me? You want *me* to try to be less annoying? How about . . . ?" I let the sentence trail away. I wasn't in any sort of position to argue or accuse. I weakly nodded my head and she answered with a smug little smile.

Chapter Fourteen

"Thanks for the ride," I said as I climbed out of the pickup truck and then closed the door behind me. The cook, Naomi, gave a little wave goodbye and the truck started off.

Loretta had climbed out of the truck first and had already walked off and into the centre. I stopped and looked. It was a big, shiny, new building. A warm light escaped through the large windows that wrapped around the front and mingled with the glow coming off the lampposts that dotted the parking lot. There were a couple of dozen cars all parked close to the exit.

Standing there, I could have been back home in Mississauga, or in the suburbs of any city anywhere in North America. Then, as I listened, I heard the unmistakable sound of waves hitting the shore and remembered exactly where I was. I looked off to the far end of the parking lot where the lights faded and saw a cluster of boulder-sized rocks, large enough to hide a polar bear. Suddenly I felt very alone out there by myself and I hurried after Loretta.

Pushing through the doors I was greeted by a gust of hot air and a blast of loud music. There were groups of kids, in twos and threes and fours, sitting around tables or standing around talking. I looked from group to group trying to find Loretta. I loosened my parka and started to undo the zipper. Where had she gone to?

Nervously I moved among the groups of kids. Mostly they were too busy to even take notice of me. A couple of them looked up, saw me, then turned back to their activities. There was a doorway marked "Gymnasium" and I wondered if maybe that's where she'd gone. I grabbed the handle of the door and started to open it.

"You can't go in there!"

I let go of the door as if it were too hot to handle and spun around. There were three boys standing there. They were about my age, and I recognized a couple of them from the cluster of kids who had been sitting by the front door. They must have followed me.

"Sorry," I apologized, "I didn't know." I turned and started to walk down the open corridor to the right.

"You can't go there, either!" the same voice called out.

I stopped and spun around. "I can't?" I asked anxiously.

"No, you can't," came the reply from one of the four. He stepped forward. He had jet-black hair, tied in a ponytail, and he was about my age and size. There was a threatening look on his face.

"Where can I go?"

"Out through the doors you came through. This centre isn't for the tourists. It's only for locals!"

The other three nodded in agreement.

"I didn't know . . . I'm sorry," I sputtered.

"Well now you do, so you better get going."

Get going? And how was I supposed to do that? "But I'm here with somebody," I said. Maybe that would make it okay.

"Who?" he demanded.

"Loretta."

"You're a friend of Loretta's?"

"Yeah." Maybe calling her a friend was pushing it, but at this point I would have claimed we were related. "Do you know her?"

"Unfortunately," he replied, and of course I could understand his sentiments. He smiled, and I felt myself relax. "You know what they say . . . any friend of Loretta's . . . is a jerkface."

The other three started laughing. In the background I noticed that a few more kids were watching what was going on and were drifting over in our direction.

"It's nice Loretta finally found herself a friend." He paused. "And judging from your parka you must be her girlfriend. Were they all out of clothes in the boys' section where you shop or do you like dressing like a girl?"

"My baggage got left in Winnipeg," I tried to explain. "Loretta lent me the parka."

"Isn't that special. You and your new friend even share clothes." He laughed. "Do you share makeup as well?"

He came a few steps closer, as did his three friends. There were more kids gathering in a little semicircle behind them. It seemed as though they were after some excitement. This wasn't looking good.

I felt myself straighten up, and I had to fight the urge to curl my fingers into fists. I didn't want to fight. I had to try to talk my way out of this.

"Do you just dress like a girl, or do you fight like one as well?"

At least that question left no doubt about where this was leading. I took a deep breath and tried to slow my racing heart. I eased the tension out of my shoulders, just the way I'd been taught.

He moved in closer until we were no more than a metre apart. I looked him square in the eyes. If I didn't show fear, maybe he'd back away and leave me alone.

"Oomph!" Air rushed out of my lungs as he pushed me forcefully backwards. I staggered and then regained my balance.

"I don't want to fight," I said.

"Well I do!"

"Come on, " I reasoned with him, "it can't be any fun fighting with somebody who isn't fighting back."

"That's where you're wrong! It'll make it easier for me to beat you up if you just stand there," he said as he pushed me again.

This time I was ready for it and he moved me only slightly back. Talking my way out of this didn't look as though it was going to work. Slowly I raised my fists and turned to the side.

"I have to warn you not to fight with me," I said quietly. I'd practised those words many times before but had never had actually said them to anybody other than my reflection in the mirror.

"Warn me?" he snapped. "Why, are you going to bleed all over me if I'm not careful?"

There was a ripple of snorts, chuckles and laughter from behind him. My back was almost to the wall and I was grateful that the circle of spectators—kids who probably were his friends—couldn't get behind me.

"Let me warn you about *this*!" he yelled as he swung his right fist at me.

I dodged to the side and his fist narrowly missed my face, passing so close I could hear the wind whistle by my ear. Awkwardly and off balance he swung his left hand now. I used my arm to turn his fist aside, stepped forward in a twisting motion and then all in one movement pushed him from behind. He toppled over and slammed into the wall.

We both turned again to face each other. Now his friends were behind me.

"You're going to pay for that!" he screamed. I could see blood flowing from his mouth.

In the rush of adrenaline I was feeling I'd pushed him too hard and he hadn't had time to bring his arms up to protect himself, so it was his face that had hit the wall. The look in his eyes was total and complete rage, and I knew that whatever he was feeling before meant nothing. Now, he wanted to hurt me badly.

Despite the tightening in my chest I had to stay calm and relaxed and loose.

He made a growling sound and then rushed at me, swinging his arms wildly. I blocked the first punch and stepped to the side, and as he roared past me I stuck out my leg, sweeping him off his feet and causing him to land with a loud thud in a heap on the floor. He struggled to his feet with the help of his friends. He still looked enraged, but now he looked puzzled as well. He couldn't understand what was happening to him. It was supposed to be *me* that was getting hurt!

"I still don't want to fight," I said. My instructor would have been proud of me.

"I'm going to beat you bad," he grumbled under his breath.

I shook my head slowly. I'd had enough of him. If he rushed me again he could count on somebody getting hurt, and it wasn't going to be me. Maybe my instructor wouldn't be *that* proud. I tensed and then relaxed the muscles in my leading leg in preparation for a front kick. I was going to catch him square in the face with this one and end it.

"All right, break it up!" screamed an adult voice.

The kid lowered his fists and took a step back. The circle of kids also retreated slightly as they parted to allow a man to step forward. He wasn't very tall, but he was thick and muscular looking.

"I should have known you'd be at the centre of whatever trouble is happening, Tim," he said to the kid.

"I didn't do anything!" he protested.

"Sure, and I guess your mouth is bleeding because you cut yourself shaving."

The kid, Tim I guess, reached up and brushed away the blood that was trickling from the corner of his mouth. He looked at his hand and then at me. His eyes were filled with rage, and I stepped back involuntarily.

"It's all his fault!" he yelled, pointing at me. "He came in here and started a fight with me!"

I opened my mouth in shock. His statement had left me more off balance than the pushes he'd given me.

"He's lying!" called out a voice. "Tim started everything!"

I looked up, as did every other pair of eyes. Directly above me, leaning over a second-floor railing, was Loretta.

"Kevin told him he didn't want to fight and Tim just came at him," she said. "Kevin didn't even hit him. He just dodged around, and Tim is so stupid he smashed into the wall!" Loretta started to laugh, and I could hear other people chuckling as well.

"Shut up, Wolfman!" Tim screamed.

"Why don't you shut up youself you stupid—"

"Enough!" the man hollered even louder, interrupting Loretta. "Did other people see it the way Loretta did?" he asked the crowd.

"Yeah, Tim started it," a girl answered, and half a dozen others added their agreement.

The man nodded his head. "Okay, everybody break it up. Go back to what you were doing."

Reluctantly the crowd started to drift away. I figured they were all disappointed because they didn't get to see the big show they'd been looking forward to.

"That's it, Tim. You're banned from the rec centre for one week," the man said.

"That's not fair!"

"It's completely fair. I told you that's what would happen if I caught you fighting again."

"You can't do that!"

"I can, and if I hear another word out of you it won't be one week, it'll be two. Any questions?"

Tim mumbled a response that I couldn't hear but I could imagine.

"Come with me and we'll call your brother to come and get you," the man said.

"He's not home . . . he's probably at the bar," Tim answered.

The man shook his head. "There's no point calling him there because he won't be able to drive. Go to my office and I'll be there in a couple of minutes to drive you home."

"This isn't the end," Tim snapped at me.

"It is for tonight," the man said.

"And you're lucky," Loretta added. "He was beating you up and he hadn't even hit you. Imagine what would have happened if he'd taken a swing!"

"That's enough out of you as well, Loretta, unless you want to be banned again as well," the man warned.

"I'll shut up," she offered, holding up her hands as though in surrender.

What did he mean, "again"? Had Loretta been banned from there as well?

Eyes downcast, Tim walked away without saying another word.

"Are your parents here at the centre?" the man asked me.

I wished they were. It would have been wonderful to have had my parents to take care of everything . . . including me.

"My parents aren't even in Churchill. They're in Mississauga."

"Then who are you staying with?" he asked.

"My uncle," Loretta said. She had come down the stairs and appeared now at my side. "And I'm helping him to stay out of trouble."

"You?" the man asked.

"Yeah, me!" she answered defiantly.

He chuckled. "I can't see anybody ever putting you in charge of the keeping-out-of-trouble department." The man turned to me. "Sorry this had to happen. This is a friendly little place. How long are you staying for?"

"Till the end of the week."

"That's a good long visit. You're welcome to come in here anytime while you're in town."

"Thanks."

He walked away, presumably to take Tim home. I turned to Loretta.

"Yeah, a real friendly little place."

"Come on, you can't tell me there aren't any jerks in Mississippi."

"That's Mississauga."

"Whatever," she snorted. "Don't you have jerks?"

"Yeah, of course."

"Well so do we. You just happened to pick a fight with the second-biggest jerk in Churchill."

I already had an opinion as to who was the biggest jerk, but I didn't think Loretta was referring to herself.

"The biggest jerk," she continued, "is Tim's big brother."

I swallowed hard. This was not good news. "Big brother?"

"Yeah, and I don't just mean older brother, which he is, but *big* brother. He's bigger than Tim . . . a lot bigger." She paused and smiled. "And I don't think he's going to be any too happy about Tim getting beaten up. Not happy at all." She started to chuckle.

I was so pleased that I'd added some joy to her life.

"Why did he call you 'wolfman'?" I asked.

"Why not? It's my name."

"Your name is Wolfman?"

"Yeah. Loretta Janice Wolfman. Do you have a problem with that?"

"Not me!"

"Because it's a native name, and if you have problems with natives—"

"I don't have problems with anything!" I protested. "It's just that I thought you'd have the same last name as Charlie . . . isn't your father his brother?"

"Yeah, but my mother's name is Wolfman. I use her name. So, anyway, what's *your* last name?"

Oh great. "Spreekmeester," I said softly.

"And you thought *my* name was strange." She laughed. "At least mine is part of my heritage."

"Well so is mine."

"And what tribe exactly are the Spreekmeesters from?"

"Not a tribe, a country. It's a Dutch name. In Holland every second person is a Spreekmeester!" I didn't think that was right, but I knew she didn't know any better. And better still, it shut her up.

"So where did you learn how to fight like that?" Loretta asked. "You looked like one of those karate guys from the movies . . . except, you know, not as good or good looking."

"Thanks a lot. It's called Tae Kwon Do. It's like karate except it's from Korea," I explained.

"Do you have a black belt?"

I shook my head. "I had a red belt."

"Had?"

"Yeah, I don't take lessons any more."

"Why would you stop doing something cool like that I'd love to learn how to take care of people who bother me. And believe me, there are a *lot* of people who bother me."

I believed her, but I also believed there were far more people who she bothered. I had to hold back the urge to laugh. In all the years I'd been taking Tae Kwon Do, this was the very first time I'd ever had to use anything that I'd learned outside of classes or sparring in a gym. It was good to know that it worked.

"So why did you quit?"

"I don't know. I guess I just got tired of it," I explained, although as I was saying it I really couldn't remember what exactly had caused me to stop. I didn't mind the classes, and the tournaments could be fun, and it was definitely cool sparring with a partner.

"I just know that if I had a chance to take karate that I wouldn't stop until I was really good and had my black belt," Loretta said. "It's good to be the best at things you do."

That sounded just like something my parents always said, and I suddenly remembered why I'd dropped out of classes.

Chapter Fifteen

I awoke with a start to the sound of a roaring engine. Wide-eyed I sat bolt upright in bed and looked around. For a split second I struggled to remember where I was. Then, of course, it all came back. I wasn't in my own room in my house in Mississauga but in a small, sort of rundown motel room in Churchill. The engine roared again, and I stumbled out of bed and over to the window.

My eyes widened even more at the sight of the vehicle making all the noise. It looked as if a school bus had mated with a monster truck and had offspring. It was gigantic: the body of a large yellow bus sitting on top of enormous tires that looked much higher than I was tall. Slowly the vehicle rolled along the side of the motel. It was as high as the building! As it passed, I caught sight of a large platform, enclosed by a metal railing, attached to the back of the bus. It came to a stop beside a set of stairs on wheels, like the kind they roll up to help passengers on and off small planes. The roar of the engine was silenced.

The door opened and Charlie climbed out. He saw me watching him through the window and gave me a big, friendly wave. He climbed down the stairs and began inspecting the vehicle, checking out the tires and looking underneath the carriage. I was amazed to see that the top of Charlie's head wasn't even close to being as tall as the tires. He could easily walk right underneath this thing without even having to bend down. This was the largest vehicle I'd ever seen, and I had to go out and have a closer look. I hurried to pull on my clothes and head out.

I rushed through the kitchen. There were half a dozen seniors either sitting at the table eating breakfast or standing by the counter sipping what smelled like coffee. I was hungry myself but far more interested in having a look at the monster bus than I was in eating.

Going outside I was instantly hit by a gust of strong wind and almost blown back in the door. Maybe it was clear and sunny, but it was still windy and cold. I zipped up my parka—at least, Loretta's parka—and pulled on my gloves as I walked. I stared up at the vehicle, which seemed to be getting larger as I got closer. Stopping right beside it I leaned back and strained my neck to look up at the top.

"Good morning!" Charlie sang out.

"Hi."

"I thought you were still sleeping."

"I was, until you drove up with this thing. It practically shook me out of bed."

Charlie laughed. "It is a mite bit noisy. Have you had breakfast yet?"

"Not yet. I wanted to have a look at this thing first."

"Pretty amazing machine, isn't it?"

"Totally," I replied in awe.

"You should eat. We're leaving in about fifteen minutes. Besides, there'll be plenty of time to look at the tundra buggy during the ride."

"You mean we're riding on this?" I asked.

"How did you think we were going to see the bears?"

"I hadn't really thought about it," I admitted. I'd had far too many things to think about. My mind had been spinning so fast that I'd had a lot of trouble getting to sleep the night before.

"The buggy is the best way to see the bears."

"That's fantastic! But . . . but why is it so big?"

"It isn't *that* big. A couple of the tour companies have bigger ones," Charlie said.

"Bigger than this?"

"Yeah, Northern Tours has one that can seat sixty passengers, or it can be converted to let up to twenty people sleep on it and eat their meals right out there on the tundra."

"But it can't be any higher than this."

"You're right there. They're all about the same distance off the ground, a little under three metres. They have to be that high to keep everybody safe. Tall enough so a big male bear on his back legs can't quite reach up and take a swing at the tourist hanging over the side to take his picture. It's bad for business if a bear kills one of the people on your tour."

I tried to picture a bear leaning against the side of the tundra buggy, stretching up with its front paws trying to get at somebody.

"And of course the tires are the way they are for two reasons. I guess you can figure out one of them," Charlie said. "We need those monster tires to pull us through mud, muskeg, streams and small ponds."

That made sense. I couldn't picture anything stopping this thing.

"And the second reason, the one people don't usually think about, is to protect the plant life."

He was right, that certainly wasn't anything I'd thought about.

"Plants have only a few months to grow up here each year. Nothing grows fast. Maybe you've noticed how small the trees are."

I hadn't noticed. Actually, I hadn't really noticed much in the way of trees at all; there were mostly small shrubs and bushes.

"Down south a tree that's fifteen years old will be as tall as a house. Up here it's hardly taller than me. The same is true for all plant life. These big wheels distribute the weight and lessens the pressure on the ground plants. When you're out there today you'll see thin lines of brown extending into the distance. Those are places where a normal vehicle has been driven. The pressure of the wheels has killed all the vegetation. Environmentalists say when you go into the wild you should take only pictures and leave only footprints. Up here we try not to even leave prints behind."

Charlie walked underneath the buggy and I trailed behind him. I'd never seen the underside of a bus before. As he moved, he kept reaching up and checking on things. It was a stretch, even for somebody his height.

"I've got to make sure everything is sound." He continued to the front of the buggy and stopped directly beneath the engine.

"This is really important," he said reaching up and tapping a piece of metal. "This protects the radiator. The bears are always trying to break into the rad."

"Why would they want to do that?"

"For a drink. Rad fluid has a sort of sweet taste to it. Once they've had a taste of it they keep trying to get more."

"That can't be very good for them."

"It's actually very bad. The stuff is poison. If they get enough it can cause paralysis or blindness or kidney failure. All of those lead to death. Luckily the bears are so big that they don't often get enough fluid to do them serious harm, although they do get sick."

Charlie continued to check things out. I had no idea what he was doing. Actually, I didn't know anything about motors or cars or stuff like that. My mother said I was just like my father that way. It was both frustrating and embarrassing for my father when he had to get something done with the car. He was used to being smart, so being dumb didn't sit well with him. I sort of enjoyed it—at least when it was him, not when it was me.

"There," Charlie said, "as far as I can tell everything is fine and ready to go. Nothing's been sabotaged."

"Sabotaged? You mean someone would deliberately damage it?"

He shook his head sadly. "Last week it was a slashed tire."

"Maybe it happened when you were out on the tundra. Those bears have pretty sharp claws, right?"

"That they do, but they don't have screwdrivers."

"Screwdrivers!"

"When we took off the tire we found the broken-off tip of a screwdriver lodged inside."

"I guess it was kids being jerky," I said. I already had one candidate for him.

"I don't think so. The other times it happened it wasn't just jamming a screwdriver into a tire."

"Other times! How many times has it happened?"

"Two others. And whoever did it really knows about these buggies. They damaged something that couldn't be fixed and had to be shipped in from down south."

"Who would do that? Do you have enemies?"

"It wasn't just me," Charlie said. "Three of the other tundra buggies in town were damaged at the same time."

"Why?"

He shook his head. "We're not sure, but we have a couple of ideas."

I gave him a questioning look.

"We have some enviro-nuts in town who don't think we should be bringing people out to the tundra to see the bears."

"Why not?"

"They say we're harassing the bears and hurting the ecosystem. We've done our best to be environmentally sensitive, but there's no satisfying some of those people."

"And they'd do that to all the buggies?"

He shrugged. "Maybe, but there's no proof."

"You said you've got another idea?"

"Yeah, this one's got a little brother. I think you've met him."

"Tim?"

He scowled. "Tim Blackburn. His older brother, Kurtis, operates a small tour company in town."

"But I thought the damage was done to all the buggies in town," I said.

"To all the buggies except his."

"How did he explain that?" I asked. "That sounds suspicious."

"He says it's because he keeps his locked up in a fenced-in area by the shack he lives in. The rest of us don't protect our vehicles the same way."

"I guess that could explain it," I allowed.

"But that doesn't mean it's the truth," Charlie pointed out.

"But why do you suspect him? Does he get some extra business when the rest of the tours can't go out?"

"Nope. I even had a couple of rich Americans who were booked with me who offered him extra money, a lot extra, to take them out, and he refused," Charlie said.

"Then why?"

"Tim's older brother makes Tim seem like a good guy. He's a mean drunk, and he's drinking most of the time. Maybe he just does it to be nasty. I feel sorry for Tim having to live with him."

"What about their parents?" I asked.

"They don't live here. The two kids showed up alone in Churchill about two years ago. Not much said or known about their past, but judging from the way they act I figure their parents ran away from home."

I laughed along with Charlie.

"What's so funny?"

I turned to see Loretta standing there. I nodded a greeting and she sort of scowled back at me.

"Glad to see you decided to come along," Charlie said.

She shrugged.

"Loretta, can you go inside and hurry up our guests?" Charlie asked,

"Sure, no problem." She turned and headed back to the motel.

"Does Loretta come with you very often?"

"Hardly ever during the school year, but I thought I'd have her come today because of you."

"Me?"

"Sure. I've seen how the two of you hit it off and I thought it would be nice for you to have a friend along."

He was right about that. I would have loved to have had Ian around, or somebody else from school who was a friend. Heck, I'd almost rather have had Tim come along.

"Thanks," I said, smiling weakly.

Chapter Sixteen

The word "hurry" and this group didn't go together. Slowly, ever so slowly, seniors shuffled out of the motel and up the stairs into the tundra buggy. I helped move their personal things into the vehicle and then assisted the cook in bringing aboard the food and gear that would be needed to feed and care for everybody for the day.

Besides having a washroom, the buggy had a stove and a fridge. There were seats along the windows—singles, so everyone could have a window seat—a few beds, and two tables situated in the very middle of the floor. Out the back door there was a large metal platform, sort of like a patio for the tundra buggy. Charlie said that the best pictures would be taken from out there. He also said that we'd need to keep our coats and boots and gloves on all day because the vehicle wouldn't be heated. Heat would cause windows to fog up, which would interfere with taking clear pictures. A couple of the seniors complained that they couldn't be in the cold all day. Charlie told us if we'd wanted to stay warm we could have stayed down south. We'd come up here to take pictures.

The engine started up and the floor began to vibrate and rattle. The cook, Naomi, had all the seniors take a seat, and we rumbled off. I looked around for Loretta. She wasn't anywhere to be seen. I walked to the back of the buggy and I could see her standing on the platform, staring out into the distance. I opened the door.

"Mind if I join you?" I asked.

"Do what you want," she said, without turning around. Another fine example of local friendliness.

"How long until we reach the bears?"

"Could be only a few minutes, could be a few hours. This isn't like some zoo where the animals are sitting there waiting in their pens. We drive until we find them."

"Do you go out with your cousin very often?"

"Nope. Best tourist seasons are in the spring for migratory birds and in the fall for the bears. I'm in school."

"So this must be nice for you then. You get out of school and you get to see the bears." I was trying to sound positive.

"It's okay," she answered. "Can I ask you a question now?"

"Sure," I answered. I was a relief not to be making *all* the conversation.

"What's it like to be rich?"

"I'm not rich!"

"Don't you live in a big house?"

"Our house isn't that big," I answered. It certainly wasn't any bigger than any of the other houses that made up our subdivision.

"What do your parents do for a living?" she asked.

"My father's an obstetrician and my mother's a lawyer."

"That's what I figured. You're rich."

"We're not, honestly. We're just normal."

"Yeah, right. Normal families send their kids away on expensive trips."

"My parents didn't pay for this trip. I won it."

"Won it? How did you win a trip?"

"I entered a newspaper contest and my picture took first prize."

"You're a photographer?" she asked incredulously.

"Yeah. That's why I came up here to take pictures of the bears. Just like everybody else."

"Where's your camera?"

"Umm . . . in my bag inside the buggy. Why?"

"It's just that people who are into taking pictures always have their cameras with them. I bet you're the only person on this bus besides me who hasn't already shot half a roll of film."

I realized that she was probably right. I'd noticed that all the other members of the tour had a camera, or multiple cameras, strung around their necks, and they'd started taking pictures even before getting on the bus.

"I'm saving my film until we get to the bears."

She shook her head slowly. "If you say so," she answered, in a tone of voice that hinted that she had her doubts. I was never very good at lying.

"You should probably avoid Tim for the rest of your stay up here," Loretta said.

I welcomed the change of topic. "I'm going to try to stay as far away from him as possible," I answered. Boy, did that make me sound like a first-class wimp. "But I can handle him, if necessary."

She chuckled. "The next time he'll be ready for your little dance moves, and he might bring something along to even things up."

"You mean his brother?" That had been my fear since I'd first heard that his brother was bigger and mean.

"Not likely. He probably didn't even tell his brother what happened. It was bad enough to be embarrassed in front of everybody, but if he told his brother he'd lost a fight he'd probably lose another one."

"You mean . . . ?"

"I'm pretty sure his brother smacks him around. He's nasty with everybody, so why would he be nice with Tim?"

"So how would he even things up then?"

"I've seen him jump somebody from behind. I heard he once tried to take off somebody's head with a hockey stick."

That was good to know. "I'll try and keep my eyes open."

"Good idea. And you'd better open them in that direction because there are some bears right over there," Loretta said as she pointed off to the side

"You're kidding!" I rushed excitedly over to the side and looked in the direction her outstretched arm indicated. I couldn't see anything "Where are they?"

"See those scrub trees?"

"Yeah?"

"Just behind them are some rocks. The bears . . . it looks like a mother and a cub . . . are lying down."

I squinted to see. The rocks were there, but I didn't see the . . . one of the rocks slowly rolled over and revealed itself as a bear!

"I see them!" I exclaimed.

"Good. That makes two of us. I don't think Charlie has spotted them. Go in and tell them and then come back out with your camera and I'll show you the best place to set up for your shots."

"Sure," I agreed enthusiastically.

I opened the back door of the buggy and went inside. "There are bears out there," I hollered to everybody as I hurried up the aisle. "Over on that side!"

"You've spotted bears?" Charlie yelled back.

"A mother and cub," I called as I hurried up to his side. "Right back there," I said pointing out the spot we had just passed by in the distance to our right.

125

Charlie slowed the buggy down and cranked the wheel hard. I had to hang on to not be thrown off my feet.

"I see 'em!" Charlie shouted, and a buzz of comments and excitement filled the vehicle.

"Way to go, Kevin! Good photographers usually have sharp eyes for spotting game, so I'm not surprised you saw them."

"Thanks," I mumbled, feeling suddenly guilty for taking the credit. Somehow, though, I felt as though I needed the compliment more than Loretta did, in case I needed to bolster my claim to be a photographer.

"Can you do me a favour, Kevin?" Charlie asked. "Grab my camera off the back counter and bring it to me. I might be able to get a shot as we come up to the bears."

"Sure, no problem." I rushed off and picked up his camera. On the way back I took a quick look at the settings and the lens he was using.

Then, after handing off Charlie's camera, I took my bag out from under the seat and got my own. I adjusted the f-stop to mimic Charlie's and hurried back outside. A number of the seniors had already had the same idea and the railing of the platform was almost ringed with people. There was a small spot beside Loretta and I squeezed in.

The buggy swung around and we came to a stop beside the bears. I was surprised that they didn't get up and run. They didn't budge, or even cast a glance in our direction.

The big bear was lying on her back with her feet sticking up in the air. Her fur was more yellow than white, and it looked straggly and dirty. The cub, which was about the size of a large dog, was brilliantly white in colour. He was lying with his head on the belly of the mother. Was he asleep?

The engine stopped, and so did the vibrations pulsing through my feet. Then the sound of the motor was replaced by an explosion of clicks and whizzes as shots were taken and self-winding cameras readied for the next picture. I brought my camera up and framed the bears in the middle of the viewfinder. They seemed so far away. I adjusted the telephoto, zooming in until they completely filled the space, and pushed the button, capturing the image of the little bear slumbering on his mother's belly. It looked as though the cub had a smile on his face, and I wondered if he was dreaming about seals.

A wave of "*aaahhh*s" washed over me and I looked back to see that the mother had rolled over and was getting to her feet. Just like a big shaggy dog she arched her back, opened her mouth wide and stretched and yawned. A barrage of clicks and whirrs came at me and reminded me to take some more shots.

The big bear looked over and then up at us. She tipped her head to one side in what I figured was a thoughtful way and started to amble over toward the buggy. The little bear followed close behind.

"Aren't they cute!" a woman gushed.

"Cute until they try to kill you," Loretta countered.

"But they look so gentle," somebody else said.

"Hah! There's hardly anything more dangerous than a mother white with a cub. Not just because she wants to protect the baby, but because she's desperate for food for herself and the cub. If you were down there on the ground instead of up here on the platform, you'd soon be up *there*," Loretta said pointing to the sky. "She'd tear you to pieces."

I felt a tingle run up my spine. I was pretty grateful to be safe.

"She's climbing the side of the buggy!" somebody screamed.

At that same instant half of the people backed away from the side railing while the other half leaned over farther. I looked down and was shocked. The bear was right beneath where I stood, stretching her paws up toward me. I gasped and jumped back, practically knocking into a couple of people, including Loretta.

"Get real, Kevin, it can't reach you," Loretta scolded me. I looked at her doubtfully.

"I'm sure," she said. "Go and take some pictures."

Tentatively I moved forward and leaned over the railing. The mother bear was still standing there on her back legs, front paws outstretched. Thick black claws extended out even farther. Her mouth was open, exposing dozens of sharp teeth. She closed her jaws with an ominous click and then a *hiss* escaped her muzzle.

I brought the camera up to my eye and was startled for a microsecond. I'd forgotten I still had the zoom on, and the bear looked as though she were right on top of me. I took shot after shot as she stretched and repeatedly opened and closed her mouth. It was hard to believe that I was this close to a polar bear! This was amazing . . . just amazing. This was one pretty cool trip I'd won.

The engine of the buggy roared to life and the bear dropped to the ground to a chorus of complaints from the tour group.

"Why'd he have to start the engine?" somebody asked. "He chased away the bears!"

"My uncle probably got a call from one of the other tour operators telling him where there are more bears," Loretta explained. "You'll see."

Of course it turned out Loretta was right. We drove for fifteen minutes before coming up to the high metal fence of an abandoned military base. There were gaps in the fence where large sections were missing and Charlie steered the buggy through one of the holes. We soon came to a cluster of buildings, rusting, with broken windows—obviously deserted. The buggy rolled onto a long strip of pavement. It looked like a runway. It was still mainly intact, but there were cracks and gaps in the asphalt, with plants pushing up through the spaces.

As we passed between two buildings I had the eerie feeling that there were unseen eyes watching us from the broken and boarded windows.

"It's a bit spooky," I said.

Loretta looked at me and slowly shook her head.

"Don't you think so?"

"Not really," she answered. "But I can see why *you* would think it was scary."

"And why is that?" The better question was why she kept picking on me.

"Because you're white."

"And if I was native I'd never get scared of things?" I demanded.

"Of course you would, but just not the same things."

"What do you mean?"

"Think about it. Where do all your scary stories take place ... castles, cemeteries, ghost towns, abandoned buildings, haunted houses."

"Your point?"

"It's always about you."

"What does that mean?"

"You whites always get spooked about places where you were but left ... you know, where you died or houses you deserted. You're afraid of your own spirits."

"And natives aren't afraid of their spirits?"

"Afraid is the wrong word. We're *aware* of spirits."

"And what does that mean?"

She looked at me as if I'd just asked the stupidest question in the world.

"We don't see spirits as something bad or wrong or hanging around to somehow harm us. Spirits just *are*. They're a part of our world, just like trees, or rocks, or the sky and water."

I still didn't understand, and I threw her a questioning look.

She sighed deeply and again shook her head. "Spirits are everywhere. Here, in the town, in my house, out in the bush, on the water. Me being scared of spirits is like you being afraid of . . . afraid of . . . air." She paused. "Do you get it now?"

"I get it." I didn't actually, but I really wanted a break from Loretta. "I'm going to talk to Charlie and ask him how much farther we have to go," I said.

Stepping inside the buggy, I was captured by the smell and sizzle of bacon and eggs cooking on the griddle.

"Smells great," I said to the cook.

She looked up at me and smiled. I hadn't expected more. Naomi was very nice and friendly but I hadn't heard her say more than a few words.

I continued up the aisle. The rest of the guests were engaged in noisy and happy conversation. Bursts of laughter, and the clicking and whizzing of cameras punctuated their words.

"Much farther?" I asked Charlie.

"They were reported just east of these buildings."

"Reported?"

He nodded his head. "When one of us spots bears we put out a call on the CB radio to alert all the other tour operators. We all cooperate." He paused. "Well, almost all of us."

I knew without asking that he meant Tim's brother, Kurtis.

"Bad enough that Blackburn doesn't cooperate, but he doesn't play by the rules either," Charlie added.

"There are rules?"

"Of course, and they're pretty simple. Don't move in too close, don't chase them—when they want to leave let them leave—and don't bait the bears."

"Bait them?" I asked.

"Lure them close with food, or even worse, throw food down to them. That may get you better shots but you're teaching the

130

bears to associate people with food. It's a small step from there to the people *being* the food."

"I thought all polar bears thought of us as food," I said, quoting back what Charlie had told us the previous night.

He smiled. "Glad to know you were listening to what I had to say. All bears are naturally dangerous. Feeding them just makes them much, much more of a risk to people."

"Why do the bears come onto the base? Are they looking for shelter?"

He shook his head. "The bears only go inside a building looking for food. There are still faint traces of food and human scent here. Except when the female is denning—having her babies—all bears prefer to be out in the open all the time, year round."

"But I thought bears hibernated in the winter?"

"Most, but white bears are different. They spend the whole winter roaming across the open ice. They're at their most active during the winter."

As we turned the corner Charlie and I both caught sight of a large male bear. He was just off to the side, lying on his belly with his four legs stretched out in all directions. Charlie pulled the vehicle to a stop close by. Just as with the female and her cub, he didn't seem to pay any attention to our arrival. Everybody shifted either to the bear side of the bus or out to the back platform.

"None of these bears seem to like to move very much," I said.

"Not cold enough yet," Charlie said. "At least not for a polar bear. That's why he's lying on his belly, to get cool. The thinnest layers of fat are on the belly. Lying like that, the snow cools the blood that flows through the stomach, and that cools the whole bear down."

"I see. Are you coming out back to take some pictures?" I asked.

"Nope. And neither should you," Charlie answered.

"Why not?"

"Because we can get some better shots of those two bears," he said, pointing just up ahead.

There were two large males standing, facing each other. As we watched, one lunged forward and swatted the other. Then both bears reared up on their hind legs and started to "box," repeatedly swinging their front paws and snarling and snapping at each other. I stared at them open-mouthed. This was incredible. It was like watching some nature show on TV—no, better it was *living* some sort of nature show.

I heard a camera clicking and turned to see Charlie, a gigantic lens attached to his camera, taking shots of the action.

"I've got to get more film," I said, noticing my roll was full.

"Don't bother . . . no time," Charlie said, grabbing me by the arm as I started to move away.

Then, just as Charlie had predicted, one bear dropped back down and started to run away. The larger of the two chased after the first for a dozen steps and then stopped. He turned so he was facing us. His mouth was wide open, his tongue hanging out to the side. Even from our distant vantage I could see him panting. Then he slumped forward onto his belly with all four legs sticking out in all directions.

"He's overheated from the fight and needs to rest."

"What were they fighting about?" I asked.

"Establishing or testing dominance. They were trying to see who's the biggest bear on the block."

"Do they ever get hurt doing that?"

"It happens, but not too often. Usually the bears only fence like that when they're close enough in size for there to be a question about dominance. If one bear is a lot smaller than the other, it turns and runs."

"And then the big bear leaves it alone?"

Charlie laughed. "They leave alone only what they can't catch. The big bears eat anything they can catch and kill, including smaller bears."

"You're kidding . . . right?"

"Nope. The only danger a cub has is of being killed by one of its own species. That's why they stay close to their mothers, so they can be protected from the bigger bears."

"But aren't the female bears a lot smaller?"

"A lot smaller, but that's where nature has helped to take care of things. The smaller the bear, the longer it can go without overheating. The big bears are fast, but they can't run as long the smaller ones. As well, I guess there's more motivation if you're a small bear."

"What do you mean?"

"Would you run faster to *get* a meal or to *avoid becoming* a meal?"

"I see your point."

"I thought you might," he chuckled. "You know, it's easy to tell you're a photographer."

"It is?"

"Sure. You're watching an incredible event—almost a tonne of bears fighting—and you want to leave the scene to go grab more film."

"I didn't want to miss the chance to get the shot," I said, still looking at the bear lying unmoving on his belly.

He smiled. "I know how you feel. Sometimes it doesn't seem like some things really happened unless I have the picture to back it up. You've never done wildlife photography before, have you?"

I shook my head. Of course I'd never done wildlife photography before; I'd never done anything before.

"The wild life in Mississauga is a different type," I said.

Charlie smiled. "Then this is your first lesson. You have to have your camera with you and loaded at all times because things happen without warning and are over almost instantly. Got it?"

"I got it," I said. I tore my eyes away from the bear and ran over to get my camera. I wasn't going to miss anything more.

It was coming up to 4:00 p.m. and the sun was almost down. I'd used up ten rolls of film and was exhausted. I slumped down on the seat across from Charlie.

"Well?" Charlie asked.

"That was amazing. We must have seen two dozen bears."

"Twenty-six."

"Is it always like this? Do you always see this many bears?"

"Nope. Sometimes less, sometimes more . . . sometimes a lot more. There aren't as many bears now as there will be in the next few days."

"You're kidding, right?"

He shook his head. "More bears each day until the weather gets colder."

"How can you keep saying this isn't cold?" Parts of me had been ranging from chilly to numb throughout the day. The only thing that chased away the cold was the heat from the excitement of sighting bears.

"Not cold enough to solidly freeze the ice on the bay. Until the ice is thick enough to support the bears they have to remain on land."

"When does that happen?"

"It depends on the year. I've seen them take to the ice as early as the middle of October or as late as the end of November. It was nearly a disaster the year they left early."

"What happened?"

"I had four weeks of tours without bears. Only thing more dangerous than a polar bear is a bunch of disappointed tourists." Charlie started to laugh.

"So what did you do with the tourists?"

"There are other things of interest around here, and we got lucky and saw a couple of bears heading out to the ice. The tourists were happy enough, I guess. They didn't know what they'd missed, and I certainly wasn't going to tell them."

We started to roll past the first few buildings on the outskirts of town. The powerful headlights of the buggy swept a wide path in front of us.

"So what now?"

"Most of the group will probably lie low around the motel. Some might want to go to the shops. You and I, we have other things to do."

I gave him a questioning look.

"Unless you've started to enjoy dressing in Loretta's clothes, we have to go out to the airstrip to meet your luggage."

Chapter Seventeen

By the time we got to the airport it was pitch black and wind was driving the snow horizontally across the tarmac. It was a replay of the night before, except this time I was sitting on the bus bumping up to the waiting plane. There were fewer passengers and they were already being loaded onto their respective vehicles.

"Your friend's brother is here," Charlie said as he pulled the bus to a stop.

"My friend?"

"Yeah, good old Tim. There's his brother's buggy. He must be picking up some people for his tour."

"Great," I muttered. "Do you think Tim's with him?"

"Maybe. He comes sometimes. Why, are you afraid something might happen?"

"No," I said defiantly, although it certainly was the first thought that had flooded my mind.

"He might not even be here. But if he is, and he gives you any hassles, just—"

"I know, I know, walk away," I interrupted.

"Walk away?"

"Yeah." That was what my mother and my Tae Kwon Do instructor always told me to do.

"I was going to tell you to deck him."

"You're joking, right?"

"Nope. From what Loretta told me you don't have anything to worry about. And don't even think about Kurtis. I'd love a chance to take care of that business myself." Charlie smiled. "Better yet, if he's here, don't even wait to see if he'll start something with you. Just go up and pop him one."

"I can't do . . ."

Charlie started laughing and I knew that this time he was just joking.

The bus came to a complete stop and Charlie threw the door open. He bounded down the steps and I quickly followed after him. We were making our way straight across the tarmac to the plane but we'd taken no more than a few steps when Charlie turned back toward me.

"Tim's here. Remember, if he hassles you . . ." Charlie made a fist with one hand and smacked it into the other.

I didn't see how he could tell that one of those parka-clad figures gathered by the plane was Tim. They all looked the same to me. Thank goodness I'd decided to leave Loretta's parka back at the motel and worn my thin jacket instead. I'd figured I wouldn't have to wait long for my parka anyway and I could live with the cold more happily than I could with any further embarrassment.

"How's my favourite senior citizen doing?" Crash called out as he came toward us.

"He's doing fine," Charlie answered.

"At least I will be doing fine if you got my luggage."

"Luggage? Was I supposed to get your. . . ?" He let the sentence trail off, and just as I was about to react in shock he and Charlie burst into laughter.

"Don't worry, it's on board."

"Thanks."

"You're welcome. Besides, I should be thanking you," Crash said.

"What do you mean?"

A smile burst across his face. "If it wasn't for you, I wouldn't have met Tammy. We're supposed to go out the next time our schedules work out and we're in Winnipeg at the same time."

I felt a rush of disappointment. I knew it had only been a silly fantasy, but it was *my* silly fantasy.

"That is, if it's all right with you, Kevin," Crash said.

"If what's all right?"

"You met her first, so, is it all right if I go out with her?"

I wanted to blurt out "No!", but I knew that wouldn't be right.

"Sure . . . no problem." I guess if she had to date somebody other than me she could do far worse than Crash. Besides, it was nice that he'd asked me. We both knew I was just a kid, but he'd treated me like I was more than that.

"Thanks, man," Crash said putting a hand on my shoulder.

"Hey, how about you stop gabbing and take care of business," called out an angry voice from behind me.

I didn't recognize the voice but I knew the attitude. I turned around knowing I'd be looking at Tim's brother. Like Tim he had jet-black hair, and he was wearing a baseball cap with a picture of a bear and the word "Wapusk," which Charlie had told me was Cree for "white bear." Tim was right beside him, and they both wore identical scowls.

"He *is* taking care of business," Charlie said, taking a step forward defiantly.

"I wasn't talking to you, McGinty," he snapped.

"Well I was talking to you. You got a problem with that?" Charlie asked.

Tim's brother mumbled something under his breath.

"What did you say?" Charlie demanded. He took another step forward. He looked as though he was spoiling for a fight.

"I was just wondering how that old bundle-of-bolts tundra buggy of yours is holding together. Has it broken down lately?" Blackburn asked.

"You little—"

"Everybody hold on!" Crash yelled as he stepped between the two men, holding Charlie back by putting both hands on his shoulders.

"Get out of my way!" Charlie demanded.

"Let him go!" Kurtis ordered as he came toward Charlie.

"All of you stop it, right now!" another voice called out.

Instantly everybody stopped and turned toward the voice. It was Captain Bishop.

"You get back on your buggy and wait for your passengers," the captain ordered Blackburn, pointing to his vehicle.

He hesitated for a split second and then walked away, muttering under his breath. He went straight to his buggy and boarded it. Tim tagged along. He'd barely even looked at me.

"You too, Charlie, straight onto the bus."

"Ah, Captain—"

"No back talk! Get going!"

Charlie looked fit to be tied, but he too turned and walked away, leaving Captain Bishop, Crash and me.

"Good thing you came along," Crash said. "It's pretty scary when I'm the most responsible one in a group."

"That's more than scary, it's downright terrifying," Captain Bishop replied. "Let's get the baggage off the plane. Start with those jokers who are going with Blackburn. I've seen more than enough of those three to last a lifetime." He turned and walked toward the terminal.

"Want me to help?" I asked.

"I was counting on it," Crash replied, and we started off to the plane.

"They really listened to Captain Bishop," I commented.

"Everybody listens to him. He's like a legend in these parts. He's brought people in and out for years, got them to hospital for emergencies in weather that was unbelievable, found lost people in the wild and flown rescue operations. There's almost nobody who lives here who doesn't owe him."

"Does Charlie owe him?"

Crash nodded. "Captain Bishop flew in the doc in the middle of a blizzard to deliver a baby that wasn't coming right." He paused. "Hard to believe that something as big as Charlie was ever a little baby, huh?"

"A baby, yes . . . little, no."

"And those who don't respect the captain are usually smart enough to fear him."

"How come?" I asked.

"When he was young he was the toughest man you might ever meet. Now that he's older, he's still somebody you wouldn't want to tangle with. As well, there's only one airline that makes regular flights into Churchill, and you have to remember who owns this plane," he said, pointing up to the aircraft. "If he doesn't like you, it's a long walk back south."

He opened up the hatch to drop down the latch to the luggage compartment, making a ramp.

"Be careful with these," Crash said as he handed me down a long, thin leather case.

"What is it?" I asked.

"Gun bag."

"Gun bag! You mean they're going to hunt the bears!"

"Hunting the bears is illegal. Against the International Polar

Bear Convention," Crash said as he reappeared with an almost identical bag. "But they are going to go hunting."

"Hunting for what?"

"Arctic fox, wolves, deer, caribou, elk, whatever they come across."

"And that's all legal?"

"Blackburn gets them the proper permits. Lots of people come up here to hunt," Crash explained. "His guests are often hunters instead of ecotourists."

"What's an ecotourist?"

"That's what you are. It's short for ecology tourists. Most of the people who come these days are here to observe nature— hike, take pictures or canoe. And I have to tell you that most of our passengers, whether they're here to hunt or take pictures, are mighty friendly. The few times we've had problems, though, it seems like it's people going on a hunt with Blackburn. Like this flight."

"There was trouble on this flight?"

"They were just loud and obnoxious. Brought some booze on board and had too much to drink. They were bothering Wendy and wouldn't listen to her. Captain Bishop had to go back and straighten them out. There, that's the last of their luggage," Crash said, handing me a large bag.

"That's not much stuff."

"There's only three of them."

"That doesn't seem like a very big tour group," I observed.

"Blackburn's groups are always small, sometimes he has only two or three people at a time. I don't know how he can make any money."

"Maybe hunters pay more."

"Maybe."

I started walking one of the big bags over toward the vehicle.

"Don't bother," Crash called out. "Leave everything right there in a pile and they can come and get it themselves."

I gladly set the bag back down.

"Here are the important bags," Crash said as he walked over holding one of my bags in each hand.

"I never thought I'd be so happy to see luggage." I put the bags down beside me.

"I'm just glad I was able to reunite you with your loved ones," Crash said. "Come here, Kevin."

Curious, I walked to his side.

"You want to see something really interesting tonight?" he asked quietly, and somewhat mysteriously.

"Sure."

"Good. I'll pick you up from the motel in about an hour and a half."

"Where are we going?" I asked.

He leaned in close. "The dump."

"We're going to the dump?" Apparently there was even less to do in Churchill than I could have imagined.

"But you can't tell anybody . . . except Charlie. He'll want to come for sure."

"Okay. And can you tell me why exactly Charlie would want to come along?"

"Because of the bears."

"There are bears at the dump?" I said loudly.

"Ssshhhhhh!" Crash hissed at me, looking around to see if anybody had heard me. "A dump to bears is like a candy store to kids. There always used to be dozens and dozens of them wandering through. There were some really unusual opportunities for photographs. At least before they put up the fence."

"Why did they put up a fence?" I asked.

"To keep the bears away. They were eating all sorts of things they shouldn't—plastic, pieces of rubber—and some got sick, even died."

"That's awful."

"There were also some close calls. People would go to the dump to drop off their garbage and the bears would be sitting there waiting. And of course some weren't too patient and would come right up to the trucks or cars. A window isn't much protection when a bear decides he wants what's inside."

I thought about how I'd felt nervous even in the tundra buggy.

"And besides, the bears were starting to become too dependent on people food. The conservationists were saying that the association with people food was what was causing the bears to visit the town itself more often. So they fenced the dump in."

"So we're going to go and watch the bears standing by the fences?" I asked.

"No, there are some bears inside the dump."

"If it's fenced in now, how is that possible?"

"There are a few bears who got in the habit of eating there over the years and figure they should still be able to. They guess a big male just bashed it down and went inside, and then other bears followed behind."

"It sounds like they should be building stronger fences," I suggested.

"They'd practically have to be built with solid concrete to keep out a really hungry bear. So, are you interested?"

"Of course."

"Good. Dress warm and bring along plenty of film, a flash and a tripod if you have one. You're going to get some shots that you won't believe. And remember, don't tell anybody. If too many people hear about it and show up then they won't let any of us into the dump. I'll pick you up around eight."

Chapter Eighteen

"Are you sure it's okay for you to come along?" I asked Loretta. I was worried that Crash would be mad at me for letting her hear about the bears, although it was actually Charlie, not me, who had told her.

"Hah," she snorted. "It's more okay for me to come along than you!"

"I was invited!" I protested.

"I don't need an invitation. Gavin and I are friends, close friends."

"Gavin?"

"That's Crash's real name. Did you think his parents named him Crash?"

"I hadn't really thought about it," I admitted. What I *was* thinking about was how I'd just got stuck spending another evening with Loretta.

"Are you sure you don't want to keep my parka?" she asked.

"Not on your life!" I paused. "Why, what's wrong with this one?"

"Nothing . . . if you like boring."

"I'll take boring any day," I offered.

"Yes, after spending some time with you I'm aware of that," she said, her voice dripping with smug satisfaction.

I was about to answer when a vehicle pulled up in front of the motel and the headlights swept over us.

"There's Gavin," she sang out, and she headed out the door, running to the waiting pickup.

I closed the door and followed, climbing in.

"Hi, Kev," Crash said. "What a surprise to have Loretta come along."

He gave me a look that made me believe that while it was a surprise, he didn't necessarily think it was a pleasant one.

"I told him how close the two of us are and that you wouldn't object," Loretta said. "Is that a new shirt you're wearing?"

"Yeah, I just got it down in Winnipeg," Crash answered.

"It looks really nice," Loretta told him.

I'm not sure what was more confusing: Loretta complimenting something—especially a shirt that was just peeking out of the front of Crash's partially unzipped jacket—or the tone in her voice. It was sort of soft and gentle, nothing like the way she normally spoke.

"Where's Charlie?" Crash asked.

"He can't come right away. He said he'd drive out himself once he'd settled all the guests in for the evening," I explained.

"I didn't think he'd want to miss a chance like this. You brought along your camera didn't you?"

"Right here, under my parka," I answered, patting the front of my coat.

"Then we're off," he said, putting the truck into motion.

"Is the dump far?"

"Not too far. It's just south of town—that way it's downwind of the town most of the time."

The truck's transmission ground noisily as Crash geared up to go faster.

Looking over I realized that there was a big space on the seat between me and Loretta. She was sitting very, very close to

Crash. And strangely it looked as though he was sitting squished against the driver's door, desperately trying to keep a little distance from Loretta. In fact, if he'd moved any farther over he would have been driving the truck from the outside.

I could smell the dump before I could see it, and then I saw lights in the distance. There was a high metal fence, and beyond that I could make out a number of small fires, smoke curling up into the night sky and disappearing into the darkness.

We came to a stop at a gate. There was a little booth just inside the fence occupied by a small man wearing, of course, a parka.

The man left the booth and came trudging toward the fence. Crash rolled down his window.

"It's closed!" the guy yelled. "The dump is closed!"

"We don't want to dump anything, Mr. Rolands!" Crash yelled back. "We came to look at the bears!"

The man shook his head. "Didn't know the news got out."

"Hasn't got far. The Ministry guys were talking to Captain Bishop and me about it over the airwaves on the flight in. Thought we'd come and have a look."

"The men from Natural Resources just finished fixing the fence," Mr. Rolands explained.

"Does that mean we missed the bears?"

He shook his head. "Three bears still inside. That just stops any more from wandering in. You've got to fix the hole in the bottom of the boat before you start bailing it out."

"But how do you bail out the bears still inside?" I asked.

"Traps," Loretta answered.

"So can we go inside and have a look?" Crash asked.

"No can do. Nobody is supposed to go in."

"But those Natural Resources men, they said I could come."

"And my boss said that nobody except them should be in the dump tonight. And he's the guy that signs my cheque and hires and fires people, so I'm going to listen to him."

146

Crash was just about to answer when Loretta practically crawled over top of him and leaned out the window.

"That's fine, Mr. Rolands. You don't have to let us in. We'll all just go back to town . . . and mention to everybody we meet that there are bears in the dump. And of course word will spread like crazy and soon you'll have dozens and dozens and maybe even hundreds of people all gathering at your—"

Mr. Rolands reached over and unlatched the gate, swinging it open so we could drive through. Loretta gave a little smile as she settled back into her seat and we drove inside. I looked back through the rear window and saw him close and latch the gate.

"Very impressive, Loretta, very impressive," Crash said.

She flashed him a megawatt smile—I hadn't even known she was capable of smiling.

We were now officially in the dump, fenced and locked in with some polar bears—bears that associated people with food—protected by a few very thin pieces of glass. This little truck certainly wasn't a tundra buggy.

We drove slowly down a gravel road, bumping up and down repeatedly as we hit the potholes. We wove between mounds of dirt and piles of garbage until we came to a large open space. Half a dozen small fires gave off flickering light and chimneys of smoke. It was an eerie scene straight out of some bizarre horror movie.

"I don't see any bears," Loretta said.

"Me either, but there's the Natural Resources truck over in the far corner," Crash said. "Let's go over and talk to them."

He put the truck into gear and we slowly rocked over to pull up very close alongside the other truck. Crash rolled down his window and the passenger on the other vehicle did the same. They exchanged friendly "hello"s. It did seem like everybody knew everybody else in this town—except of course for me.

147

"I thought you were going to keep this to yourself," one of rangers said.

"I did," Crash said. "Practically. It's impossible to keep anything from Loretta, and I had to tell Kevin here . . . I owe him big time."

"Owe him for what?"

"It's kind of a personal thing," Crash replied.

Crash proceeded to introduce me to the two rangers. The one behind the wheel was older and in charge. His name was James. The other, who wasn't that much older than Crash, was called Reg. From the way they joked around I figured that he and Crash were friends and he'd probably been the one to let Crash know about the bears in the first place.

"So what's happening with the bears?" Crash asked.

"Two of the three are already in the traps. You'd save us a trip if you could tow one of the traps for us when you leave."

"Yeah, I can do that, if it isn't too late. So where's the third bear?"

"He's playing hide-and-seek with us. We circle around one way and he goes the other. He doesn't seem interested in the bait, but I guess I can't blame him—there's so much food in this garbage everywhere that there's not much reason to crawl into the trap."

"Anything we can do to help?" Crash asked.

"Maybe. If you took your truck and circled around one way and we went the other we could maybe push him toward the trap," Reg suggested.

"Sounds good." Crash rolled up his window and we started off as the Natural Resources truck curved around in the other direction.

"Get your camera ready," Crash said to me.

I pulled it out of my jacket and started to fiddle with the

settings. I was actually starting to have slightly more than a vague idea what I was doing.

"There it is!" Loretta yelled, and I practically jumped out of my seat.

I caught sight of it through the front windshield—one gigantic bear. It was sitting on its backside, holding a green garbage bag in one paw and ripping it apart with the other.

Crash eased the truck off the road and slowly moved toward the bear's position. We closed in as the animal grabbed the bag in its mouth and started shaking it for all it was worth. Garbage was flying in all directions.

"Before we do anything else, I'm going to angle the truck so you can take pictures out your window," Crash said.

He turned the wheel and then brought the truck to a stop no more than two car lengths away from the animal. I brought the camera up to my eye. The bear practically filled the frame. Its fur, illuminated by the light of a fire that burned just by its side, was filthy dirty. It was more brown than white.

It was strange to see the bear from this angle. I was almost at ground level, and rather than looking down at the top of the bear—the way I had from the buggy—I had to aim the camera up to capture its head. I preferred being up high.

"You going to take pictures or what?" Loretta asked.

I started snapping shots.

"You'd get better pictures if you rolled down the window, wouldn't you?" Crash suggested.

"I guess . . . should I do that?"

"Sure."

"But is it safe?" I asked.

"Just as safe as with the window closed. It's not like a little piece of glass is going to slow down that bear at all," Crash said.

"How about if we move a little closer!" Loretta pleaded.

Please don't! I felt like screaming out, but I kept my mouth closed.

"This is close enough," Crash said, and I had to stifle a deep sigh of relief. "I have to have enough distance to throw it into reverse and get out of here if the bear charges."

"He's not going to charge. He's not interested in anything that isn't inside a garbage bag. I don't think he's even noticed us," Loretta said.

I had to admit that it seemed she was right. The bear was either totally unaware or totally unimpressed by us. I took the last three shots on the roll of film and quickly changed rolls. Maybe the details of photography were beyond me, but after taking over a hundred shots today I could change rolls like a professional.

All at once the bear roared and jumped into the air as if it had been stung by a bee! It turned in tight circles, like a dog trying to catch its tail. As it spun I saw a colourful dart protruding out of its side. It had been shot with a dart gun! With a big paw it smacked at the offending object and the dart went flying through the air, end over end, landing on one of the heaps of garbage.

The bear was suddenly captured in bright lights and the Natural Resources pickup truck came bouncing into view. Out of the open passenger window leaned one of the rangers, still holding a rifle—the gun that must have fired the dart. The bear turned and faced the truck. It reared up on its hind legs and then, without warning, tumbled over to the side, landing on the pile of garbage where the dart had landed. It quickly staggered to its feet but lost its balance once again, rolling onto its side. It seemed that the back leg on the side where the dart had hit was almost completely useless. Once again it tried to regain its feet but instead stumbled forward, crashing into another mound of garbage, its fall cushioned by the bags that squirted out from under it. The bear tried again to rise, but instead a quivering motion overtook its entire body, and then it slumped helplessly to the ground.

The rangers leaped out of their truck. Reg was still holding the rifle while James had another object in his hands. Reg stopped short and aimed the gun at the bear and James rushed forward. He was carrying what looked like a big tool or fishing tackle box.

"Come on, let's have a closer look!" Crash said as he climbed out of the truck. Loretta followed right behind.

I found the urge to simply stay in the truck almost overwhelming, but my sense of curiosity and desire to not look scared outweighed my fears. I climbed out of the passenger door and jogged after them, taking my place with them in a semicircle around the comatose animal. Reg still held the gun, now at his side.

"I thought you were going to try to drive it into the trap," Crash said.

"Would have preferred that, but time was getting tight. We have to clear the area before morning so people can start using the dump, and this old fella has never been too cooperative," James explained.

"You know this bear?" Crash asked.

James walked forward and pulled up one of the bear's ears. There was a red tag secured to the inside. "I first tagged him almost eight years ago. Right here in this dump. He was a regular here for four years after that, but I haven't seen him since. It was probably him that battered down the fence."

"We'd better get going," Reg interrupted. "I don't know how much of the drugs got into him before he shook the dart loose. Crash, can you come with me so we can hook up the trap and bring it over here?"

"Sure, no problem."

"Oh, and Loretta, can you hold the gun and keep my partner covered?" Reg asked.

"Of course," she said, taking the rifle from him.

Reg and Crash climbed into their trucks and drove off. I was hit with a terrible feeling in the pit of my stomach. Both Crash and the trucks were gone, leaving my security in the hands of a fourteen-year-old girl with a rifle. Then I remembered just who the fourteen-year-old girl was: the way Loretta could snarl, she could chase away a bear even if she didn't have a gun.

"Want to give me a hand?" James asked.

I stood there waiting for Loretta to answer.

"He means you," Loretta said, poking me in the side.

"Me?"

"You see anybody else around here?" she taunted.

"Well . . . you."

"I'm standing guard. I could help and you could protect us . . . oops, I forgot, you've never fired a gun."

"Could *somebody* help me?" James demanded.

"Sure." I lowered my camera and tentatively moved to his side.

He was bent over beside the head of the bear. Its eyes were closed and the mouth was slightly open, revealing the beginnings of massive yellowing teeth. I could detect the sound of its slow, shallow breathing.

"Hold this." James had placed the end of a tape measure at the very tip of the bear's nose.

I hesitated.

"Don't worry," he said reassuringly.

I heard Loretta snicker over my shoulder. I decided I'd rather have my fingers bitten off than be laughed at. I stood as far away from the bear as possible and stretched out my arm to take hold of the end of the tape. James reeled out the tape stopping at the very end of the bear's back.

"He's fairly big. Two hundred and twelve centimeters."

"That's incredibly big!" I exclaimed.

"Well, not that big. I've personally seen them over two hundred and seventy centimetres long, and the biggest ever measured was over three and a half metres."

"Unbelievable!"

"And while I can't be sure until I do all my measurements, I would estimate that this fella doesn't weigh much more than four hundred and fifty kilograms. A really big bear would weigh half as much again."

As he took the tape measure from me and started to measure other parts of the bear I tried to imagine anything short of an elephant being much bigger than this bear.

It was a mass of dirty white fur. Three of its legs were pinned underneath its body while the fourth leg extended off to the side, the massive paw turned upward to reveal pads and claws. Slowly and carefully I placed my hand against the paw. With my fingers outstretched I couldn't come even close to reaching the edges where the five thick black claws began.

All at once a shudder ran through the length of the bear. I jumped back and bumped into Loretta, almost knocking her off her feet.

"What are you doing?" she screamed.

"It's all right!" James yelled.

I nodded my head dumbly. The bear remained frozen to the ground. It wasn't going to get up and kill me.

"Jump back like that again and scare me and it won't be the bear you'll have to worry about," Loretta threatened.

"Why did it do that?" I anxiously asked.

"That was the nervous system reacting to the tranquillizer.

He still isn't going anywhere for a while yet," James explained.

"That's good to know," I said quietly, stepping forward again.

"You should get your camera ready for a really unusual picture," James said. He turned away and reached into the metal box, then pulled out a large pair of pliers.

"What are those for?" Loretta asked.

"A little tundra dentistry."

James circled to the front of the bear and started to pry open its mouth, while Loretta and I watched in amazement.

"I'm going to take out a tooth. We can learn a lot about the animal's health and habits by an analysis of its teeth."

"But doesn't that hurt the bear?" I asked.

"With the amount of tranquillizer he has in him I could practically perform open-heart surgery. Besides, I'm only going to take one of these broken-off canines. It isn't helping him much anyway, and he'll still have forty-one other teeth left."

James grasped the tooth with the pliers, holding them with both hands while bracing his feet against the side of the bear. He grunted and groaned and twisted.

"Are you going to take a picture?" Loretta asked.

"Oh, yeah." I brought the camera up and started to click away. I shifted slightly to the side and captured the bizarre image, including a close-up shot right down the throat of the bear.

James continued to try to pry the tooth loose. It didn't look like it was going anywhere. Then suddenly he flew away from the bear as though he'd been shot out of a cannon, landing with a thud on the ground a couple of metres away. He smiled and held up the pliers, which gripped the tooth.

"Just like my dentist . . . except he usually doesn't fly through the air. Either of you two ever seen a polar bear tooth up close?"

"My grandmother had a necklace made of teeth," Loretta replied casually.

"No, never," I answered, staring at the tooth, impressed.

"Here, have a closer look at it," he said, handing it to me.

I took it carefully. I was astonished by the sheer size of it! Despite the fact that the top third was broken off, it was still longer and thicker than my baby finger. I turned it over in my hands and examined it closely. I tried to imagine what it would feel like to have one of those—or worse, three dozen of them—sink into my flesh. I shuddered.

The quiet was broken by the roar of an engine and the headlights of a truck swept over us. The two vehicles drove up, each pulling what could only be described as gigantic pieces of metal sewer pipe on wheels. One truck drove just past us, swung to the side and then backed up, aiming the trailer right to where we were standing beside the prone bear. As it closed in I could see that the end of the pipe was blocked by a set of iron bars.

"You'll now see one of the main reasons we hate to use the tranquillizer gun in these situations," James said. "A bear that can't walk any more needs to be dragged into the trap."

I didn't like the sound of that.

Crash and Reg climbed out of their trucks and came to the back of the trailer. With a metallic clank the bars blocking the end were raised straight up to open the mouth of the trap. Next a ramp was lowered to the ground.

As I continued to watch, Reg walked up the ramp, bent over and went right into the trap. Trailing behind him were two ropes. My eyes followed back to the other ends of the lines— James was tying them to the front paws of the bear! I turned back around in time to see Reg feed the ends of the rope through the back of the trap.

"Now the hard part begins," Reg said as he exited the cage.

"You feeling strong?" James asked me.

"Him?" Loretta snorted.

"No problem," I told James, although I was really answering Loretta.

"Good. Follow me."

We walked around to the back of the trailer, where Crash and James were already waiting. I took hold of a rope with Crash.

"Okay, we're going to pull on three . . . one, two, three!"

The rope jerked and then stretched taut. We were pulling, but it barely budged. Hand over hand we slowly strained to pull the bear toward us. Standing behind Crash I couldn't see the bear moving, but I marked its progress by the increasingly long length of rope accumulating behind me.

"Just a metre or so!" Reg called out, confirming my hopes.

With renewed efforts we pulled. The trailer shook, and I could hear the animal being dragged across the metal flooring.

"Okay, that does it!" Reg said.

I dropped the rope and tensed and flexed my sore fingers. I could feel sweat trickling down my sides underneath my parka. It was difficult to do anything too physical wrapped up like this—I felt a bit like a polar bear after a strenuous run.

James reached into the trap and started to undo the ropes while Crash and Reg went to the front of the trailer. With a thunderous slam that rocked the whole trailer the front bars slammed shut. There was some sort of spring release that Reg had tripped to close the trap. It reminded me of a gigantic mousetrap. The ramp was raised and tied into place.

"There. Let's hook up the other trailer. We can hook a second onto the back of this one. Is it okay to keep these two away a little longer?" James said, referring to Loretta and me.

"That's no problem," Crash answered.

"Good, then Kevin will have a chance to see the jail."

"Jail? You put the bears in jail?" I asked in amazement.

Everybody laughed.

"It's not the people jail," Reg explained. "It's the polar bear jail."

"Another Kodak opportunity," Crash said. "Tell you what, how about Kevin and Loretta ride with you, James, so you can answer questions about the bears?"

That sounded great to me, but I saw Loretta's face fall. I had no doubt that she wanted to ride with Crash . . . or should I say "Gavin."

Chapter Nineteen

Loretta sat forlornly against the passenger door of the truck while I took the middle. She kept glancing over her shoulder. At first I thought she was interested in the trap trailing behind us, but I soon realized that she was actually looking farther back at the truck following us—or, more accurately, at the person driving the truck.

I thought there were very few things worse than having Loretta not like you. But I was beginning to think that having her *like* you could be worse.

"Did you feel that?" James asked.

"Yeah. Wasn't that just another bump in the road?"

"That was from the trailer, not the road. The bear's starting to move around."

"I was wondering how long it would stay out," I said.

"That's something we always wonder about. We usually get some signs—it starts moving its limbs or trying to turn its head—but once I was working with a bear that just jumped to life without any warning signs."

"That must have been awful!" I exclaimed.

"And dangerous," Loretta added.

"It was both—as well as tragic."

"Something happened to somebody?"

"Not to the people. To the bear. We had no choice. It was either kill it or risk it killing one of us."

I looked back, and in the light cast by the headlights of Crash's truck I could see the bear standing and moving around in the trap we were trailing behind us.

"It's up and moving," I said.

"Good. Just like you're always worried they're going to get up before you expect, there's also a danger that they're never going to get up. Some bears die under the influence of the tranquillizer." He adjusted his rear-view mirror so he could look back. "Obviously this one is going to be okay."

"How long will you be keeping him?" I asked.

"They're sentenced to jail until the ice on the bay is strong enough to support their weight. Could be about three weeks."

"That seems like a long time to be in a cage," Loretta commented.

"We have no choice. If we release them before that they're likely to just go straight back to wherever it was that they were causing trouble in the first place."

"How many bears do you have in jail?" Loretta asked.

"With these three, that brings us to eight," James said.

"That's a lot."

"It's a fair number. Last year there were only two. In other years we've had as many as fifteen. That's why we had to stop feeding them. When we first started to jail the problem bears we brought them food. The next year we got three bears who had been in jail the previous season actually trying to break in for a free meal. So, no more snacks."

"But they must need to eat!" I exclaimed.

"You have to remember that when they're waiting for the ice

to form they really aren't eating anyway. They can go weeks without eating, just living off their fat reserves. We just make sure they're given plenty of water. Here we are."

James slowed the truck down and we pulled up to a squat cinder-block building behind a metal fence similar to the one at the dump. A series of light standards stood around the perimeter of the enclosure and powerful beams shone down, lighting up the night.

James reached over and grabbed a remote from the dashboard. He pressed the button and the gate started to slide open. With Crash following, he drove us through, and then we all climbed out of the trucks.

All around the enclosure were large metal cages. I looked at the nearest one. Pressed up against the bars was its occupant, its large white muzzle protruding through the bars. As I walked up to have a closer look it hissed loudly and I jumped back in surprise.

"That one's not too friendly," James said.

"Can we get the trailer off my truck first? I have to get these two home," Crash said.

"But I haven't seen anything yet. Couldn't we stay a little longer?" I pleaded.

"It's already late," Crash responded.

"That's okay," Reg offered. "You're all welcome to come back any time."

"Tomorrow?" I asked.

James shook his head. "We won't be here tomorrow. We're going out to the tundra to try and track some bears."

"Say," Reg said, "I've got an idea. How about if we bring Kevin along with us tomorrow?"

"How about me?" Loretta demanded. "I'm supposed to stay with Kevin."

James shrugged. "Why not . . . there's room for two more, and you two have shown you can be helpful."

"The extra hands can only be good," Reg said.

"Fantastic!" I beamed.

"We'll swing around and get you on the way to the airport," Reg said.

"The airport?"

"Sure that's where we fly out of."

"We're taking a plane?"

"Helicopter. We'd better put these bears to bed, and you all better get to bed as well."

Chapter Twenty

"Get up, your ride is waiting for you!" Charlie announced as he shook me awake.

"What time is it?" I could tell it was still dark, but somehow it seemed to be an even darker dark than I'd expected.

"Four-thirty."

"Four-thirty!"

"Get yourself together and I'll go and grab you some grub," Charlie said as he left the room.

I got up and started to pull on my clothes. They were in a ball at the foot of my bed where I'd left them the night before. I had to smile. That would have driven my mother crazy. Not only had I not put my dirty clothes into the correct laundry hampers— white, dark and colours—I was actually putting them back on again!

That was how I'd "put away" my clothes both nights. As well, I'd gone to bed without brushing my teeth or flossing. I had to admit that my teeth did feel sort of gritty, and there was a funny taste in my mouth, but I figured that was what indepen-dence tasted like.

I slung my camera around my neck and stuffed four rolls of film into my pockets. Charlie had been kidding me the night before about abandoning the tour because I'd found a better photo opportunity. He'd said that was just another sign that I was a "real photographer." I was starting to feel guilty about fooling Charlie. Of course, not guilty enough to tell him the truth. Guilty I was, stupid I wasn't. Then again, the first rolls of film were being developed and were supposed to be coming back today. He'd see soon enough what sort of photographer I really was.

At least there was nothing phony about me trying to learn. I listened to everything Charlie said—not just to me but to everybody else. All the talk about f-stops and shutter speed and filters was pretty foreign to me. I simply listened in and then adjusted my camera to match the advice Charlie offered.

At first I'd just been using my zoom to get as close as possible to the thing I was shooting. Then I started to think about what a photograph really was; nothing more than a mechanical drawing. So I started to apply all the things I knew about art and drawing. It all made perfect sense once I figured that out. Things like composition, framing the subject, balance, backlighting, shades and shadows, and the angle of light entry. I stopped taking so many pictures and started to try to take the *right* picture.

I even asked Charlie if I could get some black-and-white film. I'd always loved sketching with charcoal, and black-and-white shots seemed like the equivalent. Charlie brought out a gigantic album filled with black-and-white shots. Slowly, and in great detail, he told me about each picture. They were beautiful. He told me that black-and-white was his first love, and then he gave me three rolls of black-and-white film and a promise to develop them himself right after I'd taken them. I should have been scared of him seeing the pictures I was taking, but I wasn't. I just wished he could see the last rolls I'd taken instead of the first.

I'd slipped on my boots and started to pull on my parka when Charlie reappeared carrying a gigantic paper bag.

"Here," he said, thrusting it into my hands.

"What is it?"

"Food."

"I'm only going for one day!"

"I'm only giving you enough for one day. Breakfast, lunch and a snack. Enough for you and Loretta."

Oh right, Loretta was coming along. But why was Charlie fixing meals for her instead of her parents?

"It's not like you're going to run into a McDonald's out there on the tundra, you know," Charlie joked.

He opened the front door and stepped outside into a stiff wind and the cold darkness, dressed only in a T-shirt. I was continually amazed at how the cold didn't seem to affect him. I zipped up my parka and ran after him.

"Let's hope the wind isn't too strong for the chopper," Charlie said.

"They can't fly in strong winds?" I asked, feeling myself almost blown back by the gusts.

"Winds, yes . . . really strong winds, no. But I doubt this is strong enough to ground them."

In the pitch black I stumbled to the truck. In contrast, Charlie seemed to glide over the ground. The door of the truck opened and the dome light came on, revealing Reg.

"Morning. Where's Loretta?" Charlie asked. There was a gruff tone to his question.

"James is picking her up. We're meeting at the airport."

"Good. Why so early, Reg?" Charlie asked.

"The helicopter is chartered out at two so we have to set out early enough to complete some hits. We want to be in the air in the right sector when the sun comes up."

"Which sector are you heading to?"

"I think south, but it all depends on the signals from the trackers."

James and Reg had explained to us the night before that they were going to be tracking signals from bears that had been tagged previously and equipped with a tracking device. This was part of a long-term project at the Ministry of Natural Resources to study the health and life-expectancy of the bears.

"Can you give me a call on the radio when you've reached the sector?" Charlie asked. "I'll drive my buggy out in that direction with the rest of my tour group. Hopefully you can give me some eye-in-the-sky directions to a hot location."

"Sure, no problem."

"Besides, it would be good if you could drop the kids off at my buggy before you headed in. That way they could still get the rest of the day on the tundra."

"Sound good. We'd better get going."

"Kevin, you have to adjust your shutter speed to compensate for shooting from a helicopter. If you don't shoot much faster, the vibrations will cause everything to blur."

"I'll do that."

Charlie leaned in the open window over top of me and tapped Reg on the arm. "Take care of my kids . . . understand?" There was a strange combination of caring and threat to the way he said those words.

"Count on it," Reg said.

We started off. I looked back and Charlie stood there watching. He didn't move; he just got smaller and smaller until he disappeared into the darkness.

"He certainly is protective of Loretta," Reg said.

"I think Loretta can take care of herself."

"She practically has to take care of herself. It's not like there's anybody else," Reg said quietly.

"What do you mean?"

There was a long pause. "Maybe I've said too much. People up here are pretty private about things."

"Who am I going to tell?" I asked.

"I guess you have a point. Besides, you're spending a lot of time with her, aren't you?"

"A lot."

"You should know that Loretta wasn't always like she is now. She was just about the sweetest, most friendly kid you'd ever want to meet."

"Loretta?" I asked in disbelief.

"Loretta."

"I can't even imagine that. You must be talking about when she was a toddler or something."

"Not that long ago. Everything's happened in the last two years."

"What happened?" I knew I had to ask that question, but I had fears about what I might possibly get in the way of an answer.

"I guess the first thing was the death of her grandmother. She lived with Loretta and her parents. Loretta was really close to her. And I think that if her grandmother was still alive, the other things wouldn't have hurt nearly as much."

"What other things?"

"Her mother up and left. Not that I can blame her, what with her father's drinking and that temper of his."

"Temper . . . does he hit people . . . does he hit Loretta?" I asked.

"Nope. He never hit *Loretta*."

Of course I knew what he meant—it was Loretta's mother who had been abused.

"Matter of fact, if he or anybody else even thought about hurting Loretta, then Charlie would shell 'em like a peanut. And you know when Charlie said 'Take care of my kids' he meant I should treat you well, but that if anything happened to Loretta, then . . . well . . . I'd better make sure nothing happens to her."

I could understand not wanting to get Charlie mad at you.

"When Loretta's mother left, she said once she was settled in she'd be sending for her. I hear she sends an occasional letter, and there's been a call or two and some presents at Christmas and her birthday . . . but otherwise nothing."

There was a long silence. I stared out the windshield and into the small patch of light created by the headlights.

"But I don't think it would matter much even if her mother did send for her."

"Why not?" I asked.

"For the same reason she won't accept Charlie's invitations to come and live with him."

"Charlie offered that?"

"All the time. But she won't go because she won't leave her father."

"But if he's like that . . . I don't understand."

"She figures somebody has to take care of him, and she's the only one left to do it."

"Are things any better?" I asked, hoping.

He shook his head. "The drinking has got worse. Some days the only time he's even home is when he's passed out. I hear that Loretta cleans him up, shovels some food into him and pleads with him to stop drinking."

I couldn't help but picture the whole awful thing in my head. I felt a sickening feeling in the pit of my stomach, and I was overwhelmed with guilt for all the things I'd thought about Loretta . . . not to mention the things I'd said to her.

"I guess you can understand how somebody could get all angry and bitter," Reg said.

I could. "At least she's better with Charlie."

"Charlie and Crash."

"That's right," I said, remembering my confusion over the way she'd talked to Crash in the pickup truck the night before.

"It's kind of sweet her having a crush on him. The part I enjoy, though, is watching how nervous it makes Crash!" Reg laughed. "If only she could be as nice to her teachers as she is to him, she wouldn't have been suspended from school."

"Suspended! I didn't know she'd been suspended before."

"Not before, now! How do you think she's free to spend time with you this week?"

"I thought Charlie took her out of school so I could have company for the week."

"Charlie's in charge of her during the suspension." Reg nodded his head slowly. "Let's keep all of this between us. Loretta wouldn't be too happy to know we were talking about her home situation."

There was no need to tell me a second time. I understood about keeping family stuff private. I didn't think making Loretta unhappy would improve her disposition.

Up ahead I could make out the lights of the airport. Having been there two days in a row, it was all starting to look pretty familiar to me. We pulled in beside another Natural Resources pickup truck. I could see James and Loretta standing beside it. Beyond that, in the distance, I could make out the outline of a helicopter.

Reg climbed out quickly, and in my rush to follow I forgot the bag of food Charlie had packed. I ran back to get it and caught up to them just as they reached the chopper

Not only had I never ridden in a helicopter, I'd never even been this close to one. It certainly didn't seem like a very big one. I couldn't help but wonder how safe it was. Maybe the winds would suddenly blow up strong enough to keep us on the ground . . .

"So what took you so long?" Loretta demanded.

I opened my mouth to explain but she didn't wait.

"Because if you were letting Kevvy-boy sleep in to catch up on his beauty sleep, you got him up way, way too early," she continued.

James and Reg chuckled. My mind started to tick off all the things I could throw back at her, but I didn't.

"Charlie packed food for both of us," I said, holding up the bag. I wondered if she'd had breakfast.

"Oh," was Loretta's only response.

"That's some bag," James commented. "It's so big, though, I'm afraid we'll have to choose between it and one of you."

"Leave him, he's just dead weight anyway," Loretta said, gesturing to me.

"*I'm* dead weight! What do you think you. . . ?" I let the sentence fade away. "Do you want me to bring the bag back to the truck?"

"Get real, Kevin, he was just joking," Loretta said. Even the dim light couldn't hide the expression of disgust on her face.

"We'd better get going. Our gear is all on board and time's wasting," James said. He hurried off to the chopper and Loretta followed. Reg reached out and grabbed me by the arm to stop me from walking away.

"That was nice of you not to get into it with her . . . maybe nicer than I could be," he said.

Maybe nicer than I can be for very long, I thought.

The engine roared to life and the blades of the helicopter started to turn slowly. Then they began going faster and making a whirring sound, and a strong gust of wind almost forced my hat off my head.

"Duck down!" Reg yelled over the noise.

I imitated him, keeping low, one hand on my hat while the other held on to the monster meal. I figured even if the wind was so strong that it threatened to blow me away I'd be anchored in place by the meal. Reg opened the back door and I climbed in beside Loretta. He slammed the door closed, shutting out an amazing amount of the outside noise. It certainly wasn't quiet, but at least I didn't have to fear that my ears would start to bleed.

Reg climbed in next to James in front, and it was then I noticed that James was wearing a headset, and sitting in the pilot's seat.

"You're the pilot?" I asked. I had just assumed that there was somebody else who was going to fly the chopper.

"Well, I've never flown before, but the pilot didn't show up so I figured I'd try it. I've seen him do it dozens of times and it doesn't look that hard," James said.

I opened my mouth in shock and . . . he had to be kidding.

Loretta elbowed me sharply in the ribs. "That was another joke . . . don't you get anything?"

"Not always," I said under my breath. ·

"Buckle up," Reg said.

I fumbled with my belt. It was all twisted and tangled. I heard Loretta's snap and I could feel her annoyance with my clumsiness.

"My goodness." She leaned over and took the end of my belt from my hands. "Did my uncle have to dress you this morning?" she asked as she snapped the buckle into place.

"Thanks," I said quietly.

"You're . . . you're welcome."

"Here we go!" James announced.

Instantly the noise of the engine and blades intensified and we tilted forward and literally jumped off the ground. I felt myself being pressed back into my seat.

"Swing left about thirty degrees," Reg barked out. He was carefully studying a box that looked like a big radio, which was balanced on his lap. I figured it was some part of the tracking system.

The chopper swung sharply and banked in my direction so I was pressed against the plexiglass door. I prayed that Reg had closed the door securely and Loretta had properly buckled my belt. I dug my fingernails into the armrests.

To my relief the chopper soon levelled out. I relaxed and looked out to the left, where a thin line of light stretched out along the horizon. This line gave way in layers ranging from light grey to dark to total black right beneath us. Then, before my eyes, the leading edge of the sun burst over the horizon. I watched transfixed as more and more appeared. It was beautiful! I went to grab my camera and then stopped. There was no way I could ever capture something that magnificent on film. I'd just enjoy it.

I glanced over at Loretta to see her reaction. She sat with her eyes down, a scowl on her face, oblivious to the wonder happening just outside. Up ahead James and Reg were too busy flying and fiddling with the tracking equipment to even notice. I tapped Loretta on the leg and she turned toward me.

"Look," I said, pointing to the incredible sunrise.

She started to scowl and then stopped herself. She looked out and her whole expression softened.

As I turned back to watch the day begin I couldn't help thinking about my mother. She often got up to watch the sunrise and would tell me I should get up with her because it was so beautiful. And I never would. I sighed deeply. When I got home I'd set the alarm to wake me really early one morning. Maybe early enough to even have coffee ready before I woke her up, and we'd see the sun rise together. Of course at that point she'd probably start to work and I'd go back to sleep.

"Another ten degrees to the south," Reg said.

"Aye aye, sir," James responded, and the chopper shifted slightly to the side.

I leaned forward to have a closer look at the black tracking box. On the top were dials and arrows and plugged into the side was a cord that led up to earphone in one of Reg's ears.

"We're right on course. The signal is getting stronger. I figure we're no more than about three kilometres away and closing." He turned around. "Kids, keep your eyes peeled. We're looking for a female bear. With luck she'll have one or even two cubs along with her."

I pressed against the window, straining to look for the bears. Down below the ground rushed by and I really couldn't see much except colour—green, blues, whites and browns. A couple of times I thought I saw something but it was only a rock or a patch of white snow against a darker background.

"There she is!" Reg yelled. "Almost dead ahead and just off to the left. And she's got a little one with her! Yee hah!"

I still couldn't see anything. The chopper dropped and I felt my stomach lurch into my throat. Before it could settle back into place we swung to one side, and it felt more as though we were sliding along a patch of ice than flying. As we banked once more I caught my first sight of the bear. A much smaller bear was standing so close to its side that it seemed as though the little one was trying to crawl underneath. We were now very low to the ground. We had to be less than ten metres up.

"Bring her around so I can get a shot!" Reg yelled.

As the machine spun around I looked up at him. The black box was no longer on his lap. In its place he was holding a rifle. He reached forward and opened up a flap on the door and poked the end of the gun through. The noise of the rotors and engine poured in through the hole.

"Hold her steady . . . steady . . ."

The gun exploded and I jumped in my seat involuntarily.

"Got her!" he yelled.

I looked down beneath the craft. The bear, a red dart sticking out of her backside, scrambled into view, followed by her cub. I was too far away to see but I could picture in my mind the look of terror that had to be on her face.

The helicopter suddenly surged upward, again catching both me and my stomach off guard. We seemed to be going straight up at a tremendous speed.

"We're backing off so she can go to sleep faster and be less stressed," Reg yelled over his shoulder. "I'll keep my eye on her. Everybody else needs to scout the area for other bears. If a big male gets in there while she's woozy she won't be able to protect her cub from him."

The helicopter banked around in a big circle with the darted bear and her cub at the very centre. I tried to make sense of the shadows and colours and rocks that littered the surface. I couldn't see any other bears, but then again, I hadn't been able to pick this one out either.

"Okay, I'm going to set her down," James said.

Quickly he brought the chopper in for a landing. There was a jarring thud on impact as the landing gear met the ground. James reached up and pushed some toggle switches and the roar of the engines faded and then died. The whirring of the rotors persisted for only a few more seconds, and after that the blades continued to turn slowly, losing momentum.

James and Reg jumped out. Both carried rifles; Reg still had the tranquillizer gun while the one James was carrying was the real thing. Loretta and I climbed out too. Reg opened up a compartment in the rear of the chopper. He pulled out the big metal box that I'd seen before at the dump. James took it from him. He then pulled out a large coil of rope and put it over his shoulder. What was the rope for?

"She's just on the other side of that rise," James announced. "Let's move!"

They both started to jog and we scrambled after them. I certainly didn't want to miss anything, but I also wasn't going to bet my life on there not being any other bears around. It was always smart to stay close to the guy with the gun.

From the top of the hill we saw the bear and cub. She was down on her side, not moving, and the little bear stood on top of her. He was making little baying sounds. We walked toward them very slowly. The cub retreated behind the body of its mother.

"First things first," Reg said. He handed the rifle to Loretta. "You ever seen a tundra rodeo?"

"A what?" I asked.

Reg smiled. "I'm going to lasso it. We have to control the little bear. If he stays by his mother's side he might harm one of us—he weighs more than you do and comes equipped with standard bear teeth and claws. Or he could run away, and then the mother wouldn't be able to find him. In that case, he'd be good as dead."

"But why the rope? Wouldn't it be easier to just shoot him with the dart?" I asked.

"Easier, but not safer. We don't like to drug the little ones."

Walking toward the bears, he took the rope off his shoulder and started spinning it around his head.

"Here bear, bear, bear . . ."

Loretta nudged me and then moved closer. "Ever notice when people are trying to get an animal's attention they call it by its name . . . like they think it understands?"

I chuckled. It was nice when Loretta was taking shots at somebody else.

I looked back in time to see the rope fly through the air. There was a loud yelp from the unseen bear. The rope snapped taut and then Reg was practically jerked off his feet. He dug in his heels but still skidded slowly forward, like a water skier being towed behind a boat. The little bear tried to run away.

"Give me a hand!" he hollered.

James, who had put down the rifle and toolbox, rushed to his side and grabbed hold of the rope. Together they brought the bear to a stop. Then they started to drag the bear away, and I could hear his claws digging and tearing into the ground as he tried to resist. They stopped when they came to a stunted tree, anchored amongst some rocks. James tested its strength. Satisfied, they looped the rope around the exposed roots and tied the bear into place. They walked back, leaving the little bear lying on his belly, panting and puffing. As they got closer I saw that the bear wasn't the only one who was tired.

"We can get to work on the mother now. Can you two keep one eye on the cub and the other on our backsides?" Reg asked.

"Sure," Loretta answered.

"Take my gun, Kevin," James said, motioning to where it lay on the ground.

"Him?" Loretta objected. "He doesn't know the first thing about guns."

"I guess everybody has to learn sometime," James said.

I picked up the rifle ... carefully ... and cradled it in my arms. I think I would have felt more comfortable and safe if I'd had the dart gun and Loretta had been holding the real rifle. The two men worked quickly, repeating most of the things I'd seen done in the dump yesterday. They began to measure and examine the animal.

"Do you know how much weight she's lost since the last time we darted her?" Reg asked me.

I shook my head.

"I'd guess almost two hundred kilograms."

"Is she sick?"

175

"Nope. When they go off to den and have their cubs they don't eat at all for a few months. This is a pretty common weight drop," Reg explained. "That's why a female with cubs is so dangerous. She's starved herself and is desperate for food."

"There, finished," James said. "All we have to do is let the little one loose and then watch over them until the mother comes to."

They put their tools back in the metal box. James took the rifle back from me and we strolled over to where the cub was tied down. He was still lying on his belly and didn't even budge as we approached. If it hadn't been for the fact that his eyes were open, I would have thought he was sleeping.

"He's playing dead," James explained. "Hoping we don't see him."

"Kevin, how about you go over there and untie the bear," Reg suggested.

This time I knew he was joking. "Sure, but only if I can give him a big hug first."

"He does look cuddly, doesn't he?" Reg agreed.

"So how do you untie him?" I asked.

"You see that length of rope hanging off the bear?"

I nodded. It was a piece about as long as I was tall.

"The knot around his neck is a slip-knot. That's the release end. One little tug and the line drops right off."

Reg and James started walking in different directions, circling around the cub. First the little bear looked at one of them, then the other, and then back again, as though he were watching a tennis match. The cub finally decided that James was more interesting and stared solely at him. Head raised, mouth slightly open, he hissed softly. James started to talk to the cub, occasionally waving his arms to help keep its attention. Reg continued to slip slowly to the other side. Whenever the bear's attention started to drift in the direction of Reg, he would freeze like a statue and James would hoot loudly to recapture his focus. Bit by bit Reg crept closer. Finally in one leap he drove forward, screaming at the top of his lungs as he flung himself toward the bear. In one motion he grabbed the loose end of the rope, the bear leaped away squealing and the noose dropped off his neck. The cub bounded across the open space at full speed until he bumped into his mother and then took refuge behind her.

"Let's get all our stuff and find a safe place to watch her recover," James said.

"Maybe this is a good time for you to bring out that food bag of yours," Reg suggested.

My stomach had been growling for a while so I was more than happy to follow that suggestion.

Chapter Twenty-One

We sat up on the rocky rise and all of us had some homemade buns, a couple of sticks of jerky and a glass of orange juice. In one direction the helicopter was close at hand, and we kept a watchful eye out for any other bears that might be approaching it. In the other direction we saw the mother slowly get up, stagger around for a while and then finally lead her cub off.

"They'll be fine now. Let's find the next bear," Reg said.

I was willing to stay longer, but at the same time I was eager to get going. This was all unbelievable. Just think, if I hadn't been there, I'd have been sitting in geography class pretending I was learning something. Instead I was actually in the middle of real geography, really learning things.

Reg and James gathered up their stuff—I grabbed what remained of the food—and we hurried off to the helicopter.

"Be sure to thank Charlie for the grub," James said as we reached the chopper. I climbed in, slammed the door and, thank goodness, was able to snap on my belt without any assistance.

James went through a quick series of checks and then we lifted off again. I felt that same rush in the pit of my stomach as we leapt into the air. I was ready for liftoff this time, but strangely the daylight made me feel even less safe: now I could see the ground as it rapidly rushed away from us.

"Move off on a southerly heading," Reg suggested.

"Are you getting a reading?" James asked.

"Nothing very strong. I'll search different frequencies until I hit something stronger and then we'll follow." Reg turned back around to me and Loretta. "We use a number of different frequencies which indicate either a specific bear, or the year tagged or the sex of the bears. That way we can track them from a distance and still know with certainty who we've found, and—"

"Action to the right!" James yelled. "Big male loping across the tundra."

The helicopter banked sharply in that direction and I was pressed against Loretta, who was pressed into her door. I still couldn't see anything, even when Loretta tried to point it out. I just pretended to anyway.

"Nope, I'm not getting any signals. Must be new to us. Shame we don't have any time to tag him today."

James nodded and the helicopter flattened out and started heading to the south again. Loretta was busy looking through her window, searching the ground for bears. I would have looked too but I didn't seem to have the knack of seeing them even when everyone else could.

Instead I started to fiddle with my camera. I adjusted the settings, changing the shutter speed as Charlie had suggested. I looked through the lens and focused at Reg. Then turned the camera to Loretta. There was something really neat about the way the brilliant blue of the sky, framed by the window of the helicopter, set off her long, dark hair. It was a perfect picture. I steadied my hand and took the shot.

Loretta heard the click of the shutter and turned to me. "What's the big idea?"

"I was just taking a picture."

"You can't just take somebody's picture without asking them if—"

"Whoa! Strong signal dead ahead!" Reg yelled.

Loretta turned back to me. There was a look of pure fury in her eyes.

"I'm sorry," I said before she could start in at me again. "I really am sorry. If you want, you can have the negative. It was just such a nice picture."

Her face seemed to soften.

"I don't see anything!" James bellowed.

"Neither do I, but the signal says we're practically on top of it. Can either of you two see it?" Reg asked over his shoulder.

We both turned and looked out our respective windows. I didn't see anything at all.

"Turn it back around. The signal is getting weaker!" Reg commanded.

The helicopter banked to the left and I suddenly had a much, much better view of the tundra below than I really wanted.

"I still don't see anything," James yelled.

"We're practically on top of it. Take a pass over those boulders. Maybe it's hiding down there."

James nodded and brought the chopper over the rocks in a low pass. We were so close to the ground that even I could have seen a bear it it was hiding there.

"Can you tell from the signal what we're looking for?" James asked.

"I know exactly who it is. It's Grampa." Reg turned back to us. "It's the very first bear James ever tagged. That was what, nine years ago?"

"Ten. And last year we put a tracker on him. We wanted to investigate the range of older bears. So where is he?"

"The signal says he's right here," Reg answered.

"Are you sure you're reading that thing right?"

Reg scowled. "Set the chopper down and we'll track it from the ground."

I didn't like the sound of that at all, but I didn't get a vote in any of this. James flew to a point in an open area off to the side of the boulders and set the chopper down. James, Reg and Loretta climbed out, and I reluctantly joined them. Reg had taken the tracking device out, along with the dart gun. Meanwhile James had opened up the compartment and removed the rope, metal box and rifle.

"Here, you carry this," he said, handing me the box. Loretta was already holding the dart gun. "And both of you stay so close to me that you're standing in my shadow."

I didn't need any further warning as I fell right into step behind him just as he fell into step behind Reg, who had the tracker in his hands, the earphone in his ear and his eyes glued to the monitor. Loretta was close behind me.

Reg wove around the meadow. First he went toward the rocks, then away, and then he circled around. He was quietly muttering to himself as he walked.

"The signal is coming from right here . . . no more than fifty paces away from where we stand."

I looked around anxiously and carefully. Maybe the signal was there but there was no bear to go along with it, thank goodness.

"Do you think?" James asked.

"Only thing I can think of," Reg answered.

"What?" Loretta asked.

"Those trackers are on a metal belt that's looped around the bear's neck. There's no way they can slip off. If the bear and the tracker have separated it can mean only one thing," Reg said.

"The bear must have died . . . and its remains have been eaten," James added softly. "Poor Grampa."

"He was old. It happens. He's gone ... but the tracking device remains. We have to try and find it," Reg said.

"That would be good. Those things are worth close to a thousand dollars each. Let's fan out and look."

We formed a line straight across with a distance of two arm's-lengths between us. Reg, still holding the black tracking box, was in the middle with Loretta and me on one side and then James on the other. Slowly we walked across the clearing, searching the ground for the tracking device. I kept one eye on the ground, the other on the horizon, and both ears wide open. I didn't want something to find me before we found the device.

"Here it is!" Loretta hollered. She reached down and picked up a thick black belt.

"Fantastic! Way to go Loretta!" James took the belt from her and gave her a big hug.

"We'd better get moving again," Reg said. We all started back toward the helicopter.

"And you still have to radio to my uncle."

"Oh, that's right. We'd better contact him right away, okay James ... James?"

We all turned around. James was still standing, holding the belt, studying it intently.

"James, what's wrong?"

He held the belt up. "The belt. It didn't fall off. It's been cut."

Chapter Twenty-Two

There was silence as James walked toward us, holding the belt in front of him as if it were a live snake.

"Maybe it opened up at the buckle and dropped off, or another bear chewed it off," Reg suggested.

"The buckle is up here," James said, sliding his hand up the belt. "And I'd like to see a bear that could chew that straight. There aren't even any toothmarks on the rubber."

Reg looked at the cut. Even I could see it was clean.

"And look at the tracking device."

"It's been bashed around pretty good. See these marks? Red paint. Whatever it was they used to try and smash it must have had red paint on it. Maybe it was an axe or hammer. It's so beaten up I can't believe it still sends out a signal," Reg said.

"You're not the only one. Whoever killed the bear must have figured they'd destroyed the transmitter," James said solemnly.

"You think somebody killed the bear?" I asked.

"Only explanation I can think of."

"But . . . but no one's allowed to hunt bears . . . Crash told me," I sputtered.

"There is some hunting allowed under the international

agreement. Native hunters can harvest a limited number of bears," Reg explained.

"Are you saying that natives did this?" Loretta demanded angrily.

"Settle down, Loretta, of course I'm not saying that. I can't imagine any native hunting a tagged bear, and even if they had killed him they would have returned the tag to us, not tried to destroy it."

"So do you think somebody could have killed it by accident?" I asked.

"It's pretty hard to accidentally kill something as big as a polar bear. You'd have to be going after it deliberately."

"But who?"

Reg and James looked at each other but didn't answer my question.

"Blackburn," Loretta said.

"You think he would do that?" I asked.

"Him, or one of those hunters that he brings in," she answered.

"Then he should be arrested, shouldn't he?"

"You need proof to arrest somebody," Reg replied. "And there's no proof. All we have are suspicions."

"But who else could it be?" Loretta demanded. "Everybody knows he drives too close, chases after the animals, baits bears, and he's ripped up tundra with that stupid all-terrain vehicle of his!"

"And those things are being dealt with. He's been issued warnings and fines," James said.

"Like that's changing the way he does things. Somebody should just go and bust him one on the side of his head and drive him out of town!"

"Things don't work that way, Loretta. We'll talk to the police as soon as we get back," James offered.

"That won't work," Reg said. "I was talking to Nick and Sean yesterday and they're both in Fort Williams for the next two days."

"Great," Loretta muttered under her breath. "Our entire police force is out of town."

"You only have two police officers?" I asked in amazement.

"Usually that's more than we need. We can always radio in for them to return, or ask for backup," Reg explained.

"Yeah, but we still have no proof it was Blackburn," James said.

"My uncle wouldn't need any proof. He'd just go there and knock a confession out of him."

"Loretta, don't go getting Charlie all fired up. The last thing in the world any of us wants is for him to end up being arrested and—"

"Hey!" Reg blurted out. "We haven't radioed Charlie our location yet. He's waiting for us! Let's get back to the chopper."

Quickly we hurried back toward the craft.

"You said it was a really big bear, right?" I asked James.

"One of the biggest."

"I was just wondering . . . what happened to it . . . you know . . . the body?"

"Probably butchered right out here on the tundra . . . skin and head separated from the body and the carcass just left."

"Although it wouldn't be left for long," Reg added. "It would have attracted scavengers pretty quick, and they'd have eaten it right down to the bone."

"But there weren't even any bones—at least I didn't see any," I said.

"Even the bones get scattered pretty quickly," James explained.

We got to the helicopter and climbed aboard. James went through the usual checklist and then the chopper revved to life. Reg immediately got on the radio.

"This is Bear-Aid One calling from sector seven. Do you copy, Charlie?"

There was only static in reply.

He pressed a button on the side of the microphone and the static cut out. "Bear-Aid One calling from sector seven. Do you—?"

"This is Charlie!" came a staticky reply. "How are the kids?"

"They're fine. Been really helpful, too," Reg answered. "We've spotted bears . . . large male, female with cubs, in this sector. Where are you? Over."

"In town."

"In town?" Reg, James and Loretta said in unison.

"What are you doing in town? Over," Reg asked.

"No choice. The buggy is down . . . two tires were slashed . . . sabotage. Over."

"Just your buggy?" Reg asked.

"All the tundra buggies. Over."

"Blackburn's too? Over."

There was no reply except a prolonged burst of static.

"Charlie, did you copy?"

More static. "I copy. It's never his buggy. Over."

Reg put the microphone down and turned to James. "This isn't good. This isn't good at all. What do you say we open up the polar bear jail for the tourists?"

James shrugged. "That would be okay."

He brought the microphone back up. "Charlie, just to keep your paying guests happy, why don't you bring them out to the jail. Over."

"These people don't pay good money to go to a zoo," he replied.

"It's better than nothing. Besides, we'll let them get close up and personal and we'll put on a real show for them. Over."

Another long period of static followed.

"Charlie?"

"I'm here. Better than nothing I guess."

"Good. Let the other crews know as well. Over."

"That will at least keep Charlie busy," James said. "Maybe stop him from doing anything he shouldn't."

"Like what?" I asked.

"Like ripping off Blackburn's head."

James clicked the microphone on again. "Um, Charlie, so we'll see you around four. We'll keep the kids with us until then. Do you copy?"

"I hear. Besides, I have nothing better to do, at least for a while. Blackburn is out on the tundra. Do you know his location? Over."

"You're breaking up badly, Charlie, I couldn't hear what you said."

"Do you know his location?"

"Still can't copy—"

"He wanted to know where Blackburn is and—"

"Sshhhh!" Reg hissed to interrupt Loretta. "Nothing but static, Charlie. Over and out."

There was a burst of noisy profanity before Reg leaned forward and turned off the radio.

"Where do you think Blackburn might be?" James asked.

Reg shook his head. "Could be anywhere. Why?"

"Just thought we could take a pass overhead."

"Why would we want to do that?"

"Just let him know we're in the area," James said. "We don't have time to track another bear today anyway. I'll swing to the east and circle the town until I'm coming in from the north . . . is that okay?"

"Fine with me," Reg answered. "Let's just get back to town. And I'd like to ask a favour from you two."

"What?" Loretta asked for both of us.

187

"I don't want you to mention the tracking device we found to anybody."

"How come?" she asked.

"It might be better that we know something that nobody knows we know. And you know how a secret is. Once you tell one person, it isn't a secret any more."

"So I can't even tell my uncle?"

"Especially not your uncle!" James blurted.

"But he won't tell anybody!" Loretta protested.

"I know he won't. With Charlie, though, it isn't what he might *say*, but what he might *do*," James explained.

"Come on, Loretta, you know how your uncle feels about those bears. Do we want to give him another reason to do something stupid?" Reg asked.

"I guess not," she admitted. "Okay, I'll keep my mouth shut."

"And you, Kevin?" Reg asked.

"I'm good at secrets."

"I know that," he said.

Loretta stared over at me. She looked as though she was trying to see right through me, to figure out what secrets I could possibly be holding—secrets that I shared with Reg, apparently, but not with her.

Chapter Twenty-Three

I stood off in a corner with Loretta while the tourists from all four tour groups wandered past the cages containing the eight bears. They weren't, as Charlie had feared, disappointed. Most seemed totally fascinated, and they were taking pictures at an incredible rate. Occasionally there'd be a shriek or outburst of laughter as they reacted to either something the bears did or more often something that Reg and James said. They were really putting on a show, giving all sorts of information and history about the bears, talking about the ongoing research and adding tidbits about the locals.

What they were saying was interesting, but not as interesting to me as what I was trying to hear from the opposite corner. Charlie and the other tour operators had gathered and were discussing the situation. I didn't dare go any closer, and I could only pick up bits of what they were saying when the voices got angry and loud. Fortunately, or unfortunately, there were enough loud parts that I pretty much got the picture. They were all looking for somebody to take their anger out on, they were frustrated that the police had not been able to do anything, and they were ready to do something themselves.

"So you have secrets, do you?"

Loretta's question caught me by surprise. "Not really," I said.

"Then what was Reg talking about?"

"I don't know . . . maybe you should ask him." That sounded like a good way out of it.

"Maybe I will. How come you're not taking pictures?"

My hand dropped to my camera. "I took all the pictures of these bears I wanted yesterday. I'm trying to be more selective in what I take."

"Like the picture of me?"

"Well . . ." I didn't know what to say.

"You can keep it if you want," she said.

"Thanks. I think it'll be a good picture. Do you want a copy?"

"I guess . . . if it turns out—"

There was a loud, angry blast from behind that stopped Loretta's comment dead in its tracks. It was Charlie. Loretta turned completely around and shot a full-blown scowl in his direction.

It was only then that I realized that during our entire conversation, for the first time, she hadn't scowled even once.

"These guys can be idiots!" she said in a voice that was loud enough to carry to her uncle and the other tour operators And they might have actually heard, if they hadn't been so loud themselves.

"Would they really do something?" I asked.

"If they say they'll do something, then you can count on it being done. Up here people don't say things just to hear themselves talk. That's what I'm worried about."

"But I thought you *wanted* somebody to go and do something."

"Just because I *want* something to happen doesn't mean I think it *should* happen."

"And what exactly does that mean?" I asked.

Loretta looked at me and shook her head. "Typical man."

I didn't know what that meant either, but I did sort of like being called a man.

"It's my uncle . . ." she began. "I wish he'd just settle down and get married. I'm tired of taking care of him. Him and my father. They're both like a couple of little boys who need to be watched all the time."

I hadn't heard her even mention her father before, and I didn't know how to respond.

"Is *your* father like that?" she asked.

I shook my head. "He's a doctor."

"I know that, but is he like a little boy? Does he do stuff without thinking and then your mother has to clean things up and take charge?"

I had to laugh out loud. "My mother is *always* in charge."

"That's how families are . . . the wife is in charge."

Loretta looked at me and her eyes widened. I think she had suddenly realized that she'd told me more than she wanted to. Reg had made a point of telling me just how little she talked about her home and what went on there.

"I have to go," she blurted out, and she started to walk away. I felt bad that somehow she'd been pushed into saying too much, and it had ended the closest thing to a normal conversation we'd ever had.

Unexpectedly, she stopped and turned around. "Do you want to come?"

Her offer really startled me. "Come where?"

"Do you have to know how interesting the place is going to be to decide if it's worth having to spend time with me?"

"No, of course not!"

"Then either come or don't come. Go and tell my uncle that you'll be with me so he'll know where you're going and that you'll be safe."

I smiled. "So you're going to take care of me?"

"Nothing new about that," she said, and she actually smiled back at me that time.

"I'll tell Charlie," I said, and then I hesitated. His discussion with the other tour operators seemed to be getting even more heated.

"*I'll* tell him," Loretta said.

She strode toward the group of men, tapped Charlie on the shoulder and spoke to him for a moment. He nodded his head in agreement and then returned to the discussion.

"Let's go."

"He said it was okay?"

"Of course. He just said to make sure I took a gun out of the bus before I left."

I shook my head in disbelief. This was the only place I could think of where teenagers were told to take a gun along when they went out to play.

Charlie's bus was parked just outside the gates, along with the minibuses and vans of the other tour operators. She popped open the door, which of course wasn't locked, and went inside. I followed up the first few steps, partially out of curiosity but more to escape the wind. Loretta was standing beside a long wooden box directly behind the driver's seat. She fiddled with a combination lock, opened it and then lifted the lid of the box. She pulled out a rifle.

"Okay, let's go."

"Go where?" I asked.

"If I told you it would ruin the surprise."

She started off quickly and I hurried my pace until I fell in step beside her. She glanced over, gave a slight nod of her head, but didn't talk. I ducked my head to block out the wind. It was coming right at us and the blowing bits of snow, ice and fine grit stung as they hit my face.

Since Loretta wasn't talking, I tried to figure out for myself where we might be going. There were so few places in Churchill that I even knew that I could figure it out simply by the process of elimination. Obviously we weren't going to the polar bear jail ... duh ... and I didn't think we'd be walking back to Charlie's motel, or else it would have been easier to just wait until everybody was finished and catch a lift. The airport was way too far away to walk to, so that was out. Maybe we were going to go shopping at one of the stores in town? I almost laughed out loud at that thought. Loretta just didn't strike me as somebody who spent a lot of time browsing in stores. Charlie had already made it clear before that we couldn't walk to the rec centre. That left only one place.

"So what are we going to be doing at your place?" I asked.

She turned her head slightly so she could see me out of the corner of her eye.

"Did you hear me mention to Uncle Charlie that was where I planned to go?"

"No. I just figured it out," I said proudly.

"Very impressive."

I could almost feel myself chest puff up with pride.

"Also very wrong."

"But if we're not going to your house, then where are we going?" I asked.

"We're not *going* anywhere. We've arrived." Loretta stopped walking.

I looked around. We were standing at the base of a high metal fence. The top was laced with three pieces of rusting barbed wire.

"Arrived where?"

"At Blackburn's place."

Chapter Twenty-Four

Lots of thoughts ran through my mind, none of which seemed to be able to work their way into words and out my mouth.

"Of course, this isn't the front of his property. That's all the way on the other side, about as far away as possible from where we're standing."

"Why . . . why are we here?" I was so proud that I'd managed to string together a few words.

"Because if we came to the front of the place somebody would see us, and that wouldn't be good."

"No, I don't mean why did we come to the back. Why did we come here at all?"

"We came here to investigate," she said as she dropped to her knees.

I didn't know why she'd done that, but I instantly dropped to my knees as well. I grabbed her by the sleeve and tugged, hard, to get her attention.

"Investigate what?"

Without warning she started to crawl along the base of the fence, repeatedly pressing her hands against the very bottom.

I crawled fast until I was right beside her. "I thought you said that you didn't think anybody should do anything stupid!"

"That's why I'm here," she answered.

"So *you* can be the one to do something stupid?"

She shot me a look, as if to say that the only stupid things there were me and my questions. "Of course not. Stupid would be busting in through the front door screaming and yelling and looking for a fight. Smart is sneaking in the back way and looking for evidence."

"What sort of evidence?"

"I don't know for sure. A freshly killed polar bear or a skin might be a good clue, don't you think? I'll know it when I see it. But first things first. This is what I'm looking for now."

With both hands Loretta peeled the fence away from the poles until a gap appeared.

"Hold this up," Loretta ordered.

"I'm not doing anything until we talk!"

She let go of the fence and it fell back into place.

"We can't just go breaking into somebody's house," I said.

"Of course we can't. For one thing, looking at all the lights on in the place, we'd be caught for sure. It would be crazy to try to bust in there."

I felt a wave of relief.

"We're just going to go and search his garage," she said. "That's where he keeps his buggy."

Before I'd even figured out how to respond, she'd pushed the fence again and ordered me to hold it open for her. It was hard to get a grasp on it with my mitts but I was able to keep it in place. Loretta took her gun off her shoulder and laid it down in the snow at the base of the fence. Then, on her belly, she slid through the gap.

I hesitated.

"Don't be scared," she said softly.

"This has nothing to do with being scared. This has to do with being stupid."

I started to slide under the fence. I got partway through when I felt myself being held back.

"You're caught on the fence," Loretta said.

I pushed harder until I felt something give and I surged forward. Satisfied, I sat up.

"Don't worry," Loretta said. "I can sew that up almost as good as new."

"Sew up what?" I asked, but then I spotted a large piece of fabric the same colour as my parka hanging from the bottom of the fence.

"My coat!" I practically yelled.

Loretta pressed a mitten against my mouth. "Ssshhh! If we get caught you could end up with a hole in a much worse place than your parka."

I didn't like that thought, but it certainly made the parka seem less important. I just hoped my mother would see it that way.

"Hold up the fence and I'll reach back and get the gun," I said.

"No, leave it out there. We know there are no bears in here. Besides, if you break into somebody's place you're better off if you're not carrying a weapon. That's the garage over there," she said. "Stay close to me."

Loretta moved slowly through the yard. All around the house the area was lit with bright lights. The garage also had bright lights mounted on the front of the building, but these were aimed toward the house as well. As we came up from the back we were in shadow.

When Loretta reached the back of the building, she hugged the wall and shuffled to the side. I followed close behind. She stopped at a window. There was no light inside. She cupped her hands around her face and pressed close to try to see.

"Hold these," she said, removing her mittens.

With her bare hands she pressed against the glass, trying to push the window up. At first it didn't look as though it was going to go, and then it jerked open. Snow and wind blew in through the opening.

Loretta started to climb into the window, starting with one leg, then tucking her head through, and drawing the other leg in last. I peered in after her. In the darkness I made out movement, and then I saw her outline.

"Do you need help?" she asked.

"I think I'm okay."

I leaned in and put my shoulders inside, then rotated my body to get my left foot and leg through the opening. It was a tight fit but I made it. I stretched as far as I could and my leg touched ground on the inside. Then I shifted my weight and brought my other leg in after me.

Loretta was right at my side. She started to close the window. I reached out to stop her.

"Shouldn't we leave that open so we can escape faster?" I asked.

"No. If anybody sees the window open, they'll come and check things out."

I let go of her arms and she closed the window. The rush of cold air and snow stopped. I took off my mittens and pushed back the hood of my parka.

Slowly my eyes began to adjust to the darkness. There was a long table, like a workbench, that lined the back wall. I took a step forward and bumped heavily into something. I brought my hands up. It was a large tire. My eyes followed up from the wheel. I was standing right by the buggy!

"Over here!" Loretta hissed at me.

I looked around. I couldn't see her. "Where?"

"Up by the front."

I kept one hand on the edge of the buggy and circled around. There were little windows at the top of the garage door, and some of the bright light was bouncing back into the garage. It was much, much brighter there. Loretta was standing at a counter over by the side. She was examining the tools that littered the workbench.

"Anything?' I asked.

"I found this hammer," she said, holding it up for me. "I can't even tell the colour in this light. We'll examine it later. Put it in your pocket."

"We're going to steal it?"

"We're not stealing. We're investigating."

"Why don't *you* take it?" I asked.

"Because my pockets aren't big enough."

Reluctantly I agreed and slipped the hammer into my pocket. I felt the extra weight pulling down on my parka.

"We'd better check inside the buggy," Loretta said.

She scampered up a set of stairs that led to the cab of the vehicle. It was almost as big and high as Charlie's machine. I had tentatively climbed up the first few steps when the whole interior of the buggy lit up. I almost fell over in shock.

"Hurry up and get inside!" Loretta hissed.

I hurtled up the steps, tripping on the top and falling into the buggy. Then I heard the door slam shut behind me and everything went dark.

"The interior light goes on when you open up the door," Loretta explained.

At least with the light off, nobody could see us—but it was doubtful whether we would be able to see anything ourselves in the darkness.

"This should help," Loretta said, and with a click a beam of light came to life.

"Where did you get the flashlight?"

"It was out on the bench. I thought it might come in handy. Let's start at the front and work our way to the back."

"And what exactly are we looking for again?" I asked.

"Things . . . remember?"

"Such as?"

"Such as, if I knew I'd tell you."

Blackburn's buggy was basically the same as Charlie's except on a slightly smaller scale. We looked beneath the seats, inside the cabinets in the kitchen area and in two large wooden boxes built in at the back of the vehicle. It was hard for me to follow the beam of light that Loretta flashed around as she searched. Whatever it was we were looking for, it probably wasn't going to be found by me.

The thing I did notice was how messy everything was. There were wrappers and cigarette butts and assorted pieces of garbage littering the floor. The kitchen counters were a mess, and under one of the sinks was an overflowing garbage can.

We reached the back door of the buggy.

"Nothing," I said. "Maybe we'd better get going."

Loretta didn't answer immediately. That was a bad sign. I figured she was thinking about where else we should search.

"I guess you're right," she said at last.

"Thank goodness," I mumbled under my breath.

All at once there was an explosion of sound. I turned around in time to see the gigantic garage door start to slide open. My eyes widened in shock and then were hit with a blast of bright light as the big overhead lights of the garage were switched on. Loretta grabbed me by the arm and pulled me to the floor of the buggy.

"Stay down," she whispered.

I heard loud voices and laughter. It seemed to be coming from all sides.

I moved my mouth close to Loretta's ear. "Did they see us?"

"If they had, don't you think they'd be in here and not out there?"

She had a point there.

"Why are they out here? What are they doing?"

"I don't know," she whispered. "Do you want me to go and ask them?"

Loretta tapped me on the arm and motioned for me to follow her. On all fours we crawled along the floor until we reached one of the large boxes along the back wall of the buggy. Slowly she lifted up the hinged wooden lid.

"Get inside," she whispered.

"What?"

"Get inside. If what they're looking for isn't in the garage, they might come in here looking for it."

I didn't need further convincing. I carefully eased myself over the side of the box, keeping low, and just squeezed in under the slightly raised lid. The box held blankets and tarps and ropes.

"Ooomph!" I gasped as Loretta climbed in, landing partially on top of me.

"Be quiet!" she hissed at me.

I strained not to make a sound as she shifted her weight and her knees and elbows dug into me further. She closed the lid and we were plunged into total darkness. Then beam of light shot into my eyes; Loretta had switched on her flashlight. Unable to protect my eyes—both my hands were trapped underneath me—I turned my head away. Loretta slid over and disengaged her limbs from me and we settled in, lying side by side. She turned the light off again, and it seemed even darker than before.

"Could you turn it on again?" I whispered.

"No. I don't know if there are any holes the light might escape through. I don't want to give Blackburn opportunity to shoot somebody else."

I guessed that made sense. Better to be undiscovered in the

dark than . . . shoot somebody else? What did she mean by that?

"It was a long time ago," Loretta said quietly.

"I don't care how long ago it was."

I heard Loretta stifle a chuckle. I couldn't believe that she could find any part of this amusing.

"You know, Kevin, I think—"

Loretta stopped mid-sentence as a few little fingers of light protruded into our hiding spot. We both knew instantly what that meant. Somebody had opened the door to the buggy and was coming on board. At the same instant, the voices became louder and I could feel the vibrations from feet walking around. They were in the buggy.

I felt my entire body go hot. I was now officially more scared than I'd ever been in my entire life. I could feel my pulse racing and I felt panicky, like I was going to run. I had to try to calm myself down. I knew just what to do.

I closed my eyes. I quietly took a deep breath and tried to make my muscles all relax. I thought of a safe place—just the way I would before a sparring match in Tae Kwon Do. Nothing could harm me . . . nothing . . . I was in control . . . everything was relaxed and calm. A slow pulse of calm started to radiate out from my chest, spreading to my limbs. I felt better.

I opened my eyes and saw Loretta, her face just inches away from mine. Her eyes were tightly shut, as if she figured that if she couldn't see them, then they wouldn't be able to see her. She looked scared—even more scared than I'd felt—but rather than making me feel more upset, that seemed to calm me. I guess somebody had to be calm.

"It'll be okay," I whispered as quietly as I could.

Loretta's eyes remained tightly shut. Had she heard me?

I wiggled one hand free and reached out and gently touched her hand. She opened her eyes. I smiled—at least I gave her the best smile I could summon up—and she tried to smile back. I wanted to tell her that they'd soon be finished, they'd find whatever they were looking for and go, they'd leave the buggy and we'd get out without being seen. We'd be okay.

Then the engine of the buggy roared to life.

Chapter Twenty-Five

Loretta's eyes widened in shock and fear, and any illusion I'd had that I wasn't scared vanished in a flash. Why were they starting the buggy? Did they need to charge the batteries? Maybe they were testing something... maybe...

The vehicle started to move. We were going somewhere! The engine roared, and my whole body shook with the vibrations coming up through the floor. At least with all the noise we didn't have to worry about our whispers being overheard. I leaned in closer to Loretta and spoke into her ear.

"Maybe he's just moving it outside."

She shook her head.

"Why not?" I asked, as we bumped and banged and swayed with the motion of the machine.

"We're going out to the tundra."

"Maybe not."

"Blackburn never takes his buggy out of the garage unless he's headed out."

Of course she was probably right. I remembered what Charlie had told me: Blackburn claimed that his buggy never got vandalized because he kept it inside. But there were always exceptions. Maybe he had to take it out to ... inspect it? Yeah, that could be. Why would anybody be going out at night anyway? But as we continued to move, it was getting harder and harder to hold on to the illusion that we were still in the yard and not on our way out to the tundra.

I was quickly beginning to feel hot. Worse, my stomach was churning. Maybe it was partially fear, but more likely it was because of the uneven motion of the buggy. Either way, the result was soon going to be the same, and losing my lunch in a crowded wooden box would just about make the experience perfect.

I pulled off my hat and unzipped my parka as far as I could. That felt a little better, but only a little. I pushed and struggled to try to right myself. Maybe if I was sitting up I'd feel better.

"What are you doing?" Loretta demanded.

"I've got to sit up," I said.

"Just stay where you are."

"I can't . . . I think I'm going to be sick."

A small belch escaped my lips, and Loretta tried to squirm away. Her slight shift freed up my lower arm and I was finally able to sit up. I quickly unzipped my parka the rest of the way and slipped it off. Loretta slid over to the side so there was a gap between the two of us. I felt a little bit better.

The buggy rocked violently and my head banged against the top of the box. I stifled the urge to yell. As I slouched down slightly to avoid another whack my eye came in line with a knothole in the side of the box. A thin beam of light floated through it. Carefully and slowly I moved forward to bring one of my eyes into position against the hole.

At first I couldn't see anything except the back of the last seat. A fat lot of good that did. I settled back. Then, off to the right-hand side, I saw another little shaft of light penetrating the box. I shifted down so I could look through that hole. It was almost perfect! I had a sightline right down between the seats all the way through to the front windshield. I could even see the lights shining on the uneven ground in front of the buggy. Oh yeah, we were definitely out on the tundra.

I detected a bit of motion off to one side and saw a man sitting on the edge of a seat. He was staring forward. I scanned the rest of the seats as far as I could but I didn't see anyone else. I had suspected that there weren't too many people on board anyway just judging from the footfalls and conversation we'd heard before the engine started in the garage.

My lookout position was uncomfortable and I was just getting ready to settle back for a while when I noticed the reddish-orange glow of a bank of heaters. Why was Blackburn heating the vehicle up like that? The windows would all steam up and make it difficult to shoot pictures. Presuming that pictures we what he wanted to shoot. I slumped back.

I wanted to tell Loretta about the heaters. I was surprised to see that while I was looking through the hole she'd been shifting blankets and tarps and had hollowed out a place where she was partially hidden.

"What should we do now?" I asked.

"Nothing."

"Nothing?"

She shrugged. "We sit here and hope we don't get caught and wait until he parks his buggy back in the garage."

"But he could be out until morning."

"He could be out until tomorrow night," Loretta said.

"You mean we have to sit in here until then?"

"We don't have to . . . only if you don't want to get caught."

"I can't sit in here for twenty-four hours!" I quietly protested. "What about food and water and . . . and a bathroom?"

"I know. There's only one thing to do," Loretta said.

"What? What can we do?"

"Go to sleep." Loretta turned away from me and snuggled down underneath the blankets.

How could she just close her eyes and try to fall asleep like that? I looked at her. Her breathing had already slowed and she looked almost peaceful. Maybe it wasn't such a bad idea after all.

My eyes opened, and for a split second I couldn't remember where I was. Then in the next instant I remembered but didn't want to believe. I looked over at Loretta. She was still there and still asleep. There was one big difference, though: the engine of the buggy was off and I could hear voices.

I pressed forward against the hole. Three men were standing at the end of the aisle, right by the front of the buggy. They were talking and laughing loudly. One of them put a bottle up to his mouth and took a deep drink. That only reminded me how thirsty I was and how good a Coke would have gone down right then. Of course that wasn't a Coke bottle he was drinking from.

One of the men reached forward and picked something up—it was a gun! It was longer and thicker than that rifle of Charlie's that Loretta had borrowed. The gun that was still lying in the snow beside Blackburn's fence. It couldn't be good for a gun to lie in the snow like that.

Two men started down the aisle toward me and I involuntarily flinched away from the hole. By the time I got my nerve back and looked again, all I could see of them was from the waist to the floor.

"Where do you keep the lights?" somebody yelled up to the front.

"In the big box at the back," came the answer.

In the big box! I reached out and tossed the corner of the blanket over Loretta's head to cover her as the lid of the box started to open. I looked up to see the red flannel shirt and arm of a man.

"Not that one! The one on the other side!" the voice called out.

"Okay." He let go of the lid and it crashed down.

I had to fight not to let any sound escape from my open mouth. A hand reached out and I startled! It was Loretta. She'd pulled the covers off her head.

"What happened?" she whispered.

I put a finger up to my lips to silence her. Just beyond our hiding spot stood at least two of the men, who were noisily removing the equipment from the other box. There were bursts of laughter—laughter that I was sure had something to do with whatever they'd been drinking. A third and fourth voice joined the first two.

"Blackburn," Loretta whispered in my ear.

I pressed my eye against one of the holes. I couldn't see anything. How could that be? A creaking sound came from right above my head and then my sightline was clear again. Somebody was standing right there. He must have been sitting on the top of our box and his leg was what had stopped me from seeing out. He moved farther away and I shifted so I could see what was going on.

The men were unloading things from the box and setting them down in the aisle between the seats. There were poles and lights. What would they use lights for?

I heard the back door open and they started to move the lights outside. Cold air flowed in. I leaned forward and took a big breath through the knothole. It filled my lungs and tasted so wonderful after breathing the hot, stale air that was captive with us in the box.

The door slammed and the voices were cut off. Looking back out I couldn't see any hint of either the people or the poles. As far as I could tell we were alone inside the buggy. Everybody was on the back porch.

"What happened?" Loretta asked again. She had shifted over so she was right beside me.

"They were going to open the box . . . they started to open the box."

"But how did I get the covers over me?"

"I did that. I didn't want them to see you."

"That was so . . . so . . . gallant," she said.

"Gallant?" She'd called me a lot of things, but I think that surprised me more than any of the others.

"What time is it?" Loretta asked.

I turned over my wrist and angled my arm until enough light hit the dial for me to see.

"It's just after one in the morning."

"That means the search has been going on for about an hour," Loretta said.

"The search for . . . ?" Of course I didn't need to finish asking that question because the answer was so obvious. They'd be searching for *us*. In the rush and fear of everything I just hadn't thought about what would happen when we didn't show up. Charlie would be going crazy!

"Even if Blackburn doesn't find us, I'm still in big trouble," she continued.

"You? What about me? I'll be in trouble too!"

She shook her head. "I'm going to tell them it's all my fault . . . that I talked you into it. But even if I didn't, everybody would blame me anyway."

Part of me wanted to just say "Yes, it is your fault, and you did talk me into it," but that wasn't completely right. Nobody had led me there at gunpoint.

"I'm just as much at fault as you. We're in this together and . . . did it just get brighter in here?" I asked.

Loretta looked around the box. I could see her as clearly as the answer to my question.

"I guess they turned on the big lights," I said.

"What big lights?"

"The ones they got out of the other box and brought outside."

"What scum!" she snarled, much louder than I would have liked. "They're spotlight hunting!"

"What's that?"

"It's illegal. They put out those lights and it attracts animals. The animals come walking right up. If you shine a powerful beam right in their eyes they just stand there like they're in a trance. I've heard that a hunter can almost walk right up and the animal doesn't move."

"That's awful. Do you think they're hunting the bears?"

"I don't know, but I do know Blackburn will lose his licence to hunt over this, no matter what animals they're after. We have to have a look," she said, and she started to raise the lid of the box.

"You can't do that!" I hissed as I knocked her arm away.

Her eyes flashed with anger as she glared at me. "We have no choice. We have to be able to see them doing it, not just think we know."

"But they'll see us for sure," I warned.

"They might not. They're all out back, and their focus is on the tundra. And because they're standing by those lights they won't be able to see us moving around inside in the dark. This is the best time to go."

I shrugged. She was probably right. I reached up and slowly pushed open the lid. I peeked through the crack and scanned the buggy. Nobody there. I pushed it higher and turned my body around so I could look over the lid and toward the back porch. I almost had to shield my eyes from the brightness. Although the lights were aimed off into the tundra, enough brightness bounced back to illuminate the landing. There were four figures, at least three of them holding rifles. They were leaning against the railing and peering into the distance.

"I've seen them doing it," I said to Loretta.

"Good," she said. She started to climb out of the box.

"What are you doing?"

"I've got to get out—"

There was a booming explosion—a gunshot—that cut Loretta off. Before I could even think, a second, third and fourth shot rang out. I watched, frozen in place, as the men quickly moved around the back porch.

"You got him!" a voice called out to a chorus of hoots and hollers.

"And now we've got you," Loretta said quietly. "We have to get somebody here. Come on, we've got to get to the radio. We'll call my uncle, or Reg and James. There'll be lots of traffic on the air looking for us, and we'll tell them."

Loretta raised the lid enough to allow her to climb out. This was stupid, this was insane, this was . . . I climbed out after her and quickly and quietly closed the lid. Loretta ducked down and slid under the seat directly in front of her. As soon as her feet disappeared I followed behind her. I squirmed under the seat in time to see her feet go under the next one. This wasn't exactly a fast or a clean way to move to the front of the buggy, but it certainly was the safest route.

"Get the ropes and winch!" cried out a voice as the back door was flung open.

Pressed against the floor but looking back under the seat, I saw somebody stop right in front of the box in which we'd been hiding! I heard the hinged lid open. If we hadn't moved we would have been discovered!

"Hurry up!" came a cry through the open door from the back porch.

"I'm hurrying!"

I heard the sound of things being removed from the box and then the lid fell shut again. I almost jumped at the sound. Finally the door closed, muffling the voices from outside.

"Whatever they shot is big," Loretta said. She was just ahead of me, peering over the top of the seat. "If only somebody could come right now and catch them."

I looked back. Nobody was looking. I circled into the aisle and around the seat so I was beside Loretta. We were right by the kitchen area.

"Grab something for us to eat and drink while I go for the radio," Loretta said.

She glanced at the back door to make sure it was closed, and then raced up the aisle. I saw her silhouette vanish behind a seat. I looked at the counter. It was littered with beer bottles, overflowing ashtrays and ripped-open wrappings. What an appetizing combination. Obviously they'd been drinking and eating during our trip out because it was even a bigger mess than before.

I needed to stay low so I reached up and tried to sort through the debris. My first few attempts came up empty—half-filled bottles of beer and a couple of empty cartons. Then gold! A bag of chips that had been opened and abandoned. I stuffed a couple in my mouth. They tasted wonderful, but they reminded me that we needed something to drink even more than we needed food. I stuffed the bag down the front of my shirt, between it and my thermal undershirt.

At the edge of the table I spied a can of Pepsi. I slipped over and reached out and grabbed it. Darn, it was open and half empty . . . which also meant it was half full. I couldn't believe I was even thinking about taking a sip from it—somebody else's, warm, flat Pepsi. I wouldn't have believed I could ever get that thirsty . . . but I was.

I brought the can to my lips and took a tiny sip. It was

warm, and it certainly was Pepsi, but it felt good in my mouth and soothing as it went down my throat. I tipped it back and took a big gulp and . . . *what the heck?* I put my fingers up to my mouth and pulled out something solid . . . a cigarette butt! I dropped the soggy butt to the floor and spat out the Pepsi still in my mouth. That was the most disgusting thing I'd ever done in my life!

"Great, you found something to drink," Loretta whispered.

I looked at Loretta and the can I was still holding.

"It's empty," I said. There was no way I ever wanted anybody to hear about this.

"Did you get Charlie?" I asked.

"I couldn't get anybody. There's no power for the radio. I think he's got all the power rigged up to run those lights."

"What are we going to do?"

"There's nothing we can do. Let's get back into hiding," Loretta said.

"But where?"

"Back in the box."

"That's no good. They'll probably return the stuff they got from there," I said.

"The other box?"

"That's no good either. That's where they got the lights."

"Maybe—"

The back door opened with a crash and we heard somebody racing up the aisle. There was no time to react or hide or—

"What in God's name?" he yelled as he skidded to a stop right in front of us. "Blackburn! You better get yourself up here!"

We were caught in his angry gaze. There was no place to run and no place to hide.

Chapter Twenty-Six

First Blackburn, and then the other three men came and stood over us. The three guys all looked like middle-aged mighty-hunter-wannabes, and judging by their expensive outfits, they had more money than brains.

"Stand up!" Blackburn ordered. He was holding a hunting rifle, but with the barrel pointed at the floor.

We got to our feet. I backed up against the wall, trying to get whatever distance I could between him and me.

"You have no right to be on my buggy!" he yelled. I could smell the liquor on his breath.

"I should have expected this from you!" he said, pointing at Loretta. "And who are you?"

"I'm—"

"He's the guy that kicked the crap out of your brother!" Loretta crowed.

What was she saying? Did she think we weren't in enough trouble, or that he wasn't mad enough already?

"What are you talking about, you little idiot?"

"Hah! You're the idiot who's going to lose his licence and be arrested!" she threatened.

"What have you seen?" he demanded.

"Nothing! We haven't seen—" I started to say.

"We know everything." Everything! And all of you are in big trouble when we get back to town," she yelled, as she pointed at each man.

For a split second they looked taken aback. What she was saying was true, and they knew it.

"We didn't know we were doing anything wrong!" one of them protested. "He said we could hunt the bears!"

"Shut up!" Blackburn ordered him.

"You're all in big trouble!" Loretta yelled.

"And you shut up too!" Blackburn snapped, and he reached out and pushed Loretta.

"Leave her alone!" I yelled as I jumped forward and knocked away his hand. I think my action caught him off guard and he didn't know how to react. I was even more stunned by what I'd done. He recovered before I did.

"You're going to regret that, kid," he bellowed, and he took a step toward me.

"You just wait till we get back to town and you'll find out all about regretting things," Loretta screamed.

"Brave talk. We aren't in town now, and there's no guarantee when, or *if,* you're going to get there," Blackburn said ominously. His voice was quiet, which made what he was saying more scary than if he'd been yelling.

A heavy silence hung in the air, as though everybody in the room was thinking through what he'd just said.

"You don't mean you're going to . . ." one of the men started to say.

"I don't know what I'm going to do with them," Blackburn said. "You two get outside while we talk it over and figure it out."

Outside? What did he mean "get outside"? I stood motionless beside Loretta.

"Get onto the porch. Now!" He placed the barrel of his gun against my side and pushed.

I leaped forward and Loretta fell in behind me. Nervously I stopped at the box and opened the lid.

"What are you doing?" Blackburn demanded.

"I need my hat and mitts and parka," I said as I reached down and grabbed my stuff.

"You won't have to worry about the cold for long!" he threatened, and then he pushed me again with the gun.

I stumbled forward, still holding my ripped parka, through the door Loretta was holding open. Blackburn grabbed the door and pulled it closed behind us.

"My goodness!" Loretta said.

The spotlights had been turned off and the deck was dark except for the light coming from the cab of the buggy. In the dim light at the edge of the deck, still encircled by ropes that led to a hoist, I could see a large bear. The white of its fur all along one side was covered with the brilliant red of its blood. Its head lay awkwardly to the side, eyes closed and mouth open.

"How could they do that to the bear?" I asked in a whisper. I pulled on my parka.

"Forget about the bear! Think about what they're going to do to us!" Loretta snapped.

"What *can* they do, turn us in to the police?"

"There's no way they're going to call the police."

"Then what?" I asked.

"He's drunk. He's always drunk. And he's mean."

"You mean he might hit us?" I asked anxiously.

"Hit us? Get real! He might shoot us!"

"This isn't funny. Quit joking around, Loretta."

"I'm not joking around, just like I wasn't joking around about Blackburn shooting somebody before!"

My mouth dropped open. I looked past Loretta and back

through the window into the buggy. Blackburn and the three men were engaged in a heated discussion. Blackburn was waving his arms around, and muffled fragments of yelled words escaped out through the door.

"We have to do something!" Loretta yelled as she grabbed my arm.

"Like what?"

"We have to try to escape," she said.

"Escape how? Escape where?"

"We have to go over the side." She was already looking over at the ground below.

I moved to her side. It was a long way down. "If we jump, we could break an ankle."

"If we stay, we could end up with worse problems than that."

"But there are bears out there! Lots of bears!"

"We can avoid them."

"In the dark?"

"There's plenty of room for everyone."

"So instead of getting eaten we'll get hopelessly lost," I reasoned.

"Give me credit. I'm not some tourist from down south! I'm Cree, and I know the tundra. I can get us back to Churchill. I can . . . honestly."

I looked at Loretta, back at the men still arguing inside, then over the side at the ground far below, and finally at Loretta again.

"Let's go."

Chapter Twenty-Seven

Loretta stared at me, but she didn't move or speak. She looked as if she were in a trance.

"Come on, Loretta, let's go!" I said. I reached out and shook her arm.

"Yeah . . . we have to go," she said, but still she didn't move.

"Come on, Loretta, how can we get down?"

"Maybe we can use the rope and hoist that they used to bring the bear up." Whatever the problem was, she seemed to be snapping out of it.

The ropes were tied and looped around the bear in some sort of complicated fashion, but there was one rope leading off the others, which led up to the hoist. I pulled at that one. There was no give. Everything was tightly bound together.

"We have to undo these ropes . . . or cut them . . . or something," I said.

"We don't have a knife . . . or time. We have to go *now*."

Suddenly Loretta climbed up and sat on the railing. I scrambled up after her and looked down. It was an incredibly long way to the ground. Loretta was dangling her legs over the side, and when she made her move she seemed to be lowering herself down rather than simply dropping.

"What are you stepping on?" I asked.

"The wheel is right here," she told me before dropping the rest of the way to the ground.

"Hey, what are you doing?" a voice yelled out.

I was so startled that I almost fell off the railing. Blackburn was standing right there at the doorway. He rushed across the platform toward me. I leaped off the railing.

"Ouuummmp!" I yelled as I hit the ground and rolled.

"Get up!" Loretta pulled me to my feet.

Half stunned, I stumbled away, led by Loretta.

"Get back here! Are you two crazy?" Blackburn screamed.

As I tried to run, I looked back over my shoulder at the buggy and tripped and fell to the ground. Loretta dropped down beside me.

"You can't go out on the tundra!" Blackburn hollered. "Get back here now!"

I tried to get up but Loretta held me back.

"We're okay here. He can't see us in the dark," she said quietly.

"The bears will get you! Come back!"

I looked up at the buggy. I could just make out the silhouette of the men on the platform.

"Please come back, kids!" one of them pleaded anxiously. "Please . . . nobody is going to hurt you!"

"We have to get farther away," Loretta whispered. "Come on." She started to crawl away, and I followed after her in the darkness.

"Honestly!" came another voice. "We're just going back to town to turn ourselves in!"

"He's telling the truth, Loretta," Blackburn called out.

They sounded so convincing. Maybe they *were* just going to give up, bring us back and turn themselves in. What was the worst thing that would happen to them, anyway?

"Loretta?" I asked.

"I don't know," she answered. "Maybe he's telling the truth . . . but I wouldn't bet on it."

All at once we were bathed in blinding light. I shielded my eyes with my hand.

"There they are!" a voice called out.

We took to our feet and tried to scramble back into the darkness.

BANG! BANG!

Shots! He was shooting at us! After being trapped in the blazing light I couldn't see anything, it was like being blind, and I fell heavily to the ground.

"Get up!" Loretta pleaded, pulling me to my feet again.

I stumbled a few more paces and then tripped over Loretta, who had fallen ahead of me. Just over from us, the beam of light was flashing back and forth across the terrain.

"Come back!" cried out a voice. "Come back or the bears will get you!"

"Still think he sounds genuine?" Loretta asked.

There was no need to answer that question. We stood a better chance going up against the bears.

"Let's go."

We got to our feet and carefully picked our way across the uneven ground. Loretta led and I followed close behind. As our eyes adapted to the darkness we picked up the pace. I wanted as much space as possible between us and them. I knew we were invisible in the darkness, but I couldn't help but think of another shot ringing out and hitting me in the back as I fled.

"We have to stop," Loretta said.

She slumped to the ground and I sat down beside her. I looked back. We'd travelled hundreds of metres but the spotlights of the buggy still swept across the tundra.

"They can't see us. We're safe," she said.

"Are you sure they won't come after——?"

The sound of the buggy's engines starting up cut off my sentence and broke the silence. The big buggy spun around in a broad circle and then started off toward us.

"We have to get to some cover!" Loretta exclaimed.

"What sort of cover do you mean?"

"Some place where the buggy can't go. Rougher ground . . . rocks . . . boulders."

"Boulders? Isn't that the sort of place bears like?"

The buggy's engine grew louder. It was moving, headed straight in our direction. The big spotlights at the back were off but the headlights were on.

"There's no way they can see us," Loretta said. "They're just coming in the direction that we were headed when we ran away. Let's move that way instead."

She led me off at a ninety-degree angle, and it was soon clear that she was right. The tundra buggy bumped along in a straight line, moving forward and past us. We sat down and watched as the buggy got farther and farther away, until first the noise of the engines and then the faint glow of the head-lights were gone.

"Which way do we go now?" I asked.

"I don't know."

"What do you mean you don't know?" I demanded.

"I don't know because I don't know where we are."

"But you said you could get us back to Churchill!"

"Stop yelling!" she yelled.

"Why! It's not like they can hear us!"

"It's not them I'm worried about," she said.

"You mean . . ." Of course I knew what she meant: the bears.

"You said you could get us back to town," I whispered.

"I can. Just not right now. Look up!"

"At what?" I asked, peering upward. "I can't see anything."

"That's my problem. It's cloudy. I can't see the stars to get my bearings so I don't really know where we are."

"But you do have some idea, don't you?" I asked, unsure if I even wanted her to answer unless it was the answer I wanted.

"Of course I have *some* idea."

I gave a big sigh of relief.

"We just have to sit tight until the sun comes up."

"We can't just sit here. Shouldn't we be moving?"

She shook her head. "We can't take any chances. If I'm wrong, we'd be moving farther away from town."

"But what about the bears? Isn't it better to move at night so we have the cover of darkness?"

"No, we're better to wait until daybreak."

"But then the bears will have a better chance to see us!" I protested.

"Remember, the bears don't see very well, day or night. They use smell and sound, and those work as well in the dark as they do in the light. It's just that *we* won't be able to see *them* as well at night," she said.

"So we just sit here and do nothing?"

"Not nothing. We sit completely silently and listen . . . for anything coming to find us."

"And if we hear something?"

"We decide then. Either we sit and hope it misses us . . . or we run as fast as we can."

"Wake up, Kevin."

I sat bolt upright. A thin layer of snow slid off me to the ground.

"Why did you let me fall asleep?" I demanded.

"It seemed like the best thing to keep you quiet. If you stayed awake I was afraid your knees knocking together would attract a bear."

"I'm not that scared."

"I didn't say you were. I meant your knees were knocking from the cold. You must be cold."

I nodded my head. I was frozen.

"I'm scared, you know," Loretta said.

"You are?"

"You'd have to be a fool not to be at least a little scared."

"But you can get us back to town, right? You know where we are now, right?"

She nodded. "I know where we are. I'm almost certain."

"Almost certain?"

"I've never been out here alone before. Especially this far out."

"We're far out? How far out?" I demanded.

"A long way. If I'm right about where we are, I think it'll take us at least six hours to walk back, if we go in a straight line without running into anything."

Or anything running into us, I thought. I stood up and stretched. As I did so I realized that I was wearing Loretta's mitts—I'd had to leave mine in the buggy. When had this happened? I took them off and handed them back to Loretta.

"Thanks," I said.

"My hands were feeling sweaty so I took them off. I had to put them some place," she said with a shrug.

She quickly put them back on, and I imagined that her hands must have been pretty cold—at least as numb and cold as most of me was feeling. On top of that, my legs felt all kinked and my back was sore. Sleeping on the damp, frozen ground with a rock for my pillow hadn't been the best bed.

I looked around. We were in a low spot protected by a few rocks, and we'd run across a fairly flat, open meadow to get there. Bright bursts of colourful flowers punctuated the dull green that blanketed the clearing. The meadow ended in a hill directly behind us. All along the rise were rocks and boulders of different sizes, some big enough to hide a bear. But there was no sign of a bear, or anything else. There was no motion except for the distant outline of some birds high in the sky. What I wouldn't have given to be high in the sky just then.

"Come on, let's go," Loretta said.

"That way?" I asked. She was starting off to the rocks.

"You think you know a better way?"

"No. But shouldn't we avoid the rocks?"

"We should, but we can't. Unless I'm wrong, this ridge runs for kilometres and it's right in the middle of where we want to go. If we try to walk around it, then we'll have to travel for another couple of hours. Okay?"

"I guess."

Loretta began picking her way up the side of the hill. I followed close behind as she moved around the larger rocks, which thinned as we climbed. She stopped at the crest and I stopped beside her. We were standing on the highest spot for kilometres. The terrain down on the far side was almost identical to that on the side we'd just climbed: slope cluttered with rocks ending in a wide open meadow. There were patches of blue—water—mixed in with the greens and browns and whites.

"I was right. I know exactly where we are. The town is that way. If it were night we'd maybe even be able to see the glow of the lights."

"That's fantastic! All we have to do is—"

I stopped talking as I saw the bear picking its way along the slope.

Chapter Twenty-Eight

"Loretta."

"I see it," she whispered back. "Which way is the wind blowing?"

"The wind? Why should I care about the—?"

Of course I should care, I suddenly realized. If we were downwind, we were okay; upwind, in trouble.

Loretta didn't wait for me to answer the question.

"I think it's blowing toward the bear. That means our scent is travelling down to it. It might be tracking us now."

As if it had been listening for something, the bear stopped abruptly in its tracks. It tipped its head back so its nose was the highest point of the animal.

"We've got to get around it and downwind. Keep low."

Loretta slowly moved back the way we'd just come, dropping below the crest of the hill. Then as soon as we were low enough that we couldn't see the bear any more she picked up the pace until she was jogging. I ran beside her. We were actually running toward the bear, moving parallel to where the bear was on the other side of the hill.

"Slow down," I panted.

"We can't. We have to make sure the bear is still following

our scent along that side and can't track us if he crosses over. We want to get downwind, remember?"

She picked up the pace even more, but now I had renewed reason and energy to keep up with her.

"I know we're past the bear now. Let's have a look," Loretta said.

She slowed her pace to a walk and began angling back up to the top of the ridge. Nearing the top she dropped to her knees and started to crawl, and I did the same. We reached the crest and peeked over. I couldn't see anything. The bear wasn't behind us . . . which meant he might be just in front of us. A cold sweat came over me. Slowly I turned to look in the other direction, praying there was nothing there.

"I see it!" Loretta whispered.

I swung my head back around. There it was, where it was supposed to be, upwind of our position. It had been hidden behind a few rocks and a depression in the ground. It was still moving stealthily, slowly, and away from where we were.

"We'll stay on this side of the ridge for a few more minutes until we're sure it won't be able to see us. Then we'll cross over and move down."

"Through the meadow?"

"That's our best bet. The bears avoid the open spaces during the heat of the day, and maybe we'll even run into one of the buggies. We can wave and shout if we see one on the horizon."

"As far as I know the only buggy working belongs to Blackburn, and the last thing in the world we want to do is run into him."

"You have a point," Loretta admitted. "But we have to chance it."

We moved along the crest and then crossed over and started to head down, through the rocks and boulders. I couldn't help but think about how that bear had been so hard to see, which meant the next one could be just as invisible. For all we knew, we were rushing away from one bear and straight into another.

Where the ground flattened out, the vegetation was sparse in some places and deeper in others. There was a pond off to the side. It looked cool and inviting, and it reminded me how long it had been since I'd last had something to drink. I cringed thinking of my last drink—a warm, flat Pepsi with a soggy cigarette butt.

"We need to get some water," I said.

Loretta nodded. "In all the excitement I forgot how thirsty I was."

We detoured toward the pond. Closing in, the ground got soft and spongy. I knelt down, bent over and cupped my hands to capture a handful of water. I greedily drank, and it was cold and sweet and soothed my parched mouth and throat as it glided down. I cupped my hands again and again and—

"That's enough," Loretta said, placing a hand on my arm.

"I'm still thirsty."

"You'll get a bad gut pain if you drink too much after not drinking for so long."

Reluctantly I spread my hands to release the water they still contained. It dribbled out and splashed back down into the pond. It even sounded good.

"I just wish we had something to carry water with us. You know, like a canteen or even an empty bottle," Loretta said. "Come on."

For hours we moved across the open tundra. The sun was bright, but it did little to drive off the cold, and there was nothing to protect us from the wind. We passed by dozens of different-sized ponds and repeatedly stopped to drink. The larger of the ponds, none of which were very large or, according to Loretta, very deep, held an assortment of wildlife. There were birds, lots of birds, and some were followed around by their babies, who were now almost as big as the parents. A couple of times we had an Arctic fox pass close by us. Loretta said they were used to being around bigger animals—like the bears, from whom they scavenged bits of their kills—so they weren't much afraid of us. Those were the only animals we saw. If we hadn't actually seen the bear earlier that morning, it would have all seemed unreal, as if polar bears were just some creation of our imaginations.

"Do you see it?" Loretta asked.

"See what?" I crowded in close to her, fearing it was another bear.

"The road."

"What road?"

"The one that runs between town and the abandoned military base."

"I don't see anything."

"Up ahead. It's that brown line cutting through the green and grey."

I used my hands to shield my eyes. "I think I see it. So we're almost okay . . . right?"

"Not yet, but closer. And maybe we'll get lucky and run into somebody driving out to the base."

"That would be amazing."

We crossed over the open space leading to the road. As we climbed up the embankment, gravel crunched noisily under my feet.

"Which way?" I asked.

"The town is that way. If we move quickly we can be on the outskirts in less than two hours."

"Or less, if somebody comes along," I said.

"Of course. Let's just not count on it."

The roadway was elevated above the level of the tundra it cut through. It was obvious that it didn't get much use any more. Grass, and even small shrubs and bushes, pushed up through the gravel, and in places it was terribly rutted and washed out so it seemed almost as rough as the tundra.

"We'd never have gone this long without seeing a vehicle before they closed down the military base," Loretta said. "There used to be trucks and jeeps and ducks zipping along here."

"Ducks?"

"They're special trucks. They look kind of weird but they can go in the water. They're really neat! One second you're driving along the tundra and then, splash, you're floating like a boat!"

"You got to ride in one?"

"A few times . . . when I was small. I was always doing things around the base."

"So, anybody could hang out at the base if they wanted to?"

"Of course not *anybody*, but lots of people in Churchill had family who worked out there, and then you could go out to visit."

"So, who in your family worked there?" I asked.

"My father. He starting working there when he was fifteen, and he worked there for almost twenty years . . . until the base closed."

"That must have been hard on him."

"It was hard on everybody!" Loretta snapped.

There was that nasty scowl on her face again. I took a deep breath and waited for her outburst.

"It was hard on everybody . . . in the whole town. The base was the biggest employer around, and the pay was pretty good as well."

"I guess it would have been difficult to get another job," I offered.

"Impossible for some people." She paused. "I guess we should be grateful for the tourists."

"Grateful for tourists? You? I thought all tourists were stupid."

"They're not *all* stupid," she allowed.

I started to smile.

"Just all the ones I've met," she said with a laugh. "And if my father ever agrees to become Uncle Charlie's partner, then I'll have to learn to be more polite to all tourists."

"I have trouble even imagining you being polite," I chided her.

"Watch it," she warned.

"Okay, okay. So why doesn't your dad join up with Charlie?"

"I think he'd like to, but first he has to meet Uncle Charlie's condition."

"What's the . . . ?" I paused. "Maybe I shouldn't be asking private stuff like that. It's none of my business."

Stupid, stupid, stupid! Don't ask about her parents. Reg had warned me. I looked straight ahead and listened to the gravel crunching under our feet.

"He has to stop drinking," Loretta said.

Her comment caught me so off guard that I didn't know what to say.

"My father drinks . . . a lot . . . it's a problem . . ." She took a loud, deep breath. "Does your father drink?"

"Only Coke. Most of the time he's too busy working to drink . . . or even eat."

"My father hardly drank at all before he lost his job. I think he'd stop if he was working."

"That would be good, wouldn't it?"

She didn't answer.

"Loretta?"

She was staring forward and just off to the side.

"Loretta?"

She'd stopped walking, and I stopped too.

"We're being stalked. Do you see it?" Slowly she raised her hand and pointed.

"I can't see anything." I didn't *want* to see anything. I just wanted Loretta to be wrong.

"It stopped moving when we did. That's how I was sure it was watching us. Do you see it, among the rocks at the end of the pond?"

"I can see the pond . . . and the rocks . . . but I don't see any—" My eyes caught sight of a large white rock among the others. "Now I see it."

"It looks to be a big male. At least that's good."

"How is that good?" I demanded.

"Large males aren't usually as desperate for food as the females and immature males, and they can't run as long without getting overheated. Remember?"

"That's right. So do we run for it?"

"The bear's too close to the road. If we try to keep going the way we're walking he'll get us."

"But he'll overheat if he chases us . . . right?"

"He will . . . eventually, but not in that distance. He's still fast, a lot faster than we can run, for short bursts. Like the distance from him to the road right now."

"We can't just stand here—" I stopped short. "He's started moving."

"I saw . . . but he's stopped again. Did you notice that line on the horizon on the other side of the road?"

I struggled to turn my head away from the bear and looked in the other direction. "Yeah, I see it. What is it?"

"That's the fence that surrounds the base," Loretta explained.

"Yeah, so what?"

"If we could get to the fence we could climb over it."

"What good would that do?"

"The fence is bear-proof. The bear can't get through it."

"But bears do get through it. I saw them all over the base," I said.

"Bears don't get through the fence. They get through the holes where the fence has come down. There might not be any holes along this stretch."

"Or there might be," I pointed out.

"We don't know. We just have to hope. And if there is a hole that lets him through, we'll just have to stay up on the top of the fence."

"He's starting to move again," I said softly.

"Come on." Loretta grabbed me by the hand.

We scrambled down the embankment so that the bear was blocked from view.

"Run! Run fast!" Loretta yelled as she dashed out in front of me.

I didn't need any more encouragement. My feet touched down on the spongy ground and I felt myself dig in. The weight of the boots made me feel clumsy and heavy. How could I be expected to run in those? I needed my running shoes if I was to . . . forget the boots! I had to think about nothing but running!

Left, right, left, right . . . breathe in through your nose and out through your mouth . . . no looking to the sides . . . focus on the finish line . . . just like running at soccer practice or for the cross-country team. I passed Loretta. Keep focused . . . keep those legs moving up and down . . . breathe in through your nose and out through your mouth.

We were coming up to a ridge that stood in our way, and now I could see only the top few strands of the fence.

"Kevin!"

I looked back over my shoulder. Loretta was way behind. I slowed my pace, and then I caught sight of the bear. I had to fight the urge to go faster again. Now the bear flashed across the road and was charging down the embankment. He stumbled and almost tumbled over before regaining his stride. How could anything that big move that fast? He was closing the distance between us.

Loretta came up beside me. I grabbed her hand.

"You have to run faster!" I commanded as I tried to drag her forward.

"I can't," she panted. Her breathing was fast and heavy. Too fast and too heavy for how little we'd run and how far we still had to go.

We started up the rise and the top of the fence vanished completely. Loretta slowed even more. She stumbled, spinning me partway around, and only my grip stopped her from falling completely. I hadn't wanted to look back because I knew what I'd see—the bear was gaining ground. We weren't going to make it at this speed!

"Come on, faster!" I screamed. I picked up my feet and pulled harder.

We stumbled up the slope. More and more of the fence became visible as we approached the top. Then as we broke over the crest the whole fence was there, just down and a quick sprint across an open field.

"We can make it!" I yelled.

We dropped over the ridge. Between the downward slope and the promise of the fence I felt a renewed energy. I tried to pick up speed but Loretta wasn't responding. It was like dragging an anchor.

"Loretta, come on, speed up!" I urged.

"I . . . can't go . . . any faster . . . I can't."

There was only one solution.

"Keep running!" I yelled as I let go of her hand and pushed her forward.

She hesitated. "But Kevin!"

"Keep running!" I screamed. "Keep moving! I'll catch up!"

She trudged forward and I skidded to a complete stop. I had to place myself between Loretta and the bear. Then the bear would target me and I'd lead him off to the side, away from her, and outrun him to the fence . . . I hoped.

My resolve began to crumble as the bear crested the ridge. I screamed as loud as I could, partly to get the bear's attention but more because I couldn't stop the fear from escaping. I started running on an angle toward the fence but away from the straight line Loretta was on.

Running through my mind was a geometry question. If the angle was too small, then I'd overrun Loretta and the bear would get her; if the angle was too great, then the bear would catch me before I ever got to the fence.

Out of the corner of my eye I saw the bear hurtling down the hill. I needed to take a shorter route.

Breathe . . . pick up your knees . . . run . . . run . . . focus on the fence. It was almost in reach. Was the bear even chasing me? I hoped he was . . . and prayed it wasn't. I took a quick look over my shoulder and my heart almost stopped: the bear was closing on me . . . he was almost right behind me!

I turned back toward the fence, toward the finish line. So close. So close. I zigged around an outcrop of rocks and I heard the sound of the bear's feet cutting into the turf as he copied my direction change.

The fence was just up ahead. I could make it! *I could make it!* But I couldn't slow down. I had to run right up the face of the fence and not stop until I reached the ground on the other side.

I leaped up and slammed into the fence with a thundering, metallic clang. My fingers held on tight and stopped me from falling back to the ground while my boot-clad feet scrambled desperately to secure footholds! I had to get to the top! I reached up and pulled myself higher, managing to force one foot through the small openings in the chain-link fence. I pushed in the other foot, reaching higher. The top was right there . . . just above my outstretched hand.

Suddenly I heard myself scream as everything shook violently. Both feet and one hand fell from the fence. I was hanging on with just one hand!

The bear had smashed into the fence!

I dug in a foot and my fingers found the links again. Propelled by fear I summoned the strength to reach the top just as the bear reared up on his hind legs and tried to swat me down. There were strands of barbed wire on the very top. I grabbed them with my bare hand and pulled my leg over. The bear slammed against the fence again and nearly shook me off. I threw one leg over the top of the fence and heard the sound of ripping cloth. I didn't care if my clothes had snagged on the barbed wire—that was just one more thing that was going to stop that bear from shaking this particular coconut out of this particular tree.

The bear stretched out a gigantic paw and swung it toward me. I drew my legs up, and the fence rocked again.

"Polar bears can't jump!" I yelled down at the bear. "You thought you had me, didn't you, you stupid bear!"

The fence rocked again . . . but not nearly so violently. Was he getting tired? His mouth was wide open and his tongue was hanging out the side. Panting, the bear dropped down to all fours. I was so happy to have even that much more distance between the bottom of my feet and the top of the bear.

"Kevin!"

I looked over. Loretta was sitting on the top of the fence about twenty metres away.

"Are you okay?" I called out.

"I'm fine . . . thanks!" She started to climb down the safe side of the fence.

"Is that such a good idea?"

She dropped to the ground. "He's not going to bother us."

The bear had walked away from the base of the fence. He was slumped down on his belly, lying in a puddle, not even looking in my direction any more. This was the time to move. I tried to pull my other leg over but it was held in place by the barbed wire digging into my clothes. I pulled harder and was released with a loud rip. Was I going to have any clothes left intact at the end of this trip?

As quietly as possible I climbed down. The rattling of the metal fence unnerved me but didn't seem to disturb the bear. My feet hit the ground and I padded along the fenceline to reach Loretta. She took my hand and led me away toward a tall, thin building—more like a lighthouse. Off in the other direction, the way we weren't heading, the outlines of many buildings dotted the horizon.

"Why this way?" I asked.

"The main part of the base is too far."

"It doesn't look that far."

"It's too far for me. I'm too tired."

Judging from the way she was dragging her feet and the paleness of her complexion I knew she was telling the truth.

"We can get inside and find a place to hole up for a while."

"What is that building, anyway?" I asked.

"It's the old air traffic control tower. I was there two weeks ago with my uncle, and I know there are some loose boards on the doorway so we can get inside. I need to rest."

"I'd like to sit down too," I admitted. I was starting to feel tired. Putting together lack of sleep, the distance we'd covered, the constant fear and the after-effects of that adrenaline rush that pushed me up that fence to escape a killer bear—yeah, I figured maybe I needed a chance to rest too.

"At least we'll be safe there. And I was thinking we could go up on the roof and start a fire. Maybe we could attract some attention. People must be out searching for us by now," Loretta said.

"Sounds good."

"Maybe we can get warm, too. That parka of yours isn't going to be much help. It's looking worse and worse."

"What do you mean?"

She dropped just behind me. "The whole back end is ripped open. It must have got caught on the barbed wire."

"Great! I knew something had ripped, but I didn't know it was that bad! My mother is going to kill me!"

Loretta started to laugh.

"What's so funny?"

"I just thought you'd be more afraid of polar bears than you are of your mother."

"You don't know my mother."

"I'm sure she won't be mad. Once she finds out it was either your parka or you she'll understand."

"Maybe she would, but if I have anything to say about it she is never, ever going to find out what happened up here," I insisted.

"She won't?"

"Not from me, and since she doesn't know anybody else in Churchill, Manitoba, there's no way she'll ever find out."

"Hmmmm." Loretta examined the rips. "Maybe I can still fix it. I'll take some of the lining and put in a patch. She might not even notice."

"You could do that?"

"I could."

"Thanks, I'd really owe you."

"You owe me? Don't you think it's more the other way around? What you did back there was really brave. It was just about the bravest thing I ever saw."

"I was just . . . I don't know," I sputtered.

"I don't even want to think what would have happened to me if you hadn't drawn off the bear."

I didn't know what to say. I felt myself turning redder than I already was from all the running.

"They *are* looking for us, right?" I asked.

"For sure. Charlie would have come looking for us the second he found out we weren't where we were supposed to be."

"And do you think they're out here now . . . searching?"

"All over the place. A couple of choppers, at least one search plane, and if the buggies have been fixed they'll all be out here as well," she answered.

"With all those people searching, it won't take that long."

"It's hard to say. That's a lot of people, but it's a lot of country. We'd better not get our hopes up too high. I just wish we had something to eat."

My mind flashed to the potato chips stuffed between my shirt and my undershirt. I'd thought about them a few times, and each time something had come up to chase the idea out of my head. I reached between the layers and with a flourish pulled out the bag.

"Breakfast is served!"

"Where did you get those?" Loretta asked.

"I liberated them from the buggy."

She took the bag and uncrumpled it. "Too bad they're salt and vinegar."

"Sorry. You want me to go back and try to get another flavour?"

"My grandmother always said the best way to learn to like a new food is to get really hungry before you eat it. I think I'll like them a lot," Loretta said.

She took a big handful of the chips, which were more like potato crumbs. She handed the bag back to me and I took some too. They tasted pretty good to me.

We came up to the base of the tall, concrete building.

"The entrance is right there," Loretta said.

What had been a door was gone, and in its place were a number of boards nailed haphazardly across the opening. The bottom few were hanging off, making it easy to get inside.

"I really need to sit down. I'm almost feeling woozy," Loretta said.

I bent down slightly to enter the building. That was when I saw the eyes glowing in the dim light.

Chapter Twenty-Nine

Loretta and I both froze in place and stood as still as statues, watching the eyes watching us. They blinked, and we blinked back.

"It's just a cub," I said, feeling a rush of relief.

"But if there's a cub, there must be a—"

A white blur charged out of the corner and took up a position between us and the baby. The baby moved forward and ducked under the mother's legs. The big bear eased forward, opened her mouth and hissed. I knew what that meant: she was getting ready to charge. Maybe I could use one of the boards lying on the ground to hit her.

"Give me the chips," Loretta whispered.

"What?"

"Give me the chips."

This was crazy, she couldn't be that hungry! Slowly I brought the bag up and she took it from my hand.

"Get ready to run," she whispered.

"Where?"

"Around the side of the building, and then we'll try to make it to the fence again."

"Can you run?"

"I can try," she answered.

The bear took a step toward us.

"Now!" Loretta screamed as she tossed the bag of chips at the animal.

Just as I turned to run I saw the last crumbs cartwheeling out of the bag as it flew through the air.

We quickly turned the corner and were headed away from the entrance.

"Oh my gosh!" Loretta gasped as she skidded to a stop.

There was another bear walking along the fence. He wasn't moving, but its head was up and looking in our direction. There was no doubt he had seen us.

"Keep running!" I yelled, but rather than heading for the fence we continued to circle around the building toward the back. Loretta was right beside me as we raced for another corner.

"Is there a second way into the building?" I asked.

"I don't know."

Just as we were about to round the corner I looked back. The bear had left the fence and was running toward us.

We raced to the back of the building and almost ran into a big bear trap. It sat on a trailer with its mouth open. If only one of those bears had run into that, we'd have been safe.

Anxiously I scanned the walls of the control tower—solid concrete, no windows, for about three storeys up.

"What now?" I asked. We couldn't go around any farther without running back into the first bear, and the second was circling around and keeping us from the safety of the fence.

"Maybe we can run for it," I suggested, pointing toward distant buildings. I was getting desperate.

"I can't," Loretta said. "I can't. Go without me."

"I can't do that! I won't do that!"

I looked back in time to see the big bear turn the corner. He wasn't moving fast, just creeping forward. He knew as well as we did that there was no place for us to run and no place to hide . . . except.

"The trap! The trap will save us!" I yelled.

"We'll never get him to go into that trap!"

"It's not him I want in the trap! It's us! Come on!"

I grabbed her by the hand and started running toward the trap, which stood in the gap between us and the bear.

"Are you crazy!" she screamed.

I didn't answer; I just pulled her harder. The bear, seeing us running toward him, stopped and for a split second even backpedalled a step or two. Obviously Loretta wasn't the only one who thought we were crazy.

"Into the trap!" I screamed as Loretta hesitated at the opening.

I pushed her with both hands and she tumbled into it. Then I climbed in and looked up at the bars. How did I get them to come down and lock us in? It couldn't be that complicated if a bear could do it. I didn't have time to think this through . . . the bear would be on us in just a few seconds, and . . .

I heard snuffling sounds coming from outside the trap. Had he somehow lost us when he lost sight of us? Maybe he'd go by the trap and we could sneak out when he passed and get to the fence and . . .

The bear appeared on the ramp leading up to the entrance to the trap. His massive mouth was open and his teeth exposed. He stood still, staring at me, as though he was fascinated and confused and intrigued by what he was seeing. This didn't make sense to him. Maybe he'd been caught in one of these before and remembered he shouldn't go inside. How long could we stand there staring at each other?

Then he charged.

I jumped back just as the bars came crashing down and the bear smashed against them. I screamed as the whole trap was rocked backwards by the force of the collision.

The bear shook his head and struggled to regain his footing. He wasn't sure what had happened, but he knew it had hurt. He reached out with a front paw and pressed it against the bars, testing. They wouldn't give. He came forward and opened his mouth and started to chew on the bars. His teeth grinding against the metal made a sickening scraping sound. I shuddered, imagining my bones between those jaws.

After a while, he stopped biting the bars and instead he slipped a long front leg between them and fished around with a massive paw. I jumped backwards, landing practically on top of Loretta. She was holding a piece of meat in her hands—the bait. Hanging from it was a thick cord that led along the roof of the trap and out through the closed bars.

"You closed the doors," I said. "It was you."

"I pulled the bait and it triggered the door," she explained. "I almost did it too late. Can you imagine what would have happened if it had come down a second later? All three of us would have been trapped in here together and—where is the bear?"

"Maybe he gave up," I suggested.

"Bears don't give up that fast."

"Then maybe he—look out!" I screamed as the bear suddenly appeared behind Loretta.

He reached in through the back of the trap with a long paw as we both jumped away. Once it was obvious that he wouldn't be able to reach us from that way either he withdrew his paw and disappeared. I looked anxiously at the front of the trap. Was he circling around again? Was I too close to that end now? I moved right beside Loretta and into a position that was as far away from both ends as possible. The trap was like a big sewer pipe. Here in the middle he could possibly reach us from both ends, but he wouldn't surprise us from either. As long as we kept on shifting from side to side he wouldn't get us.

"I think we're okay," I said.

"You think this is okay?" she said. "And just what do you think is *not* okay?"

There was a loud smash on the side of the trap. Loretta screamed and we both jumped. It sounded as though the bear had hit the trap right by where our heads were, to see if he could strike us through the metal. The whole trap was jarred. We'd been bounced slightly to the side, and I could have sworn we'd bumped slightly off the ground.

"How much do these traps weigh?" I asked nervously.

"I don't know. A lot."

"They must be heavy. Too heavy for the bear to move around or—"

My sentence was shattered as the trap tipped up and we were thrown to the other side. It dropped back down with a thud and my skull cracked against the metal. Before I could even bring a hand up to rub my head we were tilted up off the ground again. This time I braced myself for the jarring drop, but instead we kept going higher and higher until the trap turned over completely!

"Ahhhh!" I screamed as we smashed down to the ground at last.

Loretta and I were intertwined, with legs and arms shooting off in different directions. I reached up to a painful spot on my forehead and my hand came away covered in my blood. Loretta was also rubbing her head. She looked dazed.

The bear reached in again with his paw. I jumped away and pushed and pulled Loretta to safety. On its rounded top, no longer sitting on its wheels, it was free to rock back and forth.

This was just too bizarre to be happening. I suddenly realized what it would feel like to be the last two Smarties stuck in a box with somebody trying desperately to shake you loose.

The bear circled to the other end. I jumped away but Loretta wasn't fast enough. He reached in and with his long, curved claws dug into the side of her boot.

"Ayeeee!" Loretta screamed.

The hairs on the back of my neck rose on end. He had her! The bear had her! I grabbed onto her and pulled as the bear dragged her closer. It was useless . . . I couldn't stop it . . . he was just pulling me along too!

Underneath me I felt a lump and remembered about the hammer in my pocket. I pulled it out, leaped across Loretta and with one powerful swing brought it down on the bear's paw! He howled in pain and jumped back, letting go of Loretta.

She pulled back her foot and squeezed against me.

"Are you okay?"

"I'm afraid to look," she cried out. "We can't keep this up forever. Sooner or later he's going to get us."

"We'll do it for as long as we need to! We're not giving up! He's not going to get us! He's not!" I screamed.

Loretta shook her head slowly. "I just don't . . . Listen."

"What?"

"Don't you hear it?" she said softly.

"I don't hear anything . . . except . . . is it an airplane?"

"Or a helicopter, or even a buggy or something."

"Do you think they see us?" I yelled.

The increasing noise was all the answer either of us needed. Whatever it was it was almost there. I looked through the bars and saw a helicopter touch down on the tarmac and two men, James and Reg, jump out carrying rifles.

"If you don't mind me saying it . . . I think we're okay now."

Chapter Thirty

"Are you sure you have all your things?" Charlie asked.

"Everything," I answered. I had a bag in each hand.

"We just wouldn't want you to be losing your luggage twice in the same trip, that's all."

"I've got everything," I reassured him.

"Say . . . why are you wearing that parka? Where's yours?"

"Loretta let me have her old parka . . . sort of like a souvenir of the trip."

"Well, isn't that nice of her!" Charlie beamed.

Loretta looked embarrassed and her eyes dropped to the ground. What I hadn't said to Charlie was that my parka was back at Loretta's place and that she was going to mail it to me, at Ian's address, once she'd been able to fix it up.

"And remember, you'll still need to dress warmly when you come back in the spring to take pictures of the migrating birds," Charlie said.

I smiled. Charlie had invited me to make a return visit and take more pictures with him.

"I'll remember. Doesn't it ever get warm up here?"

"It always feels pretty warm to me," he offered. He was, of

course, wearing nothing but a shirt, although it was a long-sleeved shirt today.

"And I don't want to hear any excuses from your parents about you not coming back. After all, the whole trip will be paid for, flight and all, and I'll be mighty mad if you don't accept my thank-you present for everything you did."

"Don't worry, I'll be back. The second-last thing in the world I want to do is get you mad at me."

"Second-last? What's the last thing?" Charlie demanded.

"To get your *niece* mad at me." Both Charlie and I started laughing.

"You'd better hope that plane gets here soon, then, or you're going to see me get really mad!" Loretta threatened.

"Okay, I'm sorry, I'm sorry!"

The scowl on her face dissolved into a smile—a wonderful smile.

"How's your head?" Charlie asked.

"Not bad." I reached up and touched the bandage that covered five stitches. I couldn't help but smile thinking about what I was going to tell my father and mother about all this. I could just see their faces when I told them about being inside an overturned polar bear trap while fleeing a bear. But even better was going to be my father's reaction when I told him who'd put in the stitches. The doctor was away in a neighbouring community so I'd been stitched up by the town vet. I loved it!

"Here, I have something for you. A little going-away present," Charlie said. He handed me a large brown envelope.

"What is it?"

"The idea with a present is to open it and find out," Loretta suggested.

I looked at her. "Can't you come up with a better insult than that?"

She smiled and shook her head slowly.

I opened the envelope. Inside was an article entitled "The Dump." Right underneath the title it said, "Written by Charlie McGinty, photographs by Kevin Spreekmeester." On the first page was a picture of the bear sitting on its backside holding the battered green garbage bag in its front paws. I turned the page. More text surrounding another picture, this one with the same bear standing on all fours. I had no idea that shot had even come out, I'd had to rush it so much. On the final page was a column of text and two pictures of the bear, one when it was having its tooth pulled and the other when it was in the trap at the polar bear jail.

"Do you like them?" Charlie asked.

"They're great!"

"Glad you agree with me . . . and the editors. It'll be running in the April edition of *National Geographic.*"

I was stunned. "You're kidding, right?"

"Nope. I'd already contracted for a photo spread about the bears. You just provided the pictures."

"This can't be real."

"I bet it'll seem even more real when you get your cheque in the mail."

"Cheque? What cheque?"

"For the photospread. You don't think the *National Geographic* pays its photographers? The editor told me he thought I'd discovered a very talented young man. I told him you had talents in a whole lot of areas."

"Thanks." I felt myself starting to blush.

"Obviously you've got yourself some fine parents."

"Well, yeah, I guess."

"No guessing involved. A boy doesn't grow up into a fine young man unless he's had people there all along guiding him. Helping him make choices, listening to him, maybe even making him do things he doesn't want to do sometimes. Right?"

I nodded my head slowly. "They are pretty good parents."

"Maybe they'll even come along with you when you come back. They'd be my guests too!" Charlie said.

"I'd like that. I'd like that a whole lot."

I thought about how short and how long five days had been and, I had to admit that I'd missed them—a lot. I'd even missed all those annoying little things they constantly do, although I was pretty sure I wouldn't miss those things for long after I returned home.

"Do you think your parents are going to let you come back once they find out everything that happened?" Loretta asked.

"I hope. I guess it depends on how I tell them."

"You're not talking about lying are you, Kevin?" Charlie asked.

"Not lying. I'm just planning on telling them slowly, and carefully."

"Here she comes!" Loretta called out.

Off in the night sky I caught sight of the landing lights of the plane. Like legs, the lights dropped from the belly of the aircraft, cutting through the darkness and shining down on the runway. The plane touched down and taxied toward us.

"Anybody on this flight for Blackburn's tour?" Loretta asked.

"Four people. I'll let them know they'll be spending their week with me."

"I still think he got off easy!" Loretta snapped.

"He lost his licence to lead tours, he's facing a big fine, and the bank's going to take away his buggy. Sounds like a lot to me," Charlie said. "And he did save your lives when he shot at that bear."

I couldn't stop a little tingle from rushing up my spine. Those

gun blasts weren't Blackburn trying to shoot me and Loretta—
he'd been aiming at a bear that was almost on top of us. I didn't
believe it when I first heard it, but that's what all three of the
hunters had told the police. After that, because Blackburn was a
Cree band member, they'd turned it over to the tribal authorities.

"But what about all the damage he did to everybody's
buggies?"

"He's paid for more than half and promised us the rest when
he's back on his feet. He wanted to make it right."

"Yeah, right, like I believe that!" she snapped.

"I still don't understand why he did it."

"He said he wanted to keep the other buggies in town while
he hunted. And I'm sorry you don't believe it, but the important thing is that the band elders believe he deserves another
opportunity, and jail isn't an opportunity."

"Yeah, another opportunity to take a shot at me!" Loretta
snapped.

I reached out and placed a hand on her arm. "Listen to your
uncle."

"If the two of you had stayed on board, he was coming back
to turn himself in."

"That's what he says now."

"Yeah, well, he did radio in to us as soon as you two jumped
over the side to tell us what had happened. If he hadn't, we
never would have known to search that sector."

"So we should be grateful to Blackburn?" Loretta was not
buying it.

"I'm not saying that. The only people you two have to be grateful to is each other. Each of you made it because of the other."

"That's right!" she said.

"You made some smart decisions out there. The smartest one
was probably to head for the control tower on the abandoned
base instead of town."

I swallowed hard. "Yeah, that was a good decision."

"Because most people would have hit that road and then tried to take it straight into town without thinking about how the bears love that strip of gravel."

"But I wasn't with most people," I said.

Loretta looked away. We'd agreed that we weren't going to mention anything we didn't need to mention. As far as everybody else was concerned, we were always headed straight for that control tower so we could be seen by any planes making a low pass to land at the town's airport.

"I'll go and get the bus and pull it up close to the plane," Charlie said. "Why don't you two go and help unload?"

The plane had taxied to a stop and we walked out to meet it. The propellers stopped and the back door popped open. Wendy came out and waved. We waved back. I expected a flood of passengers, but instead Crash came barrelling down the stairs.

"So how does it feel to be famous?" he asked.

"Famous? How do you figure that?"

"Everybody knows what happened!" he grinned.

"Well . . . I guess everybody in town knows," I admitted.

"Not just in town! Everywhere! I guess you wouldn't know. After all, we don't just deliver passengers, we bring the papers as well."

Out from under his arm he pulled a copy of the *Globe and Mail*. There, in big bold letters, just above the fold, it read "Polar Bear Escape." My eyes scanned down the first column, stopping when they came to my name—it was even spelled correctly.

"Your parents will be so proud of you," Crash said.

"He wanted to be the one to break the news to his parents, Crash," Loretta pointed out.

"Crash? Since when have you been calling me Crash?"

She shrugged. "Things change."

"I guess they do," he said. Crash gave me a smile. "Are you going to get in trouble?"

"Maybe. But I'm not worried."

"You're not?" Loretta asked.

"It doesn't make much sense to be more afraid of your parents than you are of a bunch of polar bears, does it?"

"I didn't think so," Loretta answered.

"How long before we leave?" I asked Crash.

"About thirty minutes. You going to help me unload the plane?"

"I think it would be better if I finished reading this article, and then called home to my parents."

"Okay, Bear. Sounds like a plan to me." Crash said.

"Bear?" I asked.

"That's your new nickname. Do you like it?" Crash asked.

"Ya . . . I think I do."

"Kinda suits you," said Loretta, with a grin.

"Good. Now go and call your parents," Crash said.

"That should be some interesting phone call. Can I listen in?" Loretta asked.

"No! But don't go too far away." I paused. "The last thing I have to do is say goodbye to you."

"I should go and help Crash."

"He can do without you for a few minutes."

"Maybe, but I'm not so good with goodbyes," Loretta said.

"Come on, you have to be better with goodbyes than you are with hellos," I teased her.

"Watch it!"

I chuckled to myself. "I just wanted to say thank you for everything. Being there and helping and . . . everything. And I hope I'll see you in the spring. Will you be able to get some time off school?"

"Depends."

"On what?" I asked.

"If I can get suspended again."

I opened my mouth to object.

"Kidding, just kidding! I'm sure I can get some time off. But I have to go," she said.

"Me too. Which way is the phone?"

"Think about it, Kevin. The terminal has only one room."

"Oh, that's right."

She turned to walk away and I started off for the terminal.

"Hey, Kevin!" Loretta called out and I turned around. "They have many telephones in Mississauga?"

"A few."

"Good. I expect you to pick one up now and then and call me."

"Count on it," I said.

"I am." She flashed a smile and turned and walked away.

"And so am I, Loretta . . . so am I."